S0-AYW-618

Washington
≋County
September, 2012
WASHINGTON COUNTY LIBRARY
8595 Central Park Place • Woodbury, MN 55125

FROZEN

FROZEN

Mary Casanova

University of Minnesota Press
Minneapolis

The University of Minnesota Press gratefully acknowledges assistance provided for the publication of this volume by the John K. and Elsie Lampert Fesler Fund.

Copyright 2012 by Mary Casanova

Mary Casanova asserts her right to be identified as the Proprietor of this work.

All rights reserved. No part of this publication may be reproduced, stored in a retrieval system, or transmitted, in any form or by any means, electronic, mechanical, photocopying, recording, or otherwise, without the prior written permission of the publisher.

Published by the University of Minnesota Press
111 Third Avenue South, Suite 290
Minneapolis, MN 55401-2520
http://www.upress.umn.edu

Library of Congress Cataloging-in-Publication Data
Casanova, Mary.
Frozen / Mary Casanova.
Summary: Unable to speak or remember the events surrounding her mother's mysterious death eleven years earlier, sixteen-year-old Sadie Rose, the foster child of a corrupt senator in 1920s northern Minnesota, struggles to regain her voice, memory, and identity.
Includes bibliographical references (p.).
ISBN 978-0-8166-8056-6 (hc/j : alk. paper)
ISBN 978-0-8166-8057-3 (pb : alk. paper)
[1. Identity—Fiction. 2. Memory—Fiction. 3. Families—Fiction. 4. Selective mutism—Fiction. 5. Minnesota—History—20th century—Fiction.] I. Title.
PZ7.C266Fr 2012
[Fic]—dc23
                              2012019376

Printed in the United States of America on acid-free paper

The University of Minnesota is an equal-opportunity educator and employer.

20 19 18 17 16 15 14 13 12   10 9 8 7 6 5 4 3 2 1

This story is a work of fiction,
inspired by historical events
in Koochiching County, Minnesota.

Behind the silver-plated parlor stove in the corner, I sat up from my nest of blankets and shivered. Mama should have finished by then with customers who came for visiting. She should have come to wake me with a soft drumming of fingertips and carry me up to our bed.

Except for someone snoring upstairs and a high-pitched wind howling outside, an unusual quiet had settled on the boardinghouse.

Footsteps creaked on the staircase, step by slow step downward.

I tucked back under my blankets and didn't make a sound. As long as I didn't get in the way, Darla let us stay. When Mama didn't work, I snuggled with her upstairs. She brushed my hair, read to me, and often said, "Things won't always be this way, Sadie Rose. Someday we'll have a home of our own."

I pressed my cheek to the dusty floor and peered out between the curved legs of the cast-iron stove.

A man stepped onto the parlor carpet of swirling reds and blues. Beneath his knee-length beaver coat appeared his dark pants and polished black boots, unlike so many worn and mud-covered boots that came and went. An edge of quilt—the same light blue circles on white as Mama's quilt—hung near the bottom of the man's coat.

"Damn it," he huffed, fumbling with the handle. Before the door shut again, a gust of brittle cold whooshed in.

| 1 |

RANIER, MINNESOTA
1920

I dropped my hands from the upright Steinway and stared at my sheet music. What could I truly remember from eleven years ago? Were these memories real or the imagination of a bored sixteen-year-old? Ever since yesterday afternoon, when I'd stumbled on the photographs, my mind had been flighty as a chickadee.

I pushed damp strands of hair from my forehead and then chewed on the tip of my middle finger, a habit Mrs. Worthington frowned upon. At least for a few days—until they returned from St. Paul—I would do whatever I liked, including coming downstairs in my cotton nightdress.

"Sadie Rose? Are you well?"

I twisted on the piano stool. Past the tufted sofa and gleaming dining table, Aasta stood in the kitchen doorway, watching me, her white braids crisscrossed over the top of her head, her apron draped around her broomstick body.

"You never stop like that," she continued, the tip of her nose dusted with flour. "I wonder if something wrong?"

Every day, Aasta filled the lake cottage with scents of rising bread, cardamom, and cinnamon. And Hans, her husband and the Worthingtons' caretaker, with a rag perpetually jutting from his back trouser pocket, was always trying to teach me something new—how to caulk boards on a leaky rowboat or how to use the oil can to quiet noisy hinges. I loved the Johannsens with their Norwegian accents and fondness for herring, lefse, and buttermilk. But their comforting presence couldn't still the whirring inside me.

My mind was spinning too fast, like reels at the motion picture shows in International Falls.

I reached to the floor and picked up the slate board trimmed in oak, never far from my side. In chalk, I wrote, "I might be taking ill."

Aasta stepped closer, wiping her hands on her apron. She placed her warm, soft hand to my forehead. "Ya, you're sweaty. But weather is warm for June."

I nodded, drew a full breath, and then turned back to the keys.

"While the dough rises, Sadie, I go to grocer's. Be back soon then."

Without turning, I nodded, picking up the melody again. This time, I would concentrate. Besides, I loved Beethoven's "Moonlight Sonata." My fingers glided easily over the white and black keys. But my mind rode an invisible current. And though my eyes and fingertips found the notes, maintaining a steady and dependable rhythm, I drifted out from the parlor to the cottage's living and dining area, to the long porch with its row of wicker chairs and screened windows, and above the village and the bay's invisible border, dividing Minnesota from Canada.

Shortly after the Worthingtons took me in, they'd sent me to public school, but when I returned home in tears the first day, teased for not speaking, they decided I would be taught at home instead. Tutors were hired, including piano teachers. At first, sitting in front of the piano keys, nothing made sense; but over time, my fingers translated the black shapes and squiggly lines into notes and music. If only memories were as readable and sure.

Only yesterday everything seemed as it should be.

Until I'd found the photographs.

From September to May the Worthingtons and I lived on mansion-lined Summit Avenue in St. Paul; the Worthingtons' brick mansion, with its stone balustrades, was as formidable as Fort Snelling and hosted a constant flow of politicians and businessmen. June through August, we summered up north. But yesterday, before they'd left in their Model T for the train depot, Mrs. Worthington explained. "Sadie Rose, you'd be bored with so many gatherings. It's only five days," she said, looking up at me, yet maintaining her steely posture. "Aasta and Hans will stay overnight as your chaperones."

"Five days inside?" I scribbled on my slate board.

She nodded. "Now that Mr. Worthington's a senator, maintaining our good name is more important than ever."

Women were on the verge of having the right to vote, yet with the Worthingtons I wasn't free to read on the dock alone or stroll to the grocer's in the village or wander the fishermen's docks. I needed something to fill my hours—and for now, I would have to settle for painting flowerpots.

Though it wasn't a young lady's place to rummage in a man's toolshed, I saw no harm in finding what I needed to amuse myself. And Hans, I knew, would forgive me. I stepped outside, anxious to feel the grass beneath my feet.

Rounding the corner of the cottage, I breathed in the plucky sweetness of the French lilacs, then stepped into the toolshed. Sunlight squeezed through the dusty paned window and spotlighted the oil-stained floorboards.

"Green paint." I silently mouthed the words. Over the years, when I was alone, I practiced voiceless words.

I searched for the can of olive green paint that Hans had used on the wooden rowboat. I shaped the words, "It must be here somewhere."

The shed held everything a gardener needed to keep the yard pruned and the lake cottage proper: rakes and shovels, pots of various sizes, saws and trimmers, paint cans and paintbrushes, hammers, screws and nails. I rummaged through two dozen cans of paint, some nearly empty, others never opened. With the help of a ladder, I climbed to the top shelf and found what I needed at the very back.

"Finally," I mouthed. But when I lifted up the can, I noticed something odd: at the back of the shelf a small stack of photographs lay facedown, their edges curled and yellowing.

Steadying myself on the ladder, I thumbed through the black-and-white images pasted on black cardboard cards—all scandalous photographs of a woman with luxurious dark hair. I was shocked that Hans might look at such pictures.

In one, the woman's hair was undone to her shoulders; she reclined, eyes half-closed, in a camisole and short bloomers on a chaise lounge. In another she sat in a suds-filled claw-foot tub, head back, smiling.

The images squeezed air from my lungs, all of the same woman. Waves of dark hair and piercing light eyes—perhaps blue, or green—there was no way of knowing for sure. Hoping to find a name or date, I turned each photograph over. Nothing. I hesitated, then tucked the photographs inside my dress, grabbed the can of paint and several small paintbrushes, and left.

I spent the rest of the afternoon on the front porch with my paints, dabbing blue-winged dragonflies over green flowerpots. I took my time. Finally, before Aasta and Hans returned in the late afternoon, I cleaned the brushes with turpentine and returned to my bedroom.

Though no one was home, I closed my door and turned the skeleton key with a click. As if they were Mrs. Worthington's fine china plates, I handled the photographs carefully. I set them on my vanity table and sat down to study them. Despite the warm air blowing in through my screen window, a chill slid from the back of my ears to my toes.

Hands damp with perspiration, I held the pictures lightly at their edges.

One captured the woman in a low-cut gown, bending to a footstool as she removed stockings from her long legs.

Another caught her sitting on a rock ledge at the edge of a high dam, her camisole slightly off one shoulder, her skirt hiked up to her knees as she dangled her legs over the edge. She dared the camera with her smile.

I held the photo up to my mirror. We shared the same hair, the same oval face, the same raised collarbones. But her eyes...this woman's eyes...were full of spirit, as if she might bolt from the camera at any moment. No one owned her. I studied my own eyes...but found none of that spirit mirrored there. My eyes were dull by comparison.

I set aside the photograph.

In the last image, the woman's hair was pinned up, with wisps slipping free. She looked over her bare shoulder, her body loosely draped in floral fabric.

Fabric with a design of cherry blossoms.

Cherry blossoms.

I studied the photo more closely and the fabric of the gown. I knew the material. I'd touched it. When I was little, I loved running my hands over the cherry blossoms, feeling the silk swish between my fingers.

Oh, no.

Mama.

The ember—gone nearly cold with time—rekindled.

Red and hot and glowing.

I dropped the photograph and pressed my hand to my mouth.

| 2 |

I neared the end of the sheet music, glanced ahead one bar, and then flipped the page without missing a beat. I couldn't bear to destroy Mozart's melody with a faulty page turn. I continued on, my fingers translating the composer's notes into the present. If my fingers could do that, I could puzzle through my past and what had become of my real mother.

Five knocks—*tap, tap, tap, tap, tap*—sounded from the porch.

I quickened the tempo and played through Mozart's last bars to the end, then jumped up from my piano stool.

Aasta must have lost her key.

Outside on the top step, someone waited.

But it wasn't Aasta.

I stopped in the shadows of the living room, hand frozen to the back of the sofa.

Framed by blue sky, white lake clouds, and lake water, a young man paced on the landing, bobbing his head of sandy-gold hair as he talked to himself. The wire glasses sitting on his straight nose contrasted with his muscled shoulders.

I wasn't dressed properly to accept visitors. The man hadn't spotted me yet. Better to remain hidden until Aasta, at least, returned to the cottage. I waited for him to leave, but instead he knocked again.

This man's attire fit neither the linen-suited tourists heading out on boats to their island estates nor the local workers in their plaid shirts and trousers. His khaki trousers were rolled up above his bare ankles, and he wore moccasins rather than shoes. I spotted a birch bark canoe tied to the dock. Though he was deeply tan, he was not Ojibwa or half-breed.

Shifting my weight, I stepped back toward the stairs. At that very moment, he shaded his forehead with his hand and peered in through the porch door.

"Hello!" he shouted, as I took another step backward. "I thought no one was home. Excuse me for disturbing you."

I stopped. I couldn't pretend he hadn't seen me. It would be impolite.

"My name is Vic—rather, uh—Victor Guttenberg."

Though he was too forthright to be well bred, I was drawn to his voice, as inviting as hot cocoa with whipped cream. I stepped onto the long porch with its red-cushioned wicker chairs.

Unlatching the hook, I remembered my bare feet, with Mrs. Worthington's words in my head: "A well-reared young lady wouldn't step into public without stockings and shoes."

"I'm looking for Mr. Worthington," the young man said, as the door swung wide. "I didn't realize he had . . . Is he home?"

He was younger than most men who sought out the senator, but he was still at least six or seven years older than I was. Still, something about him made me wish I could answer with spoken words. Other than an occasional cry or moan, my voice had died with Mama years ago.

Silence. My sanctuary and my prison.

I shook my head.

Victor frowned. "I should have made an appointment," he said, removing his battered fedora, revealing a pale forehead. "I really should have written a letter ahead, but, well, you see— Ennis's proposed dams, they'll change the landscape forever.

Your father, he's friends with E. W. Ennis—he might be able to communicate some sense—when might I catch him here?"

Without my slate board, a quick answer wasn't easy. I shrugged my shoulders.

"Tomorrow?" he asked.

I nodded, even though I knew it would be three more days. I'd lied and wasn't sure why, but I wanted to see Victor Gutten-berg again, without the Worthingtons' scrutiny.

"Once I get an idea in my head...," he trailed off, then began again. "Not that I'm the only one seeing things differently, of course. There're other movements afoot, trying to conserve—to save and protect what we have. But you see, I'm living on Falcon Island...this lake means everything to me." He motioned over his shoulder to the trestle bridge, as if to prove his point that there really was a massive lake beyond, dotted with islands that stretched for miles and miles.

I pointed to his canoe and raised my eyebrows in question.

"An hour's paddle is nothing," he said, "not when I've been canoeing and mapping regions—north—for hundreds of miles." He wore a saddle of peeling skin and sunburn over his nose as proof. His white shirt was wrinkled and graying, and I wondered if he'd put it on to impress Mr. Worthington. If so, his efforts would have been lost. No one was taken seriously who didn't either support Mr. Worthington politically or work for E. W. Ennis's paper mill operation in some way. And from the water dam downriver and to the farthest reaches of the lake, Ennis employed every man, directly or indirectly, in Koochiching County.

This Victor Guttenberg...did he have any idea what he was up against?

"Will you tell him I stopped by then, Miss Worthington?"

I held up my forefinger, then hurried inside for my slate board and returned with it, scribbling as I approached the

porch door, and stepped out again. I showed him what I'd written: "My name is Sadie Rose, but not Worthington."

"Huh. I guess I heard something about you, now that . . . Rose.
So that's your last name?"

I shook my head.

"If not Worthington, then what *is* your last name?"

I erased the board with the edge of my nightdress, bit
down on my lip, and wrote the answer. Reluctantly, I showed
it to Victor.

He seemed to study the words for a long time. Then he met
my eyes and seemed to see clear through me. "You don't have
one?"

I pressed the slate board to my chest, my throat burning.

"Sadie Rose, *everyone* has a last name. Perhaps I can help
you find yours . . . and maybe someday . . . you'll help me." Then
he tipped his hat and strode down the stone steps. Nimble as
the mink that darted in and out of the dock's supporting log
cribs, Victor untied his canoe, stepped in gently, and pushed
off. Then he carved his paddle into the water, heading toward
the lift bridge that connected Ranier with Canada.

Beyond the bridge, a speck of a tugboat pulled a boom of
floating logs. With a lasso of heavy chain, tugboats corralled
thousands of cords of logs from Rainy Lake, sluiced them under
the lift bridge, and floated them downriver to the paper mill.

Victor was safely out of the tug's path, and I watched until
he disappeared.

The lift bridge was Mr. Worthington's engineering mar-
vel. With it, he'd brought shipping and trade to the county. I'd
always felt part of some greater design, too, waiting for the
Worthingtons to tell me. I was, I'd always told myself, Sadie
Rose Worthington, even though they hadn't adopted me.

But like a snag in one of Aasta's intricate snowflake sweaters, a yarn had come loose. Tug at a loose yarn and the whole might unravel, Aasta said.

First the photographs.

Part of me wanted to put them back in the shed, hide them under the paint can, and forget I'd ever found them.

But there was a second snag.

Victor's asking, wanting to know . . .

Everyone has a last name.

His words chimed in my head . . . *name* . . . *name* . . . *name* . . . until I could scarcely breathe.

Turning back to the cottage, I paused on the top step. A fresh hatch of fish flies clung to the cedar shakes, as if defying the Worthingtons' love of order. Unlike mosquitoes, deer flies, and horse flies, fish flies, at least, with their delicate oversized wings and filament tails, were harmless. I reached for one, its wings like pieces of etched glass. In protest, the fish fly wiggled its greenish elongated body, but I tossed it into the air, and it flew off.

I wasn't a Worthington. I couldn't pretend any longer. I had to find out who my mother was.

Who I was.

| 3 |

With the Worthingtons gone, I didn't bother to get out of bed
the next morning. I drifted in and out of a dark sleep, without a
reason to get up, with the photographs strewn across my quilt.
If I was neither their servant nor their daughter, then what did
that make me? A pet? I'd been forbidden to leave the house.
What did they think would happen if they granted me a little
freedom—that I'd go wild and wayward like my mother?

Yet I remembered now the softness of Mama's hands, the
way she brushed back my hair. Mama's voice was gentle and
steady. "My sweet Sadie Rose," she used to say to me. I could almost hear the pitch, like reverberations that follow long after a
piano chord is struck.

I remembered then...when the man left the boardinghouse, I'd sprung to my feet like a broom-swept mouse...

*Beyond the parlor, the door to Darla's room was closed.
When she locked her rolltop desk and went to bed, visiting
hours were finally over.*

*Desperate to see Mama, I darted upstairs, down
the hallway, and turned the glass knob to our bedroom.
Through the lace curtains, the street lamp cast a gray light.
Everything appeared the same.*

The ceramic washbasin and pitcher rested on the wash-stand.

Bedsheets gathered in rumpled waves.

But the quilt rack stood bare.

And Mama was gone.

Like flames, panic burst in me and I flew down the stair-case, nearly falling headfirst on the last step. Then I raced into the kitchen, pushed back the curtain, and scraped a hole with my fingernails in the frost-laced window.

I peered out.

The man trudged across the railroad tracks and into the blowing snow, shouldering the quilt, bulky as a sack of potatoes.

Pushing my fist to my lips, I cried into my flesh. "Mama!"

From a peg by the kitchen door, I yanked my hooded coat and pulled it over my nightdress. I searched for my boots but couldn't find them. Instead, I stepped into Ma-ma's leather lace-ups and stumbled out the back door and down the steps. With my feet pushed forward into the toe of each boot, I picked up speed, following footprints that the wind was quickly erasing.

A knock on my bedroom door sent the photos flying from my hands and across the rug. Flustered, I scrambled out of bed, gathered the photos, hid them under my pillow, and opened the door.

"Sadie?" Aasta asked. Though white haired and in her mid-fifties, she carried herself straight and tall. "I worry you sick? Staying in your room long time?" With the boldness more of a parent than domestic help, she peered into my room. "Maybe, I think, you're hiding young man?" She winked at me. "Ya?"

I shook my head in protest, but, unwilled, a smile climbed to my lips. She had a gift for that. Over the years, she'd left unexpected notes. Once, when I'd overslept—and Mrs. Worthington scorned anyone who slept past seven—I heard the rustle of a note under my bedroom door. It read, "Greet the day! No moments get away!" or the time when I'd failed my mathematics exam given by that terrible tutor and Aasta had handed me a card: "Life rewards cat who catches mice, not those that count them." In my earlier years, when Mrs. Worthington turned the task of disciplining over to Aasta, I would follow Aasta into the kitchen with my head down, as if in dread. Then Aasta would take out the wooden spoon and smack it across the potholders on the countertop.

"The Worthingtons asked me to stay here with you, but I must go early in the morning. I am asked to help on Red Stone Island. Thelma, the cook, she's worried. Ennis has big banquet." Aasta ironed her skirts with her palms, as if to ready herself for the upcoming event. "Hans will walk me to landing early and bright in the morning. Now, I'm going home for a bit, but you don't worry. I'll be back to make dinner."

I grabbed my slate board with trembling hands, spotting an opportunity, and quickly wrote: "Red Stone? Is that near Falcon Island?"

Aasta shrugged. "I just go where boat takes me. But ya, Falcon is near Red Stone, I think."

Again, I scribbled quickly. "Tomorrow—may I go with you and help?"

Aasta laughed. "Silly girl," she said, in her singsong accent, her hands on her hips. "You may be orphan, but the Worthingtons—they would not be for you working there."

I realized I was tapping my bare foot on the floor and clenching my fists at my sides, the way I used to as a child when I wanted to speak out and the words wouldn't come. I stopped myself and wrote firmly on my slate: "I can't be stuck inside here all day or I'll go crazy!"

Aasta studied me, as if by doing so she would uncover the real reasons. I held my breath, afraid the answer would be a resounding "No." What I couldn't tell her was that I wanted to know more about my mother and that I couldn't do that staying holed up like a mole.

Then Aasta tilted her head.

"Sadie, Sadie. You know I love you like you are my own. But if I say ya, you promise it is secret?"

I sniffed so loudly, it came out as a snort, and I almost laughed out loud.

"Okay, then. We'll take the six o'clock boat. I'll wake you at five, and you must wear the sensible shoes and work clothes and kerchief. I'll bring extra apron. Thelma will like more helping hands. But if Mr. Ennis finds out, he will tell Worthingtons. They would not be happy."

I nodded and smiled.

"Now I must go to Jensen's Creamery. They need butter at Red Stone. How can they run short of butter! Imagine."

I scribbled on my slate. "I'll go to the creamery for you. May I?" I hoped Aasta would bend on this simple request and added, "Please?"

To my surprise, she replied, "Ya. Okay then."

I jumped up and squeezed her hands in mine. Mrs. Worthington wouldn't be pleased that Aasta had bent the rules, but I couldn't have been happier.

The moment I stepped beyond the fenced yard, I began to breathe easier. It wasn't as if I wore a corset like Mrs. Worthington—thank God—but my life had been constrained. Suddenly I longed for a shorter dress, or pants, and not the petticoat and skirt that reached to just above my ankles. The navy cotton was loose but hot, and my heeled boots much too warm for a summer day. But at least I was free to walk to the creamery!

I was ready to taste freedom. And why not? Things were changing for women. I'd read in the *International Falls Press* and in the *St. Paul Pioneer Press* that the Suffrage movement was getting closer to its goals. Just this month the Senate passed the Nineteenth Amendment. Now, if it gets ratified by the states, women could be voting as early as fall for the next president. Away with corsets! Time for changes! That women would be treated equally under the law was only right, but it was taking forever! I had been hearing names like Susan B. Anthony, Elizabeth Cady Stanton, and Alice Paul for a long time. And alongside them, thousands of ordinary women were taking part in demonstrations, picketing the White House, and going to jail. One woman even chained herself to a courthouse door in Minneapolis, just to make a point.

And me? I almost wanted to laugh. Women might soon have the right to *vote*, but here I was, stealing the right to *walk* alone.

I loved every step of the way. I turned left at the town hall, strode past the bank and its stained-glass half-moon windows. A man in a suit tipped his hat as I passed by. "Good morning, Miss," he said.

I nodded slightly and smiled in return.

Seagulls sounded their melancholy cries, riding warm air currents as I continued down Main Street, past the general store, the White Turtle Club, and Ranier's post office.

Several taverns lined the streets, but fewer than in the past. Mr. Worthington prided himself in cleaning up Ranier after taking me in. "There were more brothels than houses," he'd say, "but during my time as mayor, we changed that."

I'd learned many of his stump phrases by heart: "Good citizens must stand up or be trampled by the corrupt." Or the shortened version: "Stand up or be trampled!"

As I crossed the railroad tracks, I pretended not to notice the boardinghouse on my left, now called Callahan's Tavern. I glanced at the gray clapboard, streaked by rust-bleeding nails. And then I forced myself to look up—up to the corner window where I'd once gazed out, half expecting my mother to peer back at me, but the windows were boarded up. At Darla's I'd heard the girls called all kinds of things: *clipper, fancy lady, lady of the night, prostitute,* and *red skirt*—since they wore red skirts around town. When I'd asked Mama once to sew me a red skirt, too, she shook me by my shoulders. "You will *never* wear a red skirt!" I'd run from her room, crying at her meanness.

"Outta the way!" someone shouted.

A horse-pulled wagon startled me, and I jumped back. I didn't realize I'd stopped to stare. As the wagon drove on, I noticed the raven he'd tried to avoid. The black bird fluffed its feathers, wings extended as it returned to pecking at its small decaying treasure.

I rounded the corner by Lou's Trading Post and Erickson's Fine Grocery, where three dogs slept in the shade of the green awning, and then stepped into the squat brick building of Jensen's Creamery. Empty milk crates were stacked to the ceiling. Behind a small counter, a chalkboard stated prices for cheese, cream, and milk (delivered and wholesale).

I rang the little brass bell and waited, studying the colorful flyer on the counter: *The One, the Only, Robinson's Touring Circus! Coming Soon!* Before I could give it more thought, the swinging doors opened.

From the warehouse stepped Owen Jensen, no longer a pudgy boy, but more of a man, especially in the plaid-shirt attire of so many northern men.

"Hey, Sadie Rose!" His brown eyes brightened as if we knew each other well, which was hardly the case, and his lips widened into a smile that—to my surprise—warmed me to my toes. He'd become lanky and oddly good-looking. I'd seen him before on the city bus ride between Ranier and International Falls—I sat in front, he always rode toward the back—and at the public library I'd spotted him with his wavy reddish hair bent over out-of-town newspapers. Job-hunting, I'd decided.

He was a year or two older than I was. I stared at his Adam's apple that jutted from his long, tan neck—then forced myself to look away.

"Can I help you?"

I nodded, and my face heated with embarrassment.

He thumped the circus flyer. "Hey, did you see this? Coming next week. You gonna go?"

I lifted my eyebrows and shrugged.

"You know, Sadie Rose, I've always wondered why you weren't in school. I mean, I know you can't talk, but—I guess it's something I've always wanted to ask you . . ."

Heat rushed to my face again. I stood there, scolding myself for not tucking the slate board into my shoulder bag. I lifted a pencil from a holder and raised it. I'd felt so at ease with Victor, so why did being with Owen feel so different? It was as if bees had taken up lodging in my head, making it hard to think.

"Here," he said, handing me a scrap of paper from a pile. "You can write on this."

Owen Jensen was a local boy. I shouldn't feel so nervous. I wrote, quite simply: "Twelve pounds of butter, please."

"Yeah, got it. That's a lotta butter. What are ya gonna do with all that? Bake ten wedding cakes?"

I scrunched up my nose.

"Oh, there's a lady who bakes wedding cakes, and she's always needing extra butter in the summer months."

I scribbled quickly: "Aasta needs to take it to Red Stone tomorrow."

"Tell ya what, I'll do one better. I'll make a note of it and run it out there tomorrow first thing. I've started doing extra deliveries with my boat. Some of those rich folks on the lake, people complain they don't tip, but they seem to loosen up their wallets soon as I start talking about my college plans."

College.

I liked the sound of that word.

"Besides, you don't want all that butter to melt on your way home." He turned to an ordering pad and scribbled something down. "Well, I have to clean out the milk coolers, so if you don't mind. I'll run your order out there tomorrow. Promise."

I mouthed the words "Thank you, Owen." And I half-wondered if he was just finding an excuse to possibly see me again.

He smiled, gave me a polite nod, then disappeared back into the creamery.

As I headed back, I almost wanted to skip. Owen Jensen. He'd stirred up some sweet warmth in me. And he'd treated me—not just as the Worthingtons' responsibility—but as me. Asking Aasta to run her errand had been a fine, fine, fine idea.

I returned toward the railroad tracks, where a cluster of workers now gathered, wielding sledge hammers and spikes. Ear-ringing clangs of steel upon steel stopped as I neared. I felt eyes following me.

The sun beat down, and the pungent smell of creosote pitch wafted up. With each step, the acrid smell became stronger, burning my nostrils.

And then one of the men wolf-whistled.

I kept my focus on the road, on my footing. I didn't want to get my heels caught in the crevices between the smooth steel. My instincts told me to keep moving.

Another crooned, "Oh, I'd love to jump that little caboose, eh?"

"She's a little vixen, that's what."

"Sweetie, got time for a dime?"

Their chuckles followed me as I walked on. I wasn't wearing anything provocative or inviting. I certainly wasn't wearing a red skirt. And yet, how quickly they'd made me feel ... dirty ... vulnerable. I wanted to say something, to tell them to mind their own business. I wanted to run home, but instead I swallowed hard, my throat parched, and walked on, head high—like a proper young lady.

I would never want Mama's life.

I wanted freedom, to keep learning, and to study music.

And to do that, I needed to go to college. And then ... I could become independent and make my own choices. I wouldn't have to wait on the whims of the Worthingtons. I could dream of performing someday as a classical pianist—or, at the very least, becoming a music teacher.

College.

It made perfect sense.

But the word floated by, out of grasp, with the dreamy improbability of a fairy tale. Owen Jensen, the son of a creamery operator, could dream of college, but what about the daughter of a red skirt?

| 4 |

When I stepped inside, the walls pressed in around me like cage bars. I paced from the piano up to my bedroom to the screened-in porch and back again, my mind drifting. Memories or imaginings flooded in...

The man was somewhere ahead, hidden in the pale night of swirling flakes.

The street was empty. Wind whipped through town and turned everything white: the boardwalk and taverns, the two-story boardinghouses that lined Ranier's dirt road, the piles of horse dung, the simple houses of fishermen, the train idling beside the depot. I leaned into the barbed wind and hurried on to the end of the block. Briefly sheltered by the bank building, I glanced up at its new bricks and a half-moon window of stained glass.

Across the snowdrifts, snow snakes hurtled at me, whirling, white, and hissing. My toes and hands turned numb, and my teeth chattered without stop. I pulled up my hood, but the wind yanked it from my grip and shrieked in my ears, scolding me for being outside and alone on such a night.

"Mama!" I cried, lips nearly too stiff for speech.

But only the wind answered.

Ahead, the man appeared, a shadow of black and white, then melted again into the storm.

A trickle of sweat ran under my camisole and between my breasts, bringing me back to June. I was sixteen. Yet my heart raced with remembering.

I followed but tripped in deepening snow and fell. Snow filled my cuffs and iced my wrists. I glanced back toward the boardinghouse, but the bank building had already faded into the storm. On hands and knees I crawled, head down, to a hollow in a snowdrift, a welcoming cave of quiet. I hunched into a ball—a tiny, tiny ball—making myself smaller and smaller, curled into myself until tears iced against the rough wool of my coat, curled in the whiteness...and slept.

I floated high above myself, my woolen coat covered by snow. Above the drifts and outside the town hall building, I looked on as a man dropped his shovel and fell to his knees beside the white mound that was me—and not me.

Mama was calling my name, "Sadie Rose...," and I saw her in the whiteness of clouds above, but just as swiftly her image disappeared, while I was caught somewhere between the cottony sky and the snowbanks below.

The memories, sharp as driving sleet, left me raw and exhausted. What I did remember with certainty was that in those early days, when Mr. Worthington was mayor and we stayed year-round in Ranier, Elizabeth Worthington had kept watch over me—in this same bedroom, pacing....

"There, there Sadie Rose," she'd said back then, squeezing icy water from a cloth and placing it on my burning forehead. "You're moaning again for your mama. Poor child. Sleep."

And I slept. Through days and nights. Sometimes I woke to think it was morning, but the house was still, except for the wheezing and rumbling in my chest.

Some days Mrs. Worthington came with Dr. Stedman. Seated on the bed's edge, he pressed his cool stethoscope to my chest and listened. When my eyes were open, I stared at the blotchy red birthmark on his cheek.

As he attended me, Mrs. Worthington swished past the window in her taffeta skirt, her corseted body sending shadows across my pillow. Ebony combs held her fine salty-brown hair in fashionable rolls and puffs. She leaned in closer to us. Her eyebrows were perfectly shaped, high and arching; in the heart-shaped face, her brown eyes seemed large. "Doctor, she's getting so thin—and she hasn't said a word. Isn't it strange that she hasn't said a word?"

The doctor peered with a scope into my ears and throat, then flattened my tongue with a device and said, "Say, 'Ah.'" But only a murmur came from the back of my throat.

After days and weeks of slipping in and out of a fever and coughing up chunks of blood-tinted phlegm into the washbasin, I began to recover.

One afternoon, Mrs. Worthington had pulled a chair close. "Sadie Rose, it will almost be like I'm your mother, but it's best that you call me 'Mrs. Worthington.'" She softened her voice. "That is, if you can talk . . . someday."

When I found enough energy to climb one morning from the high four-poster twin bed, I walked carefully down the staircase, hand on the rail. Like a tiny bird whose feathers had been soaked through after a rainstorm, I wasn't sure I could trust my limbs to carry me.

I crossed the dining room, with its cherry-wood table and matching chairs, toward the smell of fresh-baked bread beyond, wondering if I was at another boardinghouse.

Where I had lived with Mama, the kitchen always produced good smells, from cured hams to corn muffins to blueberry pancakes and sausages. Mama always said, "At least here we don't go hungry." I could picture Mama's smile, the tilt of her head, and her thick brown hair. But even in a smile, I always saw it—a hint of sadness in her eyes. It was the part of the smile that I wished I could change.

I pushed on the swinging door and stepped in.

Two women turned from a sheet of paper on a massive cutting block.

"Oh, Sadie Rose!" Mrs. Worthington clapped her hands and then held them together, fingers pointed heavenward. "Why, what a surprise! This means you're mending at last. Can you say 'Good Morning'?"

I opened my mouth to try, but nothing came out. Not even a whisper of words. How could I have forgotten to speak? I tried again, thinking my throat must be dry. But the words I knew in my brain started on a journey to my lips and somehow got lost along the way. Tears came to my eyes. If Mrs. Worthington ran her boardinghouse the same way Darla had run hers, then I better not start blubbering, or I might be asked to "pack up and leave."

"There now," said Mrs. Worthington, taking a careful step closer. "Don't worry. The doctor thinks you may have suffered some loss, but he's confident time will restore you to complete health. And this," she said, with an extended arm toward a woman as tall and lean as a signpost, "is our new cook and housekeeper, Aasta Johannsen."

A full foot taller than Mrs. Worthington, Aasta was a statuesque woman. "Once Mr. Worthington and I decided to take you in, Sadie Rose, we needed more help. The Johannsens come from Norway."

I knew enough about manners to curtsy but felt too

weak to do anything more than meet Aasta's eyes, which were blue jay–feather blue in her narrow face.

A late March wind rattled the kitchen window. I walked away from the women toward the frosty panes and looked out. Clattering and rattling, a train with endless boxcars crossed the lift bridge into Ranier. Seagulls cruised over plates of gray ice and open water where the lake and river met.

In a hushed voice, Mrs. Worthington whispered, "You know, Aasta, I've asked him to consider adoption. He agrees it's our Christian duty to give her a home, but he's not willing to go any further than that—at least for now. But I think with time, he'll come around."

"Vel—good she be here," Aasta said, looking my way.

"The seagulls have returned!" Mrs. Worthington exclaimed with forced cheeriness. "Spring can't be too far away now!"

I glanced down at my new nightgown. Across its top someone had embroidered tiny pink tulips on white fabric that ended in a ruffle at the floor. On my feet, I wore blue wool stockings. Someone had taken away my old clothes and dressed me.

"You can thank Aasta for the socks. And that's my touch on the nightdress." Mrs. Worthington smiled and clasped her hands, one over the other.

I knew that good manners required I say thank you, but my lack of words turned me suddenly shy. And everything was strangely different. I wanted the cookstove at Darla's kitchen, not this cream-colored enamel one. But I couldn't resist standing near its warmth.

"She smart one," said Aasta. "She knows what she wants." She placed her hands on the hips of her lanky frame and shook her head. "Poor girl."

"It's sinful." Mrs. Worthington spoke to Aasta. "God should have intervened long ago. Someone should have taken the child out of that house."

I shot a slit-eyed glance at Mrs. Worthington's long skirt and pointed shoes and decided she would never, ever replace my real mother. I knew in that moment what I wanted—more than anything in the whole world—the one who had whispered to me from somewhere beyond the sky.

| 5 |

A dense morning fog blanketed the village, as Hans chaperoned us to the docks. Though many women went about their errands without an escort, Mr. Worthington had insisted that the females in *his* household—no matter their social status—must always be escorted. I glanced sideways at Aasta, grateful for allowing me yesterday's freedom to walk to the creamery.

Now, not only was I getting away from the cottage, but Owen had promised to deliver butter to Red Stone Island. The idea of seeing him sent a rush of anticipation through me. And I ached with wanting to ask him more about college—about where he'd go and what he'd study—even if I couldn't see a path yet for myself.

A terrible smell hit my nose. Outside the bank building, a skunk-sprayed mutt rested on the new boardwalk, pawing at his snout. He lifted his head as we walked wide around him. "Poor dog," Hans said.

"Poor us," Aasta said, squeezing her nose.

At the end of Main Street, beyond the corner grocery store and trading post, a small crowd gathered near the docks. An Ojibwa family hovered near a canoe loaded with birch-bark baskets, beaded necklaces, and moccasins, ready to sell or trade. On the mother's back, a baby slept in a cradleboard, the carrier's exterior intricately stitched in tiny blue and red beads. I met the woman's eyes, sharing something unspoken. I waved and she waved in return. Nearby, a young boy and girl played on the strip of sandy shore as their father adjusted his bowler hat over his weather-etched face, watching the growing crowd of passengers.

Several yards distant, two young women in traveling skirts and lacy parasols chatted and giggled. Tourists, I guessed, from Minneapolis or Chicago along with the dozen businessmen in suits clustered together, their valises set off to the side in a neat row. One of them, a rotund fellow with a cane, glanced disapprovingly at the Ojibwa family. But he needn't worry. The Ojibwa sometimes showed up by canoe at our cottage and asked for medicine, or meat, or fishing line. The Worthingtons never handled such encounters, leaving such visits to Hans and Aasta, who gave the Indians what they needed. Later, in return, the Indians came back with blueberries, wild rice, venison, or fresh fish. There was no asking, no cowering, just a simple sharing. More than once, I'd sat silently drinking tea with them in the kitchen. But that wasn't something freshly imported tourists or businessmen would understand about life here.

When a deckhand, no older than I, clomped down the wooden ramp from the *Emma Louise,* the small crowd steered toward the two-story passenger boat. It looked so top-heavy that any breeze might tip it over. But looks are deceiving. Several times over the past decade, I had ridden safely on the *Emma Louise,* sightseeing with the Worthingtons. We always sat above on red-cushioned seats, with a commanding view and drinks served in glasses with ice harvested and stored from the lake's frozen season.

Now I followed behind Aasta, wearing a cotton scarf and keeping my head low. I needed to appear like a regular worker. I didn't want questions about why I was going to Red Stone, and I intentionally had left my slate board behind. My plan was to stay clear of Mr. Ennis and stick to the kitchen. I could barely contain my excitement about the chance to go to one of the islands.

I settled in beside Aasta on the boat's lower level, on a long wooden bench filled with lower-class passengers. When my shoulder touched hers, she didn't edge away from me, so unlike the Worthingtons.

The boat's horn sounded—one long blast, two short—signaling to other boats that it was getting under way. I filled my lungs with the moist air, closed my eyes, and listened to water slosh alongside the boat.

"*Vel,*" Aasta said, tidying loose strands that escaped her braids and then withdrawing knitting needles and yarn from her satchel. She handed me a pair of needles and a skein of blue yarn. "Maybe you want to knit?"

I accepted the yarn and needles. I could always start another scarf, at least for practice, though I'd never be the wizard at knitting that Aasta was. In Aasta's free time, she knitted mittens, socks, hats, scarves, and sweaters with patterns of moose, snowflakes, and stars. To be that good, you had to come from Norway and start knitting from birth.

Sitting beside me, Aasta moved her wooden needles back and forth, in and out, creating an arm of a gray wool sweater. "For Hans," she said, "if I ever finish it. *Vel,* seems we're on a little adventure this morning, ya?"

I smiled and nodded.

The boat cut through glassy waters, skirted an inside channel, and stopped at island estates to leave off passengers. Workers, as well as aristocracy, descended the plank.

Crossing an island-dotted channel, the steamer rocked back and forth as a breeze kicked up ruffled waves. I rose and held on to a post, gazing out at a cluster of islands.

"The Review Islands," said a boy of ten or eleven with suspenders over too-short trousers. He paused by our railing and pointed to a cluster of small islands. "That Goober guy who wants to close down the paper mills—he lives on that one!"

I tapped his back and he turned. I mouthed, "Who?"

"Goober. Gutten-something. That guy nobody likes."

I raised my eyebrows in question and mouthed, "Where?"

"The island with the cabin on the end," the boy said.

Falcon Island was a small pencil of land, its eastern edge a whaleback of granite, with a two-story cabin nestled in pine and spruce.

Then as the boat veered right, the boy hung over the rail and pointed toward the bow. "And that's Red Stone Island— King Ed's," the boy went on. "And sure as snot, he's got a cannon there. I ain't lyin'."

I knew better and rolled my eyes.

"I ain't! Heard him say he'd like to point his cannon that way and blow Falcon Island to kingdom come!" He imitated an explosion with a burst of his hands into the air and a puckering of his lips. "Boom!"

I peered toward our destination, then back across to the east and the pathway of shimmering water that led to Falcon Island. Victor Guttenberg's island was tiny in comparison to Red Stone Island. When I looked back toward E. W. Ennis's island, it was ten times as large, fitting for the lumber baron. A cluster of cabins and a large lodge crowned the high western shore.

I looked back at Falcon Island. Maybe Victor watched the sunrise each morning from the upper-story windows. I wondered if he was there now, and just in case, I waved.

"Who are you waving at?" Aasta chuckled. "A moose?"

I laughed, feeling caught in my silly musings, and then turned my gaze back to the water. A loon popped up only yards from the passenger boat, and then another, white spots covering their black bodies like countless stars. One started to sing; then the other took up its melancholy wail—lyrical and beautiful—filled with aching sadness. The song shivered through my body, down to my toes, and gave voice to my constant feeling of loneliness—of feeling on the outside, looking in—of never belonging. At least until yesterday, and crossing paths with both Victor and Owen.

The *Emma Louise* slowed her engine and cut to the Red Stone's north side, where a half-dozen docks greeted visitors. As the boat reversed and came to a stop, the captain called out, "Red Stone Island!"

From the dock, the island boasted a dozen buildings and a towering lodge, making Falcon Island look quaint as a dollhouse. The likelihood that Victor Guttenberg could stop the industrial plans of someone like E. W. Ennis seemed impossible—and I felt a pang of sympathy for Victor traveling in his canoe from his island home just to speak with Mr. Worthington. King Ed would no doubt consider Victor's efforts at stopping him laughable.

Aasta patted the seat beside her for me to sit back down. "We'll get off last."

Businessmen gathered their valises and carried them down the plank, only to be met by a troop of Red Stone porters. The young men seemed especially eager to help the two women with the white parasols.

"Allow me," said one teenage boy, doffing his cap.

"Ma'am," another said, bowing slightly, his long-sleeved shirt boasting the island's name, *Red Stone*.

"Certainly," said one of the women. The other giggled as they both lifted their skirts and headed from the dock and up a few steps to the island's shore.

"Trinity, it's like a jungle safari!"

"I told you, the island's complete with porters at your beck and call." She laughed. "It's the bee's knees!"

Their perfume smelled expensive, but it was no match for

the pine resin in the air. I breathed it in, pleased to be on an island of towering old trees. I had grown too used to seeing trees as logs, floating downriver to the mill. But here, on E. W. Ennis's island, ironically, the trees soared to the sky.

When I left the boat with Aasta, no porters greeted us as we stepped down the plank. This was my first visit, but the Worthingtons often boated off to gatherings on Red Stone Island. Now I could see the island for myself.

Alongside the dock, a cluster of water beetles skimmed the water, swirling and zipping. My palms became sweaty and my breath felt tight. I was stepping onto the island owned by E. W. Ennis—family friend—the man Victor was standing up to. A tight band circled my forehead and a fresh pain settled behind my eyes. I pressed the palm of my hand to my forehead, my brain swirling again.

"Sadie?" Aasta said, grabbing me by the wrist. "You're going to fall into the water! Remember, you're here as a worker. Workers are *never* idle."

Aasta turned and bustled up the stone steps to the wide path, trusting me to follow like a well-behaved dog. I nodded, adjusted my scarf, and walked after her.

I would settle in for a day of work, perhaps a life of kitchen work. If I couldn't dream of going to college, then I'd have to accept my life as it would be—with few options. But I wanted so badly to continue with my studies, my music. Not peel potatoes and hover over cook pots the rest of my life.

"No," I whispered, stunned to hear my own voice.

A voice with its own weight and substance.

My own voice.

Tears leapt to my eyes, and I covered my mouth with my hand.

| 6 |

I could barely contain myself as I worked, holding my secret close—to be shared at the right time. Soft cloth in hand, I looked around the Red Stone lodge as I polished silver. In the arch of the vaulted ceiling, a trophy moose head gazed beyond the stone hearth. Massive Oriental wool rugs covered floors. Tables, sofa legs, painting frames—everything—gleamed with fresh furniture polish. Mahogany chairs lined the table, long as a mill log. Modern electricity was something islanders had to do without; gas lamps around the lodge waited to be lit.

I set the silver spoon back in the blue velvet-lined drawer and wooden case. Already I'd peeled carrots, turning my fingernails orange.

"Done," I whispered to myself, and a thrill shot through me. It was true. The words I now willed to take voice were obeying. A miracle—nothing short of it. The Worthingtons would be amazed. Perhaps it would be enough to make them consider adopting me. If so, they would no doubt send me to college.

But for now, I reminded myself: *workers are never idle.*

I glanced through the small window of the kitchen's swinging door, where Aasta towered by several inches over the other staff. She was too busy to notice me. I stole a few moments, walked to the windows to gaze out. Large screened windows opened to a soft breeze and water. A dozen small fishing boats and larger commercial boats dotted the vast bay. I wondered if Owen was on his way, or if he'd made an earlier delivery and I'd missed him. When I saw him next, what would I say? I had no idea, but I would talk. We could have a conversation! I smiled, thinking about it.

"Sadie Rose!" Aasta whispered, tugging at my arm and startling me. "If you finished with your task, you must let me know then. I can't have you acting like . . . like the high society. And it not be good to get the questions about you. Please." She turned sharply on her sturdy shoes.

"I'm . . . sorry," I whispered to her back.

Aasta stopped with a halt, then turned slowly, her crossed arms dropped to the sides of her stained apron. Her eyebrows arched beneath her wrinkled forehead. "Sadie," she whispered. "Did you say something? Or do I lose my blessed mind?"

I nodded. "I'm sorry," I said again, this time the words coming out with more confidence.

Aasta's blue eyes filled with tears, and she placed her warm hands on either sides of my face. "Eleven years. Eleven years since you was found. Eleven years since you say a word! Oh, the biggest miracle! A blessed miracle! I never thought to see this day. They say you once chattered like little sparrow before you—"

I reached for Aasta's hand. I wanted to ask her more. Who'd told her about me once chattering? Someone from the boardinghouse? I tried to speak, but my words iced over. I mouthed Aasta's name, but my words were frozen. Was I to lose the gift of speech as soon as it had come back? My head felt thick and spongy as deep moss and pain needled the back of my eyes.

At the edge of my vision, a man loomed closer in a three-piece, pinstriped suit. I edged closer to Aasta as E. W. Ennis drew near us.

His height and broad shoulders matched those of a draft horse. Eyes the color of sky-tinted snow peered down at me from a broad, pink-sunburned face and well-set Roman nose. His breath wafted the hairs of my scalp and his cologne pinched my nose as he gripped my elbow in his pliers-like hand, not hard, but firmly enough to know I wasn't leaving without his say-so.

"Sadie Rose." His voice was commanding, warm, and frighteningly deep.

His hand steadied me, and for a moment I was glad. My vision turned fuzzy, something that happened from time to time since I was found in the snow. The doctor had said I'd outgrow it someday. I could only hope.

"I just stepped in and couldn't help but overhear. I'm not sure if I'm more stunned to find you here on Red Stone, posing as a maid, or that you have found your voice. I did hear you speak, isn't that so?" He looked to Aasta, as if she would confirm his conclusions.

Unable to contain her smile, she clasped her hands and held the flat of her thumbs to her lips and nodded silently.

I felt unsteady. Nauseous. I knew he expected me to answer, but I was speechless.

"Aasta," he continued, "I don't think the Worthingtons would like to know that Sadie Rose is working here, would they?"

"No, but Mr. Ennis, your cook she asked me to help, so I think Sadie Rose can come with me, just for the day."

"I see. I have no problem with your working here, Aasta, but I'm not sure that Walter and Elizabeth would like Sadie Rose acting like she needs to earn her keep. They have taken her in out of good Christian charity, not for her to be a servant."

I didn't understand why Mr. Ennis should be concerned if I helped out. Maybe he knew more than I did about the Worthingtons' intentions. Perhaps they were considering adoption after all.

"People may question their generosity...wonder why she's being forced to find paying work. It might not serve the senator well."

"Ya. I see." Aasta nodded.

"Escort her to the guest room on the north wing. We keep it open, for emergencies, someone gets sick, that sort of thing. And Sadie Rose," he said, patting my shoulder, "you do look a little pale. I suggest you stay there—rest—until Aasta is finished here today."

In the guest room of the Red Stone lodge, I napped and dreamed of a girl that was and wasn't me.

> *From her cave in the snow, she waited for the wind to stop. In her muted shelter, she felt contained. Safe. But she knew she couldn't stay long. She had to find her mama. She lifted her head for a quick look around. The jail building and meeting hall blended in with the white and whirling wind. And that's when she saw her mama, sleeping, facedown on the snow-covered sidewalk, the drift covering her bare legs like a warm blanket. Move, the girl told herself. You must get to Mama! But she couldn't move her fingers or toes, her arms or legs. Her whole body was immovable as stone.*

When I woke up, I lifted a washcloth off my eyes and expected to be in my bedroom. But then I remembered. I'd been ushered at Mr. Ennis's direction to the guest room. I lay with my head near the window, beneath a candy-striped blanket, and was startled to notice a young woman sitting across from me on the other twin bed.

Her hair was cut into a fashionable short bob, with waves

of pale blonde falling toward green eyes. She was one of the two young women from the *Emma Louise.*

"Hi," I heard myself say and lifted myself up on my elbow, amazed with the ease the word took shape and lifted into the air, but my head throbbed with the slightest movement, and I lay back down again.

"You're not feeling well?" The young woman leaned forward, and I recognized the soft perfume and smell of fresh soap from earlier on the boat. "Aasta, that's the woman's name, yes? She told me you're supposed to rest. So you're the girl the Worthingtons took in years ago? I met you once, but I doubt you remember me—a Fourth of July party with lots of people. You were quite absorbed in a book, as I recall, as if nothing else in the world mattered." She laughed, her voice sweet and clear—and a little too loud for my throbbing head—and chatted on.

"Well, you're to be in my care until Aasta's done with the banquet." Unlike many well-to-do women, this young woman's face was unusually tan from the summer sun. She apparently didn't believe in living under parasols or indoors to protect an ivory complexion.

"I'm not sure I'm the best chaperone," she said, with a wag of her finger, "but I'll try." She laughed and jumped up, her dress strikingly short—all the way up to her knees. She must have changed clothes on the island. Mrs. Worthington wouldn't approve of her flapper style, but I envied how daring it looked. "I'm nineteen—only a few years older than you. So frankly, I'm not sure I'll be the best influence on you. But I promised to look in on you."

"Your name?" I asked, stunned again at my own voice, at its timbre and that it rose from my throat into real words.

"Trinity Baird," she replied, then lifted an eyebrow into an exquisite arch. "But I always thought you *didn't* speak. Guess I was wrong. So a little about me. I summer on a nearby island with my family, who, quite frankly, are dreadfully boring."

She shrugged her shoulders. "Say," she began, leaning closer conspiratorially, "maybe you and I—once you're feeling better, that is—maybe we might try our hand at friendship. I have two older sisters, and when they come home to visit all they want to do is sip tea, embroider, and make plans for their weddings. Me? I just learned to *dive* this summer! And not just from the end of a dock, mind you, but from cliffs here on the lake. It makes your blood turn cold, but when you fall through the air for those thirty feet—it's almost like flying." She spoke briskly, and my head continued to tighten and pound, trying to keep up with her. With everything.

"Speaking of flying, you know that I met the Wright brothers in person, and Wilbur took me on a short spin? It was swell! I'm telling the God's honest truth, even though when I was at the hospital they tried to tell me I'd just imagined it. But—oh. I see from your expression you probably don't believe a word of what I'm saying, but I'm serious about the flying. And diving, too. Victor Guttenberg taught me."

My mind caught on his name like a hook. How coincidental that I'd just met him.

"But, oh, maybe that kind of adventure doesn't appeal to you at all. It's just that I've heard rumors that you're a little unusual, too, and well, I'm not exactly what my parents always want me to be either, and I thought—"

My eyelids felt heavy.

"Oh, I'm sorry," Trinity continued. "Here you're not feeling well and I'm chitchatting away. But I've been so unbelievably bored, you *cannot* imagine. So do forgive me. And my cousin who traveled north with me, well, you might as well put an anchor around my foot and drop me off the end of a boat. She's just *that* much fun."

I felt a smile spread across my face and I laughed, which made my head hurt more.

"Well, finally, a sign of life!" Trinity exclaimed, as if she were a midwife who had just wrestled an emerging baby from the womb and delivered it into the world of the living.

| 7 |

Trinity left, and I drifted in and out of sleep. When the clattering of pots and dishes and the murmuring voices died away, and mosquitoes buzzed in their evening chorus outside the screen, Aasta returned.

"Sadie Rose," she said, standing beside the bed. "It's time we go home then."

I eased my legs out from under the blanket and sat on the edge of the bed.

Aasta brushed the back of her hand across my forehead. "The steamer will be here soon." As I began to stand, the sharp pain behind my eyes returned, and I squeezed my eyes shut.

"Sit. Let me rebraid your hair. It's not good." She undid my braid, then started over again, tightening the braid as she talked. "I feel bad you get such pain. Lucky Mr. Ennis didn't get a doctor. Then word of your being here will fly like bird to Worthingtons. Now," she said, standing and examining my appearance, "we better go, ya?"

Along with the other workers, we boarded the *Emma Louise* for the mainland. And as we settled on our bench and the steamer pulled into the open water, I looked back at Red Stone. On the island's high western edge sat a black cannon. It appeared to be aimed directly at Falcon Island across the bay. The deckhand boy had been telling the truth after all.

I knit, mostly to please Aasta, and tried to imagine life on my own. In the past two days, I'd lived more than I had in the past eleven years. It was as if I'd been asleep and was for the first time awakening to the world around me.

As the steamer chugged across a quiet lake of golds and blues, seagulls hovered above the boat's frothy wake. From the top deck, passengers flung chunks of bread, which seagulls caught in midair. I thought of some of the village children who would be grateful for extra bread…and I might easily have been one of them. The Worthingtons had scraped me off the streets. Every day under their roof, I'd felt I owed them for my very existence…but how could I ever repay such a debt?

I looped the thin yarn of blue wool over the tips of my knitting needles, adding to the stubby beginnings of a scarf. Aasta had heard me speak, and yet she sat there knitting, as if it hadn't happened. We rode in silence and I was glad.

As we traveled west toward the descending sun, light threw shards on the water, blindingly bright. Everything was too sharp, too vivid. I let my eyes close and rested my head on Aasta's shoulder.

A few passengers away, two kitchen women spoke. "Y'know, Dimples, the circus is coming next week. Gonna have to dip into my penny jar to take the kids."

The woman named Dimples replied, "Oh, my kids would never forgive me if we didn't go. It's the highlight of our year!"

Eyes closed, my first and only circus played out before me. It was the summer after I'd been taken in. The Worthingtons drove their automobile—though it was surely close enough to walk—and parked in the field across from the railroad tracks. Smells of dung and sweat rose over the trampled, dusty dirt.

Robinson's Touring Circus returned every year by train, and villagers wore the anticipation on their faces of something exciting about to unfold. I'd gripped Mrs. Worthington's hand as we were swept in with the crowd and past the ringmaster, who shouted, "Death-defying feats! Superb artists! The Wonders of the World brought to your door!"

But when a clown clomped toward our wooden bleacher, I became terrified. His shoes were too long, his nose too red, his white face and painted red smile too scary. I'd started crying, and Mrs. Worthington leaned over and said, "It's just a clown, Sadie Rose. Clowns are friendly—and funny. He won't hurt you." And I had cried all the harder, until Mr. Worthington, who sat on the opposite side, eventually backhanded my head. "Stop that. This is a circus. None of that blubbering now. We're going to enjoy ourselves."

And I'd stopped, stinging from his reprimand. But despite the lone elephant doing its tricks on a small green platform, despite the vendors selling popcorn and peanuts, despite the glittering trapeze artists swaying overhead from ring to ring and bringing "Oohs" and "Ahhhs" from the audience, despite the ballerina-style riders in sequins and pink ribbons on white horses...all I wanted was to go home. After that, with each passing year, I'd stayed away.

But this year could be different.

As the steamer neared Ranier's docks, I already knew who might be the perfect companion. Trinity. Our new wall phone at the cottage was a party line. Islanders did not have such conveniences. But I could post a letter and send it to her. Perhaps she would reply via the mail boat. A thrill danced through me.

When we returned, I sat with Aasta and Hans in the kitchen.

"Sadie," Hans said, "Aasta tells me you can talk."

I smoothed my floral cotton dress across my thighs and nodded. "Yes," I said softly.

He jumped up, pulled out his chair, and with one hand on the chair back, danced a little jig around the chair. "That's wonderful! I knew you could. I always say to Aasta, just you wait and see. Someday, someday!"

"Hans, settle yourself," Aasta scolded. "You scare Sadie when you act like silly child."

Hans sat down and exaggeratedly folded his hands in his lap and bowed his head.

I chuckled.

And then Hans started to laugh and Aasta joined in as well. There were few times when I could remember enjoying their company as much. Even so, the day left me exhausted, and I excused myself to my bedroom.

The next day, as Aasta was doing lunch dishes and Hans was busily repairing a lamp, Victor Guttenberg came knocking. At the sound, I rose from the piano just as Aasta opened the swinging door from the kitchen. "I'll answer," I whispered.

Aasta smiled back, and I knew she was as happy to hear my voice as I was to use it. But now with Victor, I clammed up, unsure that I could trust my voice, and grabbed my slate board and chalk.

Aasta—bless her—returned to the kitchen.

"Good morning, Sadie Rose," Victor said from the other side of the screen door. "Is Mr. Worthington at home?"

I shook my head, then wrote on the slate board. "He will return Friday evening."

"Oh, I thought—I heard there was a meeting yesterday on Red Stone, and I assumed... Sorry to disturb you. Friday then." He turned and strode down the walkway to the dock, where his canoe was tied.

A train rumbled as it started across the lift bridge.

With an impulse new to me, I followed him to the dock. He undid the ropes from the cleats, stepped lightly into his canoe, and pushed off.

Then he looked at me, standing above on the dock. What did I want? I couldn't name it. But an urgency built in my chest.

"What is it?"

My shoulders scrunched up. I opened my mouth to speak, but my voice was gone. I shook my head and turned to the slate crooked in my arm. I scribbled the words quickly. I turned the board to show him what I'd written.

A fish stirred the water at the dock's end.

He read it aloud, squinting, "Ah, what does that say? Can I—um—come with you?" Then he studied me, from my bare toes and navy skirt, to the crisscrossed ties of my ivory blouse. "With me?" he asked, tilting his head.

I nodded.

"I'm not sure I should say yes, but why should I say no, either?" he mused aloud. "And you don't speak?"

I didn't move but held myself in check, afraid at what I'd begun. What if he misread my intentions? And what were my intentions? Yet there was something about Victor that made me trust him. As if he belonged to no particular class, no particular group, but moved through life as a genuinely free person.

"Your parents aren't home," he said, dropping his voice to just above a whisper, apparently understanding that voices travel across water. A conversation on the lake could be heard a far distance away. "And I don't want to get you in trouble. So tell me. Why do you want to join me?"

I wondered if Aasta and Hans were watching me now from the house. If so, with the train's clanking and droning as it crossed into Canada, they wouldn't be able to hear Victor. More likely, they weren't watching at all.

With the hem of my skirt, I brushed away the white chalk

from the board and wrote again. "To leave here and canoe for a few hours only." This time I wrote smaller, the letters tight and sharply cursive.

"Fair enough," he said. "And I need to practice my arguments. I'll make you a deal, Sadie Rose. You sit in the bow and pretend to listen. If you do that, I'll paddle until you say to turn back."

He paddled back alongside the dock and motioned me in. "Now, keep your weight low and centered, or you'll tip us."

When I'd settled on the cane seat, facing the bow, Victor began to whistle a tune from behind. I sat, head high, and gripped the sides of the birch-bark canoe.

"Do you swim?" he asked.

I glanced back and shrugged. I swam, but I was sure I wasn't the kind of swimmer Trinity must be with her ability to dive off tall cliffs.

"Well, then, I'll do my best to keep us upright. If we should go over, just grab for the canoe. But I'll try to be just like the Voyageurs. You know, the Hudson Bay Company used to hire men who couldn't swim—figured they'd take fewer risks that way with valuable cargo."

I nodded, happily expecting to be given many mini-lessons as we went.

Behind us, the Worthingtons' cottage—gambrel roof, wrap-around screen porch, and its carefully planted tulip garden and hedges of lilacs—gradually shrank away. I wanted to feel the cottage was mine, too—but it wasn't. Still, it was the closest thing to *home* I had. I vowed to return soon, so as to not disgrace the Worthingtons. I owed them that much.

A slip of the paddle sent droplets of water along the back of my neck and blouse, and I laughed out loud. A laugh, such a simple thing, and yet this was new for me. I smiled at the sound of it.

"So you can laugh, but you don't speak . . . ," Victor said.

I almost told him about my recent discovery, but I didn't yet have it in me to try to explain or to talk freely. I shrugged again, letting his words hang in the air, unanswered.

He paddled on under the lift bridge as the Duluth, Winnipeg, & Pacific train creaked and rumbled overhead. The DW&P was the pride of Mr. Worthington and E. W. Ennis. It started running in 1909, the same year the Worthingtons had taken me in. I'd looked on when they'd cut the red ribbon at the lift bridge and cracked a bottle of champagne on the tracks. I recalled the smell of lavender from Mrs. Worthington's perfume. "You and I are more alike than you know," she'd said. "We wait for things to turn our way."

If I just waited for things to turn my way, then what? She'd shown me that path, and it left her life in her husband's hands. Mrs. Worthington claimed she wanted to adopt me, but he was against it, and so...I was stuck between worlds. Limbo. I had grown accustomed to an educated life, to music and culture, and yet if I wasn't adopted, I had no hope of continuing my schooling. And what kind of work could I expect—a mute from a questionable background? But now...now that I could speak...

Water droplets occasionally struck me, but they dried quickly in the warm air. As Victor whistled, he kept beat with his paddle in the water. I glanced back and watched. The flat of the paddle cut through the air, parallel to the water, then with a turn—sharp as a blade—it sliced into the water and, with Victor's force, pulled back, creating its own frothy wake, until he lifted the paddle again, cutting, slicing, pulling us forward.

We rounded the fishing docks where commercial fishermen—who netted by day for walleye, northern, sturgeon, burbot, and whitefish—tied up their boats at night to return to their simple homes and shacks, often crammed with lots of children. Now the docks were empty, save the *Betty Jean*.

"She landed on a rock shoal in last week's thunderstorm," Victor explained, pointing at the trawler with his paddle. "She needs repair, but she's a beautiful boat."

Sitting in Victor's canoe, I sensed a warm breeze shifting.

Already the world looked different.

The houses and boathouses beside the water, even the *Betty Jean*, appeared like toys—miniatures. The canoe became the world, and everything beyond seemed small and insignificant.

| 8 |

I could just as well have taken the train from Ranier to New York City, my actions felt that daring.

And delicious.

But the farther we traveled, the more doubts slid in beside me, sharing my caned seat in the canoe. What had come over me? I was riding in a canoe with a shoeless man—though one glance at my own feet reminded me I was no better. Mrs. Worthington would call such actions "scandalous" and "brazen" and warn me that I'd become "the shame of the town."

I held the slate board in my lap and wondered what to write. I should write something sensible like, "I have changed my mind. Please deliver me home," or some such. Instead, I pushed the slate board under my bum and sat on it, tilted my head back, and gazed up.

Clouds sprang like enormous popcorn puffs above the lake.

"Lake clouds," Victor said. "They form above the vast water. The lakes up here form a chain that flows eventually to Hudson Bay. That's the way it should remain, too—flowing—not dammed up at every opportunity. Itasca State Park was established in 1891—two *decades* ago. Why shouldn't we be protecting what we have here in the same way?"

I pivoted to meet his eyes, but he was studying the shoreline as he paddled, not me.

"You'd think," he started, "operating the biggest, most profitable paper mill in the world might be enough. That building two dams, one at International Falls and another at Kettle Falls, would be more than adequate, but not for a man like Ennis." Victor stretched out his hand toward the northern shore, the southern shore, and the islands beyond. "See all this? If he gets his way, this will all be underwater about twenty-five feet, or even more. Means we'd be floating in a giant claw-foot tub. No islands, bays, or inlets."

I tried to picture such change, but it seemed impossible.

"*If* he gets his proposal passed. He's not one to back down. That's why ordinary folks need to rally together and stand up to him."

Telling E. W. Ennis "no" was not something people did. He controlled the water—maybe even the skies. It was said he'd left St. Paul and his accounting job at a lumberyard to tromp the wilds of northern Minnesota with a guide. Snowshoed the whole way, which I doubted. More likely he took a train as far as he could, then hired dogsled teams to get him to the region. He dreamed of the world's largest paper mill and set about making it happen by sending timber cruisers to survey each and every square mile. He laid claim to virgin towering pine and logged it before anyone else knew of his discovery.

I thought of Mr. Worthington and the way he ducked around Mr. Ennis, carefully choosing his words.

"Call me a fool," Victor said, "but this is a battle that must be won. My island is wide open for people of all sorts to visit—artists, poets, journalists, scientists—anyone I can interest in coming up here to appreciate the wilderness we have." He orated on. "Can you believe, Sadie Rose, that with the already unregulated lake levels, those who own lakeshore find their cabins flooded year after year? And with the constant fluctuations in water levels, birds and animals..."

I had heard so much of Mr. Worthington's political arguments over the years that, frankly, I'd learned to tune out most political talk. But Victor was different.

As he paddled and practiced his arguments, I let my mind drift along with the water and words. The shoreline whispered its own message through the treetops, from bough to bough, sending it through the soft feathery needles of white pines to the stubby-needled, wind-bent jack pine, whose hard cones would only open up and reseed through intense fire. We passed logged shoreline where only stumps remained, leaving the forest floor unprotected and powdery dry from harsh sunlight.

On the lake before, I had watched shore and islands drift by from the passenger boat, but traveling by canoe was completely different. Everything was close up. We passed log cabins, shacks made of mismatched boards, and an occasional two-story home or cottage. It was as if I were seeing Rainy Lake for the first time, breathing in its every scent, observing every curve and line, alerting Victor to any rocks or deadheads in our watery path.

"That's Baird's Island," Victor said with a nod. Stands of Norway pine towered on two islands, like either end of an hourglass, joined by a narrow beach. He paddled along its southern point, where a tiny log cabin with flower boxes of red petunias perched at the water's edge.

"And there's Trinity's studio. She's a painter."

Trinity was more complex than I'd thought. An artist, with a space of her own. I couldn't imagine such luxury. What would it be like to have a studio? If I had one, mine would hold a well-tuned piano, stacks of sheet music, and countless books. Someday, I vowed, I would visit her at her studio.

A few islands later, we rounded a peninsula, then headed northeast toward a cluster of islands. In the distance and across the bay I spotted Red Stone Island and Ennis's lodge. But it vanished as Victor maneuvered the canoe around the cabin on the point and into the shelter of a horseshoe bay, a natural port with high granite walls between two islands—and the island the dock boy had pointed out from the steamer.

"Falcon Island," he said. "I wanted to show it to you."

A mix of dread and delight flooded through me. I couldn't possibly step foot on his island. Alone with him.

With far less fanfare—no porters or waiters or dockhands— Victor paddled his canoe to his dock as dragonflies silently hovered above. He jumped out of the canoe, tied it up to iron rings, then shook out his arms, and stretched.

Perched on the harbor's outcropping of rock, a small slab building looked down on the dock. His cabin, I assumed. A wave of guilty tension passed over me. If the Worthingtons found out I'd stepped foot on a man's island, unchaperoned, they would certainly ship me off.

"The library," Victor said proudly, tilting his head toward the small building and offering me his hand. A library? *Say no. Stay in the canoe,* my training told me. But I climbed out, without spilling into the water.

"I keep ordering books," he said, palms up, as if apologizing. "I know, you're thinking—a library, out here in the middle of nowhere." He smiled, then looked away boyishly. "People have no idea what wilderness means. They haven't experienced it. Therefore, they don't know how deeply they need it, and I don't mean just for physical health." He thumped the side of his head with his forefinger. "This kind, especially."

I left the slate board in the canoe and stepped across the plank that connected the floating dock to the shore. Lichen clung to the rocky shore in pale yellows, greens, and blues. A white-throated sparrow seemed to sing—*I'm somebody, some-body, somebody*—from overhanging branches, its song promis-ing yet melancholy.

Victor cleared his throat, ran his hand back through his sandy curls. "I was diagnosed with scarlet fever and a bad heart several years back," he said. "I was starting at Harvard—only sixteen—admittedly, one of the younger students," he added. "The doctors said that I'd benefit from summers in the wilder-ness. When I finished my degree in landscape architecture, Mother and I ended up here."

I glanced around and breathed out a sigh in relief. If his mother was here, then there was no scandal. If Aasta and Hans or the Worthingtons questioned me, I would have to bend the truth and say I would *only* have gone to Falcon Island under such circumstances.

"She's in Red Wing now," he said. "Visiting friends."

"Oh." A tremble tiptoed down the small of my lower back.

He stepped onto a rocky path, and at a distance I followed. "I've ordered thousands of books and had them shipped here. I have all the reading and learning here that I could ever hope for. And just like a goose in the fall that doesn't know to leave when the first freeze strikes, I just stay on and on." He nodded toward a shed filled with neatly stacked and split wood. Em-bedded in a stump, an ax took a temporary rest. "Only, I didn't freeze in the ice." His eyes twinkled like sunlight on water.

Ahead through birch and pine trees stood a two-story cab-in with countless paned windows. A screen porch wrapped around one side. Two wicker rocking chairs sat on the other side's veranda. A stone chimney clung to one side of the struc-ture. The doorframes, steps, and window frames were painted spruce green and rusty orange.

But I stopped. I couldn't follow him into his home—alone. All at once I knew that I was risking too much. And though everything about Victor put me at ease, I'd heard stories of what could happen. I lifted my skirts, turned briskly in the path, and cleared my throat in an Elizabeth Worthington sort of way to let him know that I was heading back.

But before reaching the dock, I turned to the library. I had to take a quick glance inside. So many books in such an unlikely place as this. The squat building sat on my left, astride the rocky ledge above the inlet.

"Sadie?" Victor called from a distance, as if surprised I hadn't followed him.

I pushed open the library's heavy wooden door, and then the screen door, and was met with the papery smell of hundreds of books. From floor to ceiling, books lined the walls. A table in the middle held one large book with gilded edges: *Leaves of Grass.* I turned its pages, turned to the illustration of a nude man and woman. . . .

The door yawned on its hinges. Silhouetted against the western sun, Victor pressed one hand against the doorframe, potentially trapping me. "Ah, Whitman. One of my favorites," he said.

I felt my face burn. Embarrassment crept like a cat up my neck, licked my ears, and settled across my shoulders. "Yes," I whispered. My lips on fire with that single word, my throat scalded with self-awareness.

Victor dropped his arms to his sides, tilting his head in bewilderment. Then he crossed his arms and studied me. "You have me confused. Perplexed." He pointed to the canoe just yards below the library and tied up to the dock. He didn't look at me as he talked. "You carry a slate board. You pretend that you can't speak. I've played along with you, and now you start talking." He drew a sharp breath.

I wanted to explain. I wasn't playing games. I wanted to tell him—but tell him what? Why I'd said my first words in the past two days in more than a decade? I didn't *know* why! But

I knew it must have something to do with finding the photographs and stirring up the past. My stomach danced and twisted, tumbled and twirled until I feared I would throw up on Whitman's lovely book.

I forced my way past him out of the library and into the safety of the sunlight. But a thin, sour liquid spilled into my mouth, and my stomach ratcheted upward in my chest. I barely made it to the edge of the dock before I lost my composure.

After kneeling on the edge of the dock and rinsing my mouth with lake water, I sat back, arms wrapped around my knees. I stared at the water.

"Time to go," Victor said. He untied the canoe and I climbed into the bow. I held the slate board in my hands, wanting to write an essay to clearly explain my inexplicable behavior. But how could I explain anything? The past few days had turned me inside out. I was like a garter snake, working off an old, dry skin, unrolling it like a sock as I slithered forward, temporarily blinded, but moving toward what, I had no idea.

My throat was burning with emotion as I sat in his canoe. Victor kept up a steady, determined pace, and I felt stupid and vulnerable and completely confused. I would return, head to my room, and hide for the rest of my life. I was a freak and should be a feature act in a circus show. How could I possibly go my whole life—or since I was five—and not speak? How could I then, in only two days, start spilling words? I squeezed back tears. And here I'd been given a chance at friendship, a chance to escape my world, and I'd ruined it—with one word.

When the canoe touched the Worthington's dock, I yanked my skirts above my knees—*Oh, bother with ladylike behavior!*— and scrambled onto the dock. Without so much as turning to wave good-bye, I ran up the steps and concrete sidewalk and disappeared inside, hoping Victor Guttenberg would never have to set eyes on me again.

| 9 |

"Sadie Rose!" Aasta said, jumping up from Mrs. Worthington's wicker rocker. She blinked awake from an obvious nap.

"Where have you been? And what's wrong?" she asked, tucking loose hairs back into her crisscrossed braids. "I was just cooling down here, then you come crying. Did he—did he harm you?"

She pointed to the canoe setting off into the bay, then shook her finger at me. "Mr. Worthington is not one to stand by and do nothing. If you were harmed in any way, he will do something about it. You can be sure. And you bet my Hans, he will be mighty angry, too." She smacked her fist into her hand. "He'll do that, he will."

Tears spilled. "No, Aasta. He didn't hurt me!" I pressed past her and headed straight upstairs for a rib-racking cry.

"With your head pains again," Aasta called up the stairs after me, "you should be staying in the bed—not running around! I let you go to creamery, but that doesn't mean I open the gates wide. You best rest now, then."

The cage walls of my bedroom closed in around me. I wanted to make my own decisions, not be ordered around. I ached to be free and have a life of my own. It was as if I was always bowing down with gratitude for being allowed to breathe, bowing down in deference that someone had given me food and clothing.

And alongside those feelings, I felt like a child learning to walk. Learning to speak.

All night, I was awake. I spent hours studying the photographs of my real mother. I sat with them at the vanity, then put them in the drawer only to take them out again a short time later. I stretched across my four-poster bed and spread the images out on the quilt. If Mama hadn't died, where would my life be now? I wondered if I, too, would be working as one of "the girls." *A madam. A lady of the street. A red skirt* or *clipper*— terms that had faded. But one term would never change.

Prostitute.

I undressed before my mirror.

I wondered as I studied my full breasts and pink nipples, the dimples above my backside, the navel. This body was mine, and I appreciated the way it had changed from a girl to a woman in just the past few years. Though I didn't at all enjoy monthly menses—rubber belts, cotton pads, and the deep, aching cramps—it was still *my* body. What if I had no other choice but to rent it out for use? To make money by allowing anyone who had the right coins or bills to do with me as they wished?

I looked at the photographs. My mother had been a beautiful woman. Surely she must have had other options.

"Why, Mama?" I whispered.

Why did you accept this as work? *Why* didn't you find a different way? She must not have thought she *had* other options. And did I? Didn't I have to stay under the roof of the Worthingtons, doing as they requested, acting like their pretend-daughter, waiting for the day when they would tell me to leave? Did I have options? I didn't have money of my own. I didn't have skills, other than playing the piano, reading, and occasionally painting. Who would pay me for these abilities? If I were kicked out, within days I would have to consider whatever employment I could find to put food in my belly.

Dawn came and the sun flickered above the horizon sometime before five. Finally, I lay back, closed my eyes, and let such questions float in and out of my mind like the breeze wafting the lace curtains. I wished I could speak with Hans about the photographs. But any questions would only embarrass him. Clearly, he'd hidden them—to him, they were merely girly photos.

The person I needed to find was the photographer. And there was only one portrait photographer in the area, a Mr. Foxridge. He was well respected, taking portraits of individuals—like Ennis and Worthington—and families. It was unlikely he had anything to do with these lurid images. But maybe he knew...something.

His studio was in downtown International Falls, three miles away.

That day at breakfast—in the kitchen instead of the dining room—I put down my fork. When a quiet fell, I tried my voice again, this time with a question. "Aasta," I said, "at Red Stone, you said you'd heard I used to talk like a little sparrow."

"Did I?" she said, looking away to Hans, who scolded her with a wag of his head.

"You did," I answered. "Who—who told you I talked a lot?"

She nodded. "Sadly, I wouldn't know that because... *vel*... we started our work here when the Worthingtons found you. They needed help. But I know people here now, and one day I went to find Darla, the woman..."

"—of course she was a woman," Hans added, with a wink at me.

Aasta shushed him with a pretend swat in his direction.

"Before she moved her business to Kettle Falls, I asked her about you, and about your mother. And that's when I learn that you talked once like a little sparrow. That's what that Darla said."

"And that's why," Hans said, "we always lose hope."

"*Never* lose hope," I said, correcting his English.

He smiled wide. "Ya! Never lose hope."

"Maybe now," Aasta said, "you can help us with the English somedays. Ya?"

"Yes," I said. "Of course. And Darla, is she still alive?" I tried to picture her in my mind, a large woman with a pile of red hair pinned high.

"Ya, she still way up the lake at Kettle Falls."

"Kettle Falls," I said, wondering how in the world I might get there someday to see Darla. I wondered if she might remember me, or be able to tell me anything about my mother. "Aasta, did you learn anything more about my real mother?"

Aasta jumped up from the table and started clearing away the plates and bowls of heart-shaped waffles, fruit sauce, and eggs—as if she hadn't heard me.

"There is not much to say," she answered, her voice distant. "Now, we better get tidy around here then." She turned to the washbasins. "The Worthingtons come back on tomorrow's train."

"But it's Wednesday. I thought Friday was when—"

"Change of the plans," said Aasta, her back to me. "They called when you were gone on the lake with that young man."

So that was why she was in a huff. Maybe she was worried that I would turn out just like my mother. Better not to bring her up, a subject that was clearly not to be discussed. Better to never have been born, it seemed, than to end up as a prostitute. And better for me, they seemed to think, to pretend that I had been born into the arms of Elizabeth and Walter Worthington.

| 10 |

I played the piano for hours that morning, my eyes skipping over the notes, my fingers flying over the keys. But the only thought circling in my head, round and round like a turkey vulture, was that I had to find out more about my real mother—her life and especially her death. It was as if I were frozen, stuck in a state of barely living, and I couldn't tolerate it any longer.

What I knew was that I had to get to International Falls and find Mr. Foxridge. I would take the city bus, officially labeled the Motor Inn Bus Line, a squat, five-seated vehicle on thick, fat tires that left regularly from the community building for fifty cents round-trip.

But Aasta and Hans hovered around the cottage like a pair of mallard ducks watching their brood—of one. I watched the hours tick by through the early afternoon. I read, perused the Worthingtons' bookshelves, sat back at the piano, and hoped they would leave on an errand. I decided, finally, that I would have to lower myself to lying. When Hans was busy repairing dock boards, I stepped into the kitchen, pressing my palm to my forehead. "Aasta, I'm going to rest for a while."

"Head aching, ya?"

I nodded and left. Instead of turning to the staircase, I slipped silently out the door toward the road and walked briskly to meet the bus at the community building. I felt spurred on, like a horse ridden by an impetuous rider, propelling me forward without caution, heedless of unforeseen holes.

By four o'clock, I was walking down the boardwalks of downtown International Falls, my wide-brim hat shading my face. Several Model Ts rolled by, swerving around dung and mud holes. Horses leaned into their traces, pulling delivery carts, wagons, and buggies. Men gathered outside taverns, smoking, heads tilting with curiosity as I passed. My goal was not to be seen by anyone who would recognize me and report back to the Worthingtons. But I so rarely left home, I realized, that most likely I would be taken for a tourist passing through, or perhaps a working girl, new to town.

The First National Bank dominated a Main Street corner. I glanced in. Behind teller windows of ornate steel scrollwork was a massive walk-in vault. But I wasn't interested in the bank. I aimed instead for the nearby door with the half-moon sign overhead that read:

QUALITY PHOTOGRAPHY
Mr. Fred Foxridge

I climbed the narrow, steep staircase to the second floor. At the top, a dim light lit the hallway. Pleased with myself, I stopped at the first door on the left, its sign stating the hours, MONDAY–FRIDAY, 8–4. Oh, no…I checked my pocket watch. It was three minutes past four. I'd come too late! And I didn't know when I'd get another chance to return downtown with the Worthingtons returning tomorrow.

Halfheartedly, I knocked anyway.

"Enter!"

I stepped into a small windowless waiting room with two overstuffed chairs and a wooden smoking stand. Its inset ashtray of amber glass overflowed with cigarette butts. On a coffee table stood a ten-inch metal elephant, its tail a metal crank. I couldn't help myself. I sat, leaned forward, and turned the crank. From the elephant's belly rolled a fresh cigarette onto two metal prongs.

From behind the dividing wall, a man shouted. "It's past four! I'm closed!"

"I know. Sorry to bother you. I—I just have a question."

"Take a seat! I'm in the darkroom. I'll be out in a minute."

I sat back in the chair and waited, my hands clasped ladylike over my leather handbag on my lap. From the hallway came the creak and slam of doors and a pattering of footsteps. The door to the photography studio opened and in flew a young boy, suspenders over patched breeches. "Papa! Mama says the baby could come tonight! Tonight, Papa!"

"That's good, Pete. Don't worry. That's what she thought last night, too. But you tell her I'll be back soon."

The boy stuck his tongue out at me, then twirled away back into the hallway. "Mama!" he shouted, before his voice was silenced by a closing door.

Finally, Mr. Foxridge stepped out, a wiry man I guessed in his thirties, dark hair cut fashionably short on the sides, longer on top, with a mustache that drooped on either side of thin lips. "Okay, what?"

I didn't trust my voice to explain things right. I reached in my handbag, handed him the stack of six images, and waited.

He raised his eyebrows at the photographs, sorting through them quickly, as if they were a deck of cards in need of reshuffling. His eyes bore into me. "And?"

I cleared my throat, willing my voice to be my ally. "Did you take these photographs? Did you know her?"

He sat in the chair kitty-corner to mine, drew a cigarette from the elephant's belly, lit it, and inhaled. I waited for him to say something. He exhaled toward the ceiling. Smoke circled like an uncertain halo above his head. "Yes...and yes."

I willed myself to sit still. I waited for more.

"Her name was Bella Rose. Sort of a sad story, really. I first met her when she was forced to sell her late husband's photography equipment. Good equipment, too. She was pregnant. Needed money. So I bought it and got my start." He waved his arms wide. "And here I am today, in large thanks to her."

Mama had a husband. A photographer who died. I wanted to get up and leave, to try to absorb this information. But while I was here, I needed to learn as much as I could. "And Mr. Foxridge," I asked, feeling like a fledgling newspaper reporter, "what can you tell me about the photographs?"

He tapped the top image. "She was a looker. I was getting started, and so was she, as a, well, you know...So I came up with the idea of taking her picture and some of the other girls', and selling the photographs outside the area. Gotta tell you, I made some quick cash. So did the girls."

He looked me over. "Not that I do that kind of work anymore. But if that's what you came to ask about...turn your head to the left."

Reluctantly, I did so.

In the long pause that followed, I felt his eyes trace my body.

"You're a looker, too. Occasionally, I make exceptions. If that's what you came for, I'm sure I could find some time—it would be after regular business hours, of course...Good, now turn to the right."

I did as he asked. But if he thought I'd come to pose for such photographs, he had it all wrong.

"Oh, crap." He sprang to his feet, gave the photographs and me one last glance, as if to be sure, then shoved the photographs into my hand. "You're her kid, aren't you? Damn it. I should have seen it right off. How stupid can I be? You look just like her."

"But if you knew her, can you tell me anything more about her, please?"

"Kid, I'm not getting near this or you with a ten-foot pole." He opened the door to the hallway, nearly pushing me out. "You better get going now, young lady."

Stunned by his brusque dismissal, I stood in the hallway. Rather than finding answers, my mind flooded with more questions. Why wouldn't he tell me more? He had been willing to talk until he found out I was her daughter. Was I scum to him, or was there something else that worried him? I couldn't breathe. I couldn't make sense of the pounding in my head. Barely noticing anything along the way, I stumbled along the boardwalk and soon caught the city bus back to Ranier.

I glanced toward the rear of the bus, hoping against hope to see Owen. I would sit beside him and tell him about my search—about my strange encounter with Mr. Foxridge. But a man and two women I didn't know filled the seats.

To my amazement, I returned home without incident. I entered the house quietly, pressed through the swinging door, and found Aasta setting the kitchen table for three. "Oh, you're up from your nap. You feel good, then?"

I lied. "A little better. Yes."

On Thursday afternoon, by the time the Worthingtons returned on the first passenger train, I bristled at their return and my loss of newfound freedom. It was as if I'd found a lovely piece of colored glass on the beach and kept it in my pocket these past few days, only to have it taken away.

Chugging ever so slowly, creaking and squeaking, the train from St. Paul rolled toward the Ranier depot. I had debated about when would be the best time to let the Worthingtons hear me speak. Greeting them, I decided, would be a good surprise. I'd practiced in my bedroom. "Hello, Mr. and Mrs. Worthington," I'd say clearly. "Can you believe it? After all these years, my speech has returned!"

But just as the train wheezed its last breath and settled onto the tracks, Aasta grasped my hand and squeezed it. "Use your new words with care," she whispered, not meeting my eyes. As if anticipating my bewilderment, she added, "Some things better left not said." And then she scanned the passenger car windows, almost as if she hadn't said anything at all.

I squeezed Aasta's hand in return, to let her know I'd heard the advice. Still, it was strange. What in the world was our good housekeeper talking about? If I were to begin speaking, wouldn't this be the very *best* thing the Worthingtons would want for me? It opened up worlds of possibilities. Schooling with others. Perhaps going on to college someday. More acceptance, undoubtedly, and entry into their social circles.

Words were powerful.

With Victor, I'd angered him by speaking. I'd startled Aasta into a flustered silence when I brought up the topic of my real mother. And now she was advising me to be careful with what I said. And Mr. Foxridge couldn't get rid of me fast enough.

Words set things in motion.

Aasta's counsel sounded reasonable, but I couldn't understand why she was advising caution. It made me think of the newspaper accounts of the recent war in Europe where mines were laid in the ground that soldiers only found by stumbling upon them, losing limb and life. All I wanted was to use my voice—to learn about my mother.

Stepping from the passenger train, her hair slightly off-center, no doubt from napping on the ride north, Mrs. Worthington exclaimed, "We passed a completely derailed train as we left the cities. What a mess of supplies! Oh, to leave all that bustle behind! And what a sight for these sore and tired eyes. Sadie Rose," she said, wrinkles crinkling at the edges of her soft gray eyes. "And Aasta. I trust all is well."

"*Velkommen!* Very good. Though I think, Mrs. Worthington, Sadie did miss you, truth be told."

I smiled, then kissed Mrs. Worthington's cheek.

Mr. Worthington followed, toting a traveling coat under his arm. Just as he neared us, Einar Grayson, a villager known for his love of debating, snagged his arm. He'd been by the cottage before to air his views.

"Say, Senator! You gonna set up a blockade against that rabble-rouser?" He brushed his pockmarked nose with the back of his hand, then waved a flyer in front of Mr. Worthington's nose. "See this? It's that Victor what's-his-name stirring up trouble."

My ears perked up, and I listened closer to this man with suspenders hanging like oversized pocket chains from his trousers. "Says we'll lose our quality of life if the dams go through. Well, you ask anyone around here, and I'll tell ya—! Quality of life comes from having a job! This weasel gets his way, we'll all be out of work, and not just loggers. Mill workers, farmers, shopkeepers. Everybody."

Mrs. Worthington waited, and I listened, watching from the edges of my vision. Days ago, I wouldn't have cared what issue a villager brought up for debate with Mr. Worthington. It never concerned me. I knew better than to insert myself in the issues of city, county, and state. But things had changed. Now I knew Victor. He was well spoken, knowledgeable, and cared deeply about the waterways and wilderness. No one had ever talked about it before as something that might be lost.

"It's time to set a snare for that meddler," said another man with sharp cheekbones who was wiry as a heron with tufts of thin, white hair. "Same as I set 'em for rabbits. Get that wire between two trees just so—" He motioned like a conductor with crossed batons, then flung his arms wide. "Then snap. You break its little neck."

Mr. Worthington clamped the man's shoulder and, lowering his voice, said, "Bigby, you better head back to the bush where you belong." He forced a laugh. "We're more civilized than that."

Bigby. The name caught in my chest. But I had no idea why.

"Back in the day," Bigby began, spitting out a brown stream of tobacco. "Back in the day, I remember—"

Mr. Worthington steered him from the group. "Head on now, Bigby. Your boat must be leaving soon, yes?"

The wiry man snorted and headed toward the docks.

I felt my blood drain into the cobblestone. This was no idle game of politics. These men were serious about their differences with Victor. I thought to tell him what people were saying. Warn him, but to do what? To back down and back away? No, I couldn't do that. But I could advise him to be careful.

Suddenly I wanted to talk. To risk whatever might come of it. I reached toward the man with the pamphlet and almost said, "Please . . . may I see it?" But my mouth didn't open.

Einar's eyebrows squirreled upward. "What? You want this?"

Mr. Worthington put his arm on my shoulder. "She doesn't speak, but she's curious about the flyer, that's all." He smiled benevolently down on me, in a theatrical way I'd experienced before. "She's my biggest supporter."

"Oh, the mute. I've heard about her."

I cringed.

Hans stepped forward. "Einar, how can you be such the rock-head idiot? Sadie Rose can *hear.* Every single word. Now say you're sorry before I tell your wife on you."

The man lowered his eyes like shades half drawn. "Sorry,

Miss," he said. "You go ahead and take it. It's only good for burning anyway."

On our short drive home in the Model T—the Worthingtons in front, and I in back between the Johannsens—I whispered in Hans's ear. "Thank you for standing up for me." I used a little Norwegian I'd learned. "*Tusen takk.*" A thousand thanks.

He patted my hand in return.

At home, I immediately tucked the flyer in with the photographs to study later and then joined the Worthingtons on the porch, with the hope to learn something more from their conversation about the debate over the proposed dams.

Aasta held out a tray with three tall glasses. I lifted a glass of lemonade, topped by a mint leaf, and brought it to my lips.

"Not that we didn't have a lovely gathering on Summit," Mrs. Worthington said, "though the talk along the avenue is all about why Scott Fitzgerald moved away—no one can figure it out. I mean, his first big success as a novelist, telling everyone he could a little over a year ago, and now, well, everyone feels somewhat betrayed." She shrugged her petite shoulders. "But, oh well. There's still nothing quite like being up here on a summer day. Oh, Aasta, thank you!"

"With all your complaining, dear," Mr. Worthington said, pacing across the wooden floor, "you'd think the train ride north was eighty days long. I started to think you really didn't want to return at all."

"It was dizzyingly hot, and you know I don't handle the heat well these days." She fanned herself. "I love it here, I do, but it does take some agility to straddle both worlds. With the likes of those men who greeted you at the depot, this isn't exactly the hub of high society, is it, darling?"

But Mr. Worthington was already in another world, staring off across the water toward the lift bridge, likely contemplating pending legislation or some upcoming committee meeting. He never had been one to talk very much.

"And, Sadie Rose, what did you do to keep busy while we were gone?" Mrs. Worthington asked, picking up a *Ladies Home Journal* and opening the pages.

Slate board in my lap, I wrote with chalk. "I painted flowerpots, read, helped Aasta, and practiced the piano."

"Oh, that's nice. Do show me the pots when you get a moment, will you?"

I nodded, then picked up the novel at my side, *My Ántonia*, the most recent of Willa Cather's novels. Normally I would have finished it in two days. I opened the book and pretended to be immediately lost in its pages. But my mind wasn't connecting with the words. Instead, it danced around unanswered questions. Questions about life before the Worthingtons. Questions about my real mother, real father. Questions about where my life was going next. My visit to Mr. Foxridge had caused the tides within me to shift. And it was not a gentle force, but an unsettling current that churned from my toes to the very strands of hair on my head.

I had intended to speak to the Worthingtons, but the moment had been lost. Mrs. Worthington was paging through an article about table decorations. Mr. Worthington lit a cigarette, then exhaled a stream of smoke from his nostrils.

I'd never smoked, but I would bet anything that Trinity did. Or had at least tried it. That's who I realized I would love to talk to. I sat uncomfortably aware of my snug-waisted dress, matching stockings, and lace-up shoes and longed to stroll barefoot instead, to wear a shorter dress like Trinity's, and to cut my long hair into a chin-length bob.

Tucked between my thigh and the edge of the wicker settee, the slate board's wooden frame pressed against me. I would never have to use it again, just like Dickens's Tiny Tim tossing off his crutches at the end of A Christmas Carol.

But I wasn't ready.

Not yet.

I needed my crutch, just a little longer, even if it was now a lie.

I picked up the board and wrote, "I want to go to the circus with my new friend, Trinity."

At the sound of chalk on slate, Mr. Worthington turned, expectantly. I lifted the board so he could read it, and then toward Mrs. Worthington. They glanced at each other.

"Only Trinity around here," Mr. Worthington said, "is Major Baird's daughter. Now I realize that we cross paths with the Bairds, but I don't want you thinking that you will actually be friends with their daughter."

I tilted my head. What was he saying?

"He doesn't mean it like that," Mrs. Worthington chimed in. "He means, Trinity Baird is from the East Coast, and her family summers here. She's quite educated. Smith College ... studies art in Paris. Not that you're not bright enough, Sadie Rose, but she comes from an entirely different world, dear. If you were our own daugh—" She exhaled and sat up taller, her bosom rising and then falling. "Well, from what I've heard, she has some high-minded ideas about the roles of women. More than a bit of trouble, I'm guessing. Besides, Sadie Rose. The circus?" She laughed halfheartedly. "That's the last thing I'd ever expect you'd want to see again. I mean, last time, well—"

Mr. Worthington finished her thought. "You wet your dress, you were so afraid of the clowns."

Setting her magazine down sharply, Mrs. Worthington huffed. "Why embarrass her with such details?"

I frowned. I hadn't remembered until they brought it up.

Why did only scraps and pieces of memory appear, never the whole fabric stretched out for me to study? I felt embarrassed and out of step with everything and everyone.

"We took you home early," he continued. "But that was a long time ago. You can go if you want to. But Sadie Rose, I suggest you let go of the idea of a true friendship with Trinity Baird. I suppose that girl was strolling past our house while we were gone. Is that it?"

The perfect alibi.

I wasn't about to tell them about my heading off to Red Stone Island to work with Aasta. I wasn't about to tell them about my other adventures to Falcon Island and to Mr. Foxridge's studio in International Falls.

With a broad smile, I nodded. Then I added quickly on the slate: "Yes. She was strolling by. She seems swell."

| 11 |

The next evening, close to our dinner hour, Mr. Worthington groaned from the living room. "Good Lord! Not him."

I was in the kitchen near Aasta, knitting on a stool while she peeled potatoes to fry up later with breaded walleye. I glanced for the umpteenth time out the window, certain Victor would come since it was Friday—the day I'd told him that Mr. Worthington would return. The sun arced toward the northwest, and Victor was already down at our dock, tying up his canoe. As a train clanged and sang, crossing the bridge into the States, Victor rolled down his pant legs, tucked in his shirt, and ran a hand through his blond hair. Then, shoulders back and talking to himself—he walked up the slope toward the cottage.

I slipped from my stool, disappeared from the kitchen, passed through the dining room and living room, and stepped out onto the front porch. Mrs. Worthington was sipping lemonade and writing another of her lists. Mr. Worthington had one hand on his vest, the other around what I assumed was his favorite beverage, ice and whiskey. He never openly admitted to drinking alcohol, but we all knew better.

"The last thing I need is to hear from this fellow," he said, gulping back his drink and setting the empty tumbler on the end table. "A canoe trip to Hudson Bay and this guy thinks he knows everything. Now he's acting like he understands politics. I might even be sympathetic with his cause, but it's a fool who thinks he can cross Ennis."

As if I hadn't heard any of this, I slipped to my chair and opened up my novel again. I reminded myself that I never wanted Victor to see me again. But that seemed like ages ago. As he approached, I wanted to say out loud, "Oh, I know him already." I shifted in my chair, brought the book closer to my face, and pretended disinterest. I was certain Mr. Worthington wouldn't invite Victor inside our home; that would be like offering shelter to Ennis's enemy. And he'd never do that.

Opening the screen door, Mr. Worthington stepped out onto the landing, as I had predicted. "I was expecting I'd hear from you, young man," he said, "since you were the first topic on the lips of villagers here when I stepped off the train. Some of them are getting mighty nervous about your getting in the way of progress."

"Senator," Victor began, from the bottom step, "I'd like a minute of your time."

"Step in, step in," Mr. Worthington said, holding the door open. "Frankly, I'd rather not draw attention to your being here."

Inside? If the Worthingtons found out I'd been out canoeing with him and visited his island, they'd treat me the way bounty hunters dealt with wolves. Heat traveled to my face, reminding me that I hadn't left Victor on good terms. I'd stormed away in my confusion. I'm sure he had no keen interest in seeing me again.

I squirmed and finally jumped up from my chair, ready to disappear from the porch, but Mrs. Worthington stayed me with a hand signal. With reluctance, I sat back down.

"Young man," Mr. Worthington said, standing a half-foot taller than Victor, "this is Mrs. Washington, my wife, and our foster daughter, Sadie Rose."

"We met the other day," Victor said with a smile. "I hoped to catch you at home, Senator, but instead I ended up meeting Sadie Rose. We went for a short canoe ride."

My face burned. Why was he doing this? Didn't he understand that I'd taken great risks to go out in the canoe with him? The Worthingtons would be furious. I tried to silence him with a glare.

Mrs. Worthington stared at me over her reading glasses. "Sadie. What is this? You left the house while we were away?"

I looked at the floor and nodded, then I snatched up the slate board and wrote. "I was bored! It was harmless."

"Well, then you already know Sadie doesn't speak," Mr. Worthington added. "You took out a vulnerable young woman without our permission?"

I braced myself, waiting for Victor to inform Mr. Worthington otherwise, but he merely glanced my way with a flicker of understanding that I took to mean, *I'll help you, and you help me. Deal?*

"You overstepped your bounds, young man. If you were looking for another advocate for your cause, you'll be wasting your time here. Not to mention that I do not appreciate the impropriety of your taking such liberties with our dear girl. If anyone saw . . ."

Victor laughed. His shirttail dangled ridiculously behind him. "It was a harmless paddle on a summer day. Nothing more. The reason I came to your home is the same reason that I'm here today." He shifted his focus back to Mr. Worthington.

"Senator, I would like you to reconsider supporting the construction of sixteen dams. Already, with only a single dam, the water levels fluctuate to such extent that fish camps, docks, and dwellings get flooded out. Nesting birds that depend on more consistent water levels, such as the loon, are gravely affected. For countless reasons, it is not in the best interests of your constituents. I'd like to talk in more depth and bring some points to your attention, if I may."

With a glance toward the water, Mr. Worthington crossed his arms over his suspenders and crisp, striped shirt. "I may share some of your feelings and opinions, Mr. Guttenberg, but I assure you, my hands are tied." He turned to Victor. "My mind is clear. This is a frontier begging to be developed. Not so long ago, Ranier was nothing more than taverns and brothels."

I flinched. Though they'd never discussed such things with me directly, I had picked up enough by listening in on conversations. Ranier had thrived during its height of lumber cutting and log drives. When laborers were given a few days off and a little pocket change, they spent it on having a good time.

Suddenly, just as I'd done countless times as a child, I wanted to crawl into the small space behind the ornate, silver-plated woodstove in the parlor room—where it was always warm with a soft blanket, a place where I could stay out of sight for hours at a time. *I saw Mama's face: wide eyes, rounded cheeks, a finger to red lips, whispering, "Don't come out, Sadie Rose, until I come back downstairs. Promise?"*

Mr. Worthington talked on. "When I first came here from Duluth, I hadn't planned on becoming mayor. I made cleaning up Ranier my highest priority, a respectable place to raise children and start a business. Do you think the people here are interested in slowing down development? Not from what I'm hearing, and believe me, I *do* listen to the people. You know how vast this wilderness is? How much of it waits to be tamed and settled? It's not only the lumber to be felled, but hydropower to be harnessed. And that translates into *jobs* and *community* and *civilized* society. You bet I'm behind Ennis's proposal. It's coming, sure as the Model T."

Victor massaged his jawbone with his thumb and pressed his forefinger to his lips. Compared to Mr. Worthington's skin,

Victor's had deepened with sunshine and the outdoors. Like a gentleman, his white shirtsleeves were rolled down and buttoned fast to his wrists, but as he lowered his hand, I noticed thick calluses.

"Senator, have you considered that wilderness is part of what the human *soul* longs for and needs?"

Victor began to pace along the screened windows. "Have you considered that once you allow these dams to be built that all the delicacies of this region—the tiny islands and inlets, the family cabins and docks—will be flooded and turned into an industrial tub. And for what end? Money, jobs, and greed?"

I smiled inwardly. Parts of this speech I'd already heard in the canoe.

"We have a treasure here—a treasure that will be lost forever if Ennis gets his way. And I'm curious, Senator," he said, pausing to pivot and direct his gaze toward Mr. Worthington, "how much does E. W. Ennis contribute to your senatorial seat?"

Mr. Worthington flared up. "That is out of line and of no concern of yours, young man. We'll just have to agree to disagree. That's democracy. You're never going to please everybody." He opened the door. "Thanks for sharing your concerns."

I hated to see the way Mr. Worthington dismissed Victor so easily. Victor had made a good point about wilderness speaking to the human soul. Hadn't I felt myself opening up just by being out on the water with Victor? And what about his tiny island home, with its lichen-colored rocks and pines rooted into crevices? Would it be erased once the series of dams were fully operational? Usually, Mr. Worthington gave residents whatever time they needed to voice their concerns. He waited for them like a fish on a line until they were all played out, too tired to add one more complaint, and then he cordially said good-bye. It was a talent of his. Here, one of the most educated residents was being dismissed.

As Victor stepped outside, an anger in me built, and I jumped up from my chair and blurted, "But Mr. Worthington, wait—"

Mrs. Worthington's notebook and pen dropped to the floor.

Mr. Worthington pivoted slowly. His handsome face, with his straight nose, intelligent gray eyes, and sharp jaw—his face, which bore increasing tightness and creases of worry on his broad forehead—slackened completely in shock. What little color his skin held seeped away.

From the steps and through the open door, Victor flashed me a smile. "I'll be back to continue our discussion, Senator. Perhaps next time, Sadie, you'd like to join in and share your opinions, too, especially now that you've found your voice. I wouldn't be following my civic duty to let the topic rest." He stepped outside and nearly bounced down the walkway to his canoe.

I wished I could disappear somewhere—far from the Worthingtons and their inquisitive stare. It was as if I'd just dropped a beautiful vase to the floor and was found standing amid the shards.

"Sadie Rose?" Mrs. Worthington whispered. "You—after all this time?"

I answered with a nod. I wiped my damp palms across the sides of my skirt. "Victor helped me." I wasn't sure why I felt the need to lie and suddenly pin the reason on Victor, because it was as much the photographs as any reason.

"Victor helped you?" Mr. Worthington repeated. Then he stepped closer and towered over me. "What's that supposed to mean? He's been tutoring you? Giving you lessons?"

Picking up the slate board, I wrote, "I can't explain."

"No," Mr. Worthington said. "If you can speak, then—" He reached over and yanked the board away from my grasp. I wanted to tug back, to refuse to give it up—my protection all these years. My heart beat as fast as hummingbird wings, and I lifted my hand and pressed it below my collarbone.

"Is there something more going on between you?"

"Walt," Mrs. Worthington soothed.

But he ranted on. "You run off with whatever man shows up? Can we not leave you here under the guardianship of Aasta and Hans and not worry about you? You are here only out of our generosity, I hope you know. If you decide to start cavorting with the likes of . . . What happened exactly between you two, anyway?"

"Nothing," I whispered.

Then he rubbed his cheeks with the palms of his hands, took a deep breath, and started again, this time in a softer voice. "You can speak? This is, well, something I never . . . You were thought to be dead when they found you."

I opened my mouth. This time I willed the words, one by one. "I can talk . . . a little . . . at a time."

My voice sounded like another person had stepped into the house. It wasn't a stranger's voice, for I'd heard it in my head, but now it was solid and weighty. Like the ax that Hans had let me try out yesterday beside the woodshed. "It's not lady's work, y'know. You could lose a knee if you are not so careful." I'd talked then, too. "Please, Hans." And he'd smiled, his dimples showing through white stubble. On my first few tries, I'd missed completely, but then, with my knees bent and legs planted wide, I brought the ax back while fixing my eye on the upright piece of birch. When the ax came down, it split the wood into two with a satisfying crack. The pieces fell to the ground and the ax remained solidly wedged into the cutting block. In the same way, I could direct my words like a weighty tool. It was a thing to be used with care and skill.

Such a thing—a voice.

"Well," Mrs. Worthington said, standing up and leaning over

me. She hugged me, something so rare that it brought tears to my eyes. "After so many sessions of working with you, Sadie. After so many years of trying to help you sound out words—to speak." Her eyes grew moist. "Oh, this is something to truly celebrate! Who knows what possibilities this might bring into your life. Perhaps college. Marriage. It's amazing. And that Victor, to think—" Then she clapped her hands together. "Well, then, this calls for something special!" She hurried off toward the kitchen. "Aasta!"

"Indeed. Something special," Mr. Worthington said, but there was no warmth in his voice. He stepped closer, leaned down, and kissed the top of my head. Then he turned away toward the living room. "I'm sure as soon as Elizabeth returns, you'll want to chat as females do. I must get to my committee notes before tomorrow's meeting." And then he was gone.

Eleven years of not speaking, I would have expected that I'd want to speak with the flow of a waterfall. Instead, I remained fixed to my chair. No, words were more like the ax. Or maybe a chest of coins. I would rather sit on the chest than start spending the coins without thought. I opened the pages of my novel, as if I were guarding a treasure that could be stolen away, until Mrs. Worthington returned with her questions.

| 12 |

For nearly an hour, I talked with Mrs. Worthington on the porch. "Sadie, I confess, I'm hurt that I wasn't the first one you talked to. But I am delighted you're speaking—I truly am!"

When she asked everything she could about the canoe ride, I replied, "I canoed with him to Falcon Island. Then we came back."

"Are you sure?" she leaned forward, her eyes large in her tiny frame. "Did anything else happen? Is there something you're leaving out? This is the point in your life I have always worried about. You're starting down the path toward woman-hood. I've wondered what kind of strange ideas you may have picked up from your early years. I've *fretted* so about your sensibilities, worried that you might be damaged in your God-given sense of morals."

I wanted to say, "If God was so worried about my morals, then why did He allow me to be born at a brothel in the first place?" I began tapping the edges of the wicker chair with my fingertips. "No."

"Did anyone see you with him?"

I willed my fingers to stay still. "No, I don't think so."

When I began to feel like a parrot showing off its limited vocabulary, Mrs. Worthington snatched my novel and said,

"Just read aloud, then, so I can hear your voice. It's such a lovely voice, Sadie Rose. It's like moonlight on water. No, it's like honey in a soothing cup of warm tea. After all these years of wondering what your voice might sound like, I just need to sit here with you and listen. Just a few pages, please?"

I obeyed. And oddly, I listened as I read, too, as the words fell from my lips with less stops and starts, with more cadence and ease. It was like abandoning the piano for years and years, only to finally sit down to it and find it still in tune. All the keys still worked, the white keys and the black keys, the major and minor chords. Only the musician was rusty, but the instrument itself had retained its original qualities and timbre.

That evening, before settling in the dining room, I stepped into the kitchen, which was filled with the smells of baking onion and beef. On the counter, in an earthenware bowl, rising dough pressed up against a cotton towel, ready to be punched down. Unopened jars from the root cellar were lined up on the counter. Aasta wore a red scarf over her hair as she stirred a pot on the cookstove.

"Everything has changed," I said.

"Ya," Aasta said. "You come here."

I stepped beside her. Dots of perspiration gathered above Aasta's upper lip and on her brow. The day was humid, the air weighted.

"Everything has changed," Aasta repeated, "and nothing has changed. You're still the same as ever, ya?" Then she turned, stopped stirring the wooden spoon in the pot, and kissed the top of my head. "*Uff da.*"

Later, the dining room table was set with the floral tablecloth Mrs. Worthington had brought home from Italy, along with lead crystal Waterford goblets, blue and white Wedgwood china, and freshly polished silver. And it was set for not three, but five places. Mr. Worthington sat at the end nearest the window, as usual, and his wife sat on the other side of the oval table, but across from me were two empty chairs. "Who is joining us?" I asked.

At that, Aasta and Hans stepped into the dining room, but this time they were not in their work attire. They wore their Sunday-church best. Hans's face was freshly shaved, with a red nick on his chin as proof. His hair was slicked to the side, and he wore a black vest, softened from time, over gray trousers. And Aasta beamed in her holiday best: her *bunad* from the Sunnmøre region of Norway, with its brightly embroidered threads over a navy vest and long skirt. At the neck of her white blouse sparkled her silver *solje* pin.

"The Queen of Norway has arrived," Aasta said with a laugh. I'd only seen her dressed in her native costume at Christmas and Easter.

Hans pulled back Aasta's chair for her to sit, and then he sat beside her.

"Let us pray," Mr. Worthington began. "Bless us, oh Lord, with these Thy gifts...."

Though Aasta still got up and down to serve the meal, I couldn't have been happier to have them at the table with us. For the first time in my life, I felt part of a family.

Along with roast beef, potatoes, and carrots, Aasta put out a spread of pickled beets, codfish balls, freshly picked asparagus, and Parker House rolls (Mr. Worthington's favorite, ever since he visited the hotel by that name in Chicago). For dessert, Aasta proudly set down a golden double-layer cake with a single burning candle. "A Golden Cream Cake," I said, tickled at my free-flowing words, "for a golden celebration!"

Before slicing into the cake, Mrs. Worthington lifted her water glass. "To Sadie Rose!" she said, beaming proudly. "Who can speak!"

Glasses clinked, and I couldn't keep from smiling as they added their cheers.

I knew I needed to say something. Anything. I felt suddenly shy from all the attention. Finally, the simple words came. "Thank you."

I felt almost like the Worthingtons' daughter. Perhaps it was my lack of voice that had earlier made them hold back. Maybe my muteness had been an embarrassment. Now, it seemed, things were going to change. Even Aasta and Hans seemed part of the family.

With his fork, Mr. Worthington examined the slice of cake on his dessert plate.

"Walt, what is it?" Mrs. Worthington asked. "Are you feeling unwell?"

He looked up, then with a smile shook off whatever was bothering him. "Oh, I'm fine. It's just so startling, that's all. I've been so intensely focused on the November election that it doubly takes me by surprise." Then his eyes met mine. "I'm so very happy for you. I truly am." Then he added with a forced smile, "And after so many years of being silent, be careful, Sadie Rose, what you say."

Mrs. Worthington twisted her diamond ring. "Yes, I'm afraid he's right. We're a respectable family, and every effort must be used to maintain that respect. Good grammar and polite speech are so very important, Sadie. Not that you worry us, but the last time you could speak you were, well, at a different level of society. We've done our best to raise you up with good standards and quality tutors so you could be afforded a good education."

"Sadie Rose," Mr. Worthington added, setting down his fork and forming a steeple with his long fingers, "to whom have you talked?"

I felt as if I were on trial. "Why, no one really. A word or two to Victor and to Aasta. Why?"

"As a family, each of us must watch what we say, especially

in public. Rumors can kill someone in political office. Newspapers would love to take down a senator over any little gossip." He didn't take his eyes off me. "And for that reason, and for your own good, I must forbid you from speaking with the likes of Victor Guttenberg and that flighty Trinity Baird."

I swallowed carefully. What was he saying? I was going to be denied friends?

"God knows it's not that they lack education," he continued, "either of them, but they really do not understand how the real world works. Associating too closely with them can only lead to trouble. And I've steered this ship too carefully to run aground this election season."

"But I—"

Mr. Worthington put up his hand to silence me.

"Mr. Worthington, please," I said.

"Don't argue," he said, leveling me with his gaze.

Hans and Aasta continued to eat as if they didn't hear the conversation around them, but I knew they were listening to every word.

Mrs. Worthington took a bite of cake, then continued: "He's right. They could corrupt your mind and your morals. I've heard enough talk..."

My face heated with frustration.

"Sadie Rose," Mr. Worthington said, reaching over and pressing his hand down over mine, "we want to protect you. I ask you to trust us on this and exercise the greatest care, especially now."

Words piled up inside me. I'd never had my own friends. The Worthingtons had kept me tethered at home with tutors. The only friends I had were employees or relatives of the Worthingtons. I could see it clearly now, as if the curtains to a dark, stale room had finally been drawn. They'd kept me out of view, holed up here or in the house in St. Paul like some kind of cripple. A liability.

"He's right, Sadie dear . . . ," Mrs. Worthington added.

I thought of Trinity and Victor. They *were* different. They didn't care about what everyone else thought. They thought for themselves.

Whatever spirit of celebration I'd felt now faded like a spent candle. What good was it to have a voice if I wasn't able to exercise it? I wanted to speak up. And I knew I could. Instead, I looked down at my plate. The dining room walls, covered with frocked floral paper, closed in around me until I felt it hard to breathe.

"May I be excused?" I whispered.

Mr. Worthington nodded. "Of course, but if you want to live in this house, you will follow our orders. I hope we're clear on this."

"Excuse me," I said and pushed my chair back with a scrape. My throat was hot and tight, and I hurried upstairs to my room and locked my door. Then I threw off my shoes and dress and withdrew the photographs from the drawer.

I flopped on the bed, blinking back tears, and studied the image of my mother smiling from the edge of a dam. My mother had been a prostitute. There was no pride in that. But there must have been some good in her, too. She'd loved me. Was I better off under the unfeeling care of the Worthingtons? If I did exactly as Mr. Worthington was now demanding, I was certain I would shrivel like a plucked mushroom left to dry.

| 13 |

With a pair of sewing scissors tucked into the pocket of my robe, I stepped into the bathroom. In front of the pedestal sink and mirror, I brushed out my long waves, then, calculating the amount of natural curl in my hair, held sections straight down between my fingers and carefully cut.

Long dark locks fell to the floor around my feet. I knew it wouldn't please Mrs. Worthington, but I didn't care. My hair would reflect that I was becoming a modern young woman. When I was finished, I turned my head and studied my new bob, angled slightly longer toward my chin. It was swell. The cat's pajamas. I smiled back. Then I swept the floor, feeling lighter. Then I turned on the bathwater in the claw-foot tub to enjoy a leisurely bath.

I couldn't wait to show Trinity.

When I returned to my room, I stared at the photograph of Mama sitting near the dam. There was only one dam that I knew of—other than the one downstream at Ennis's paper mill—where my mother might have posed for the picture. Long ago, it seemed, I had traveled by boat for hours to a large two-story building in the middle of nowhere that must have been the Kettle Falls Hotel. My memory of it was threadbare. Climbing off the passenger boat, I'd held Mama's hand. Water poured over the dam and thundered near the docks, as if it might suck me into its swirling, spitting waters. Mama lifted her red skirt as we walked through mud toward the hotel's wide set of entrance steps.

I stretched on my bed. The evening air drifted in through my screen window; it was humid and warm, carrying the sounds of boys talking about fishing as they walked by on the road.

For a brief moment, my throat hot with emotion, I touched my forehead to the photo. But I held back. I didn't want to spend the evening crying. I was like the earth after a long winter, thawing under the warmth of the sun. I was filled with questions, ready to explore and discover—to be alive—fit to burst with restlessness and unformed questions.

If I could just talk things over with Trinity. I couldn't hold everything inside a moment longer.

I formed a plan. I'd row to Baird's Island, which I figured I'd manage to find since I'd passed it the other day with Victor. Trinity had seen the world. She knew about living on her own. And she said she wanted to be friends. She'd help me.

With a sense of purpose, I gathered up the small stack of photos, wrapped them in the red cardigan Aasta had knit for me last March when I'd turned sixteen, and changed into sensible clothes for the next morning's journey: a loose blouse, a mid-ankle navy skirt, leaving my feet bare.

Then I pulled my bedcovers up over myself, closed my eyes, and drifted off.

The sun was always quick to rise in the summer. It woke me as it climbed over the eastern horizon and the roof of the town hall. I rose, tucked the sweater-wrapped photos under my arm, and tiptoed past the closed door of the master bedroom and down the stairs.

From the kitchen, pans clattered. Aasta was talking with someone—probably Hans—or to herself as she prepared breakfast.

The path to the front porch and the lake beyond lay unobstructed. Without a creak, I eased out the screen door. Hoping to draw no attention, I acted as casual as possible and headed down the steps to the dock.

In the bay, a tugboat worked its way under the bridge, heading toward the lake's open water. A pair of mergansers took turns diving, then bobbing up with their crest-feathered heads.

The family's wooden cruiser was tied up on one side of the dock, the rowboat on the other. I wished I knew how to drive the cruiser. If I did, I could make it to Baird's Island much faster. But I'd have to settle for the rowboat. Mr. Worthington couldn't dictate my friends. I had to see Trinity, the one person I felt I might be able to talk to.

The photographs seemed to burn against my memories. I needed to find out more, to talk, to ask questions, and see if anyone knew anything. And in the process, perhaps, just maybe I would find out more about how Mama died—and more about my father, the photographer.

If such things were knowable.

I would visit then return home before dinner—if I hurried. They would assume that I was holed up in my bedroom— a squirrel in its nest—sulking. With renewed determination, I untied the green rowboat, settled onto its middle seat, and pushed away from the dock. With my back to the bow, I rowed toward the lift bridge, alternatively glancing up at the two-story cottage and holding my breath, hoping the Worthingtons would not spot me.

Beneath the bridge, I rowed furiously against the current, controlled by the dam downstream. To my fortune, the water that day flowed less swiftly. The river momentarily held my boat motionless as I rowed, but I leaned harder into the oars and pushed ahead into the lake's open water, sweat running down the small of my back and under my camisole.

Hours seemed to pass as I rowed, keeping far enough from shore so that no one could easily identify me. As a breeze picked up, chopping the water into small waves, my hands and shoulders complained, but I kept rowing. Occasionally I stopped, even though the waves pushed me back toward Ranier. But I'd eventually pick up the oars again, clasp them with determination, and pull all the harder.

A motor rumbled close, then idled nearby. I turned and was surprised to see a small cruiser with an enclosed bow. Behind the windshield and forward steering wheel sat Owen Jensen. Owen with the bobbing Adam's apple, the brown eyes flecked with gold, the smile that he probably gave every girl he met. His plaid shirtsleeves were rolled to his elbows.

He waved. "Ahoy, fair maiden!"

I'd voyaged well beyond the Worthingtons' view, well beyond the landing docks at Ranier, well beyond the strength in my arms. My palms were sore and red; my shoulders pinched with hot and burning pain. I stopped rowing.

"Sadie Rose! Whatcha doin' way out here? Didn't recognize you at first. You look different—but in a good way." He steered his boat until it was parallel with mine. He lifted his cap in greeting, then snugged it back over wavy hair, which glinted more red than brown in the rays.

I nodded out of habit, forgetting for a moment that I could answer with words.

"I'm rowing. And I cut my hair."

"What?" He jolted his head in surprise. "You can *talk*? But I thought—well, you never were at school because you didn't speak, that's what everyone said—"

"I couldn't," I replied, tapping my right foot against the wood planks of the rowboat's floor. I willed myself to stop. "Until recently."

"Well, shoot, that's great! So where you headin'?"

I looked ahead to uneven shapes of green: islands, peninsulas, bays. I thought I'd know how to find my way to Baird's Island, but from this spot in Sand Bay, everything looked like an endless landscape of varying hues of green and blue. It had seemed so simple when I'd sat in the bow of Victor's canoe, with the mainland staying pretty much on the right, and the larger body of water—and Canada—to the left. Now I realized it wasn't that easy. I had to aim for something, or I'd end up lost.

"To visit Trinity," I said. "I thought I knew how to get there but—I think I'm lost."

"Well, I can tell ya she's not at her island, cuz I just came from Falcon Island. When I left, she was there visiting. I deliver to Victor and his mother once a week. If you'd like, I can give you a tow."

I didn't want to let go of my vision of arriving by my own strength but relented. Though tracking Trinity down at Victor's island seemed a little strange, I wasn't about to turn back. "If you don't mind. Yes."

"So you better climb in my boat."

Mrs. Worthington's words rolled through my head: "A young lady should never get in an automobile with a young man unchaperoned." I supposed a boat wasn't much different.

"Besides, it'll go better if we get the weight in one boat and pull yours empty."

My shred of propriety floated away like a seagull feather, and as Owen held the two boats side by side, I climbed into his boat and settled on the long wooden seat beside him, without touching. The wooden steering wheel glistened from polish and the boat's floor was spotless, without the usual refuse of empty bottles, dirty rags, buckets, and loose ropes in so many boats tied up at harbor. Two long, wooden boxes lined either wall of the boat's interior.

"Not fish coolers," he said. "They each hold an ice block and dairy. This is my delivery truck, of sorts."

In no time, Owen had a rope tied to the rowboat's bow. "Keep an eye on it while I steer." The rowboat floated atop the frothy wake like a bobber.

"So you're friends with Trinity, then?" he called above the Evinrude's drone.

I didn't know how to answer. Friends? Hardly. But what answer could I give that would satisfy him? "Sort of."

"Y'know, Victor's not real popular around here." Owen raked his hand through his waves of russet hair. His eyebrows were red, too, but a lighter, sun-bleached color. "But he's not bad. Just has different ideas, that's all."

"What are your ideas, Owen Jensen?" A surge of energy filled me. I enjoyed sitting nearly shoulder to shoulder. To be able to converse with someone was so freeing. Ask questions. Answer if I wished. Lightly engage with words as people do. The slate board had made me feel secure. It was a wall that kept me safe, yet it had also kept others from getting too close.

"Ha! You want to know *my* ideas? That's pretty funny. 'Better to be seen, not heard,' my dad says. But hey, you asked." He glanced away from the water and looked at me. "You're serious?"

I nodded.

"First," he said, "get the heck outta Ranier. My dad says I have to take over the creamery, but if I do, I'll be stuck here forever. I'm saving my tips, and someday I'm taking a train outta here, going to college, and someday starting my own business."

"To where?"

"Don't know yet. A big city somewhere. Just not here."

The sun was still climbing, brightening the sky into deep

blues against puffs of white. Ripples of heat floated above the horizon. Birch trees dotted the shoreline.

A loon floated near, then dived and disappeared.

"What kind of business?"

"Not sure yet. I'll keep you posted."

A delicious wave passed through me as I ventured again beyond the confines of the Worthingtons' home. How could I have gone so many years without getting to know others closer to my own age? I was a sailboat on its first voyage, hoisting the sail inch by inch up the mast, feeling each shudder as the wind flapped and filled the white unfolding.

We motored between two long islands, then to a cluster of pencil-thin islands, and Owen slowed his motor and glided between the familiar granite islands and into the protected dock at Falcon Island. Sun baked the orange and green lichen-covered rock on which the library building sat. Below it, the dock awaited us. Two fishing boats were tied up, and Victor's canoe was flipped over on the dock, spine up to the grand sky.

| 14 |

From the tiny library overlooking the dock, Trinity Baird emerged. Her hair was wet to her head, her red wool swimsuit hugged her breasts and circled her hips in a stripe of gray. When she spotted me, she smiled and waved. "Sadie Rose! You cut your hair! It's the cat's meow!"

Right behind her, Victor called. "Well, hello!"

"Hey," Owen said, jumping from his boat and tying up. "Sorry if we disturbed anything!"

Heat rushed up my neck, feeling we'd intruded on something improper. Improper. I sounded just like Mrs. Worthington.

"Owen Jensen!" Victor called. "The creamery boy. What brings you to my fine shore twice in one day?"

Talk, I reminded myself. Try to act normal.

I blurted out, "How's the water?"

"Oh, it's divine!" Trinity exclaimed, sleeking her wet bobbed hair with her hands. More tan than usual for a woman of her social standing, Trinity perched on the high point of the granite rock wall, arched her hands over her head, and did a perfect dive into the deep water of the harbor—within feet of my rowboat, still tethered to Owen's cruiser.

When she surfaced, she cooed. "How was that, Victor?"

"Sprightly," he replied. Then he made his way down to the

dock and began to secure my rowboat. "Now that you're here, you two, do stay. Margaret has been busy making custard that I'm sure she'll insist we all try."

"Margaret?" I asked, as Victor extended his hand as a gentleman to help me from Owen's boat.

"My mother," he answered. "Came in yesterday from Red Wing."

Trinity pulled herself up onto the dock. "That's why we're wearing suits," she whispered, then laughed like a wind chime.

Victor shrugged. "Speak for yourself, Trinity. Some of us like to hold on to a little dignity—at least for appearance's sake." Then he slapped Owen on his shoulder, who was taller by at least ten inches. "Thanks to your delivery, Margaret has been pleasant all morning. How can I thank you?" He winked.

Owen's gaze kept slipping off to Trinity, who leaned back, her chest to the sky, as she squeezed water from her hair.

I felt myself fading away in her presence. I suddenly wanted to leave as much as I wanted to stay.

"Victor," Trinity said, her hand on her hip, "what do you think? Air-dry under the sun? Or do you have a towel I might borrow?"

But Victor was already heading toward the cabin on the eastern point. "I'm going to give Margaret a heads-up on company."

When Trinity looked at Owen and me, I smiled thinly. I understood. We'd come at the wrong time. It was clear as rainwater that Trinity had her sights set on Victor Guttenberg.

Trinity leaned into me and whispered softly in my ear, "I'm crazy about him. Does it show?"

Lying, I shook my head.

"Good!" she said aloud. "Now, before Margaret calls us in for dessert, follow me!" Without checking to see if we wanted to follow, she led us from the dock to the top of the rock wall and the tiny building with red petunias in its window box. She

opened the library door, allowing half a doorway for me and
Owen to squeeze past her. I figured Owen didn't mind.

Trinity danced with her arms arched over her head and fingertips meeting, as if she were a ballerina, twirled twice, and
then pulled down a hefty book titled *The Great Rebellion* by J. T.
Headley. From the space left behind, Trinity withdrew a silver
flask.

"So that's what you two were—," Owen said, cocking his
head slightly, his arms crossed in amusement.

"Sadly, not Victor," Trinity said with an exaggerated down-
turned lip. "He says he doesn't mind what I do, but he doesn't
care for spirits of any kind. Alas. His loss. He's too busy being..." She lowered her chin. "Serious." Then she smiled mis-
chievously. "To rebellion!"

She twisted off the flask's top, tipped back its contents, and
made a puckering face. Then she offered the flask to Owen,
who obliged. His Adam's apple bobbed as he swallowed, and
though he sputtered and coughed, he kept it down. "*Uff da!*"

"Sadie," Trinity exclaimed, "you're next!"

I felt caught off guard, as if I were heading out on recently
frozen ice, so thin and so fresh that you barely knew it was beneath your feet and you could break through at any second. I
was scared. But I was determined not to turn away from what
might be a little fun for once in my life. Accepting the flask, I
weighed the metal in my hand. After the way Mr. Worthington
had treated me, trying to command me to stay imprisoned in
the house, I felt I had every right to drink liquor—legal or not.

I lifted the flask to my lips and closed my eyes.

"It's whiskey," Trinity said, "straight from a blind pig at Kettle Falls."

As I tilted the metal flask, ever so slowly, my mind filled
with the image of my mother's lifeless body. *Propped in the corner. As her frozen fingers thawed, the whiskey bottle slipped from*

her grasp and lay broken on the floor. Over the years I'd heard Mrs. Worthington explain her death in hushed whispers, "Drank herself to death. So many do, you know."

"We don't have all day," Trinity said, with teasing friendliness.

I pushed the flask away and tried to dispel the haunting memory with a shake of my head. "Sorry," I said. "I just—not now."

My throat was on fire, with wanting to explain. But how could I explain what I barely knew myself. That my mother had been found in the snow with an empty bottle of whiskey? That she'd been stood up in the council chambers as someone's idea of a joke? That I'd been there, apart from my body, watching?

"Not to worry," Trinity said. "It's okay. You're still young, Sadie. Just please don't tell on us."

I flinched. "Of course I won't tell on you. I'm not a snitch."

A bell rang out. Ding, ding, ding!

"That would be Margaret," Trinity said. "We better not be late, or she'll have our heads on platters for lunch." She made a slashing motion across her neck and then tucked the flask back behind the book. "There. Better."

That day, to my surprise, Owen seemed to find no reason to hurry back to his delivering job. Instead, he settled right in with us.

Together, he, Trinity, Victor, and I sat outside on a blanket and ate egg-salad sandwiches on porcelain plates and drank lemonade out of matching teacups.

"Margaret," Victor said, waving to his mother, who was built like an icebox, her neck thick and sturdy. "This is Sadie Rose."

I nodded. "Nice to meet you."

Margaret Guttenberg nodded at me. "And you."

"And you know the others," Victor continued. "Sit and join us, Mother. For heaven's sake, it's okay to take a break."

"No, you visit," she ordered, her hair falling in a braid across her broad back as she left us near the shore. "I have catching up to do around here."

We ate and talked, though in truth—I said the least of any of us. When I asked Victor about his father, I learned that his father had left him and his mother, and that he and his younger brother were raised with the help of a stern grandfather.

"Where's your brother now?" I asked.

Victor looked toward the water. "He's been gone a long time. Died when he was little—hit his head in a fall."

"Oh. I'm sorry I asked."

He waved away my concern. "Don't be sorry. It was a long time ago."

I wished for a bit of silence to acknowledge Victor's loss, but Trinity didn't miss a beat and jumped in with, "Did you hear about the fellow who drowned at Kettle Falls?"

Owen nodded, but I shook my head.

"He was walking the dam, drunker than a skunk."

"That's what I heard," Owen said. "Fell right in and they had to wait 'til the rapids spit out his body. That's some current there."

"It's a crazy place!" said Trinity. "I mean, you never know what you'll see. It's a whole little village out in the middle of absolutely nowhere. Fishermen, fancy ladies, traders, Indians, businessmen—"

"And gamblers," Owen added, "drinkers, and blind piggers. They hide their stills all through the woods behind the hotel. That way the federal agents can't pin any business on the ho-tel itself. But everyone knows that Darla and her husband do a bustling trade. Someone's loss is always someone else's gain in this world."

Trinity's blonde hair glistened as it dried. "I love the bustle of that place, but I've only been there twice with my parents. Sometime I'd like to just sit in that saloon and watch."

"It's quite a place now," Owen said. "They even have electricity—out in the middle of the wilderness."

"Long as they keep their generator going," Victor said.

"Trinity, you want to go there, you can catch a ride with me sometime. Or just take the steamer from Ranier," Owen offered. "Leaves at 6 a.m., gets you to Kettle Falls by 1:00. You could go there every single day of the week, stay an hour, and catch the return trip back and be home by 8:30 or so in the evening. Think your parents would mind?"

"Ha," Trinity said. "Last year I smoked and drank with artists and poets in cafés along the Seine. Cat's pajamas! And then—then I return here for the summer and I'm treated like a child again, and held captive to my parents' sense of decorum. I'm so tired of trying to act like a lady!" She picked up the glass, exaggerated extending her pinky finger. "Victor and Owen, you are both so lucky to be born male."

Suddenly, with the talk of Kettle Falls and Darla, I remembered my photographs, tucked safely away in my sweater in the bow of Owen's cruiser. I stood, my legs tingling from sitting for so long. "Excuse me," I said. "I'll be right back. I want to show you all something."

The impulse was so strong. It was as if I had this one chance and I needed to share my burden, to let them in on who I was. They might reject me, but it was a risk I had to take. I couldn't carry this secret alone any longer.

I returned, holding the photos close to my chest, hesitating.

"Well, what've you got there?" Owen said.

Trinity laughed. "Are you going to show us or keep us guessing?"

Though I was embarrassed, I set the photos down in the center of the blanket.

For a few quiet moments, they studied the photographs. I

waited anxiously, wondering how they would react. For all I knew, they might each turn away from me.

"Like shock therapy," Trinity finally whispered, meeting my eyes. "The jolt shifted something in you, don't you think?"

Victor looked at me. "This explains a few things. It helps."

Owen lifted the picture of Mama sitting on the rock ledge, dangling her bare feet and smiling. "This one," he said. "This was taken at Kettle Falls right near the dam. I was out to the hotel last week, delivering blue cheese for a guest. Thirty miles by boat—just for blue cheese. But that place is always hoppin' with customers. Darla's always asking me if I want a job out there." He shrugged. "I'm busy enough as it is."

The notion of going to Kettle Falls, meeting Darla, and asking for a job cropped up like new shoots of grass. With that notion and showing them the photos, a dull pain bloomed suddenly behind my eyes, and my vision began to blur. I closed my eyes, willing away the beginning of another headache.

"Sadie, sheesh, you don't look good," Owen said. "Maybe you better get out of the sun for a while."

"No, I'm—"

But he was already leading me by the hand to the shade of a nearby tree. "Too much sun, that's my diagnosis. I'll get you a blanket to rest on and a glass of water. You'll be good as new."

I wanted to protest but eventually gave in and rested. Maybe it was too much sun. Or maybe it was far more complicated than that.

| 15 |

On the picnic blanket, I raised up on my elbow, only now I was beneath the shade of trees. I wasn't sure how much time had passed.

Owen sat beside me on the blanket and looked up from a book. "Good afternoon."

I sat up slowly, avoiding any sudden movements, pulled my skirt edge down, which had crawled above my knees.

"Nice legs," he said with a nod and a smile.

It was improper, I was certain, but I liked knowing Owen appreciated them. A "thank you" might sound too forward. Better to say nothing at all.

"Sadie Rose, I'm going to have to get goin' soon. I've one more delivery before my ice melts, but I wasn't going to leave you here alone with your rowboat."

My tongue stuck to the roof of my mouth, dry as hardtack. I cleared my throat. "I can go anytime. But I'm so thirsty."

"This way, Miss." He stretched out his arm for me to take hold, and I did. Beneath his rolled-up sleeve, his arm was bony yet muscled. He led me to the stone walkway and the Guttenbergs' pane-windowed cabin. We stepped inside.

Beside the empty hearth, Victor and Trinity sat in rocking chairs, like an old couple.

"Greetings," Victor said, setting a photograph of moose on the floor. "I was just showing images from my last expedition. Amazing how the moose will ignore me, until they hear the click of my camera."

Trinity tilted her head at me. "Feeling better?"

I tried to smile. Here I'd come uninvited to the island, trespassed perhaps on their time together, and then managed to get ill. Again. Mrs. Worthington always guessed my headaches—along with my lack of speech—were related to my high fevers as a child. No matter the reason, it was embarrassing.

Aware that I was missing something, I looked around the cabin lined with book-filled shelves. Off at one end, Margaret stirred something on the cookstove.

"Oh, don't worry," Trinity said. "I put them over there." She pointed to the bench next to the entry door. The photographs lay neatly stacked on my red sweater.

As I collected them, Margaret turned from the kitchen, hands on her wide hips. "Victor showed them to me," she said.

I shot Victor a glance. I hadn't given him permission to show them to the rest of the world.

"Come here," Margaret said. "Sit down at the table." She turned to the cookstove and returned with a water-filled pan that held small bowls of golden custard. "So, your father...," she continued, setting the pan on the counter, and then turning to me.

I sat up straighter, expecting she knew more about my real father.

"He's up for reelection again in November, yes?"

Disappointed, I nodded, hands fidgeting in my lap. "Yes." Across from me at the kitchen table, Owen bumped his knees into mine.

"And how do you like being the senator's daughter?" Margaret Guttenberg continued.

I shrugged. "I'm not really his—"

Margaret wagged her finger. "No, I realize that. But they have taken you in, so you are as much a daughter as the Worthingtons will ever have. That's beside the point."

I pressed my spine against the wooden slats of my chair. That Victor's mother knew even this much startled me. Did everyone in Ranier, whether they were lake visitors or locals, know more than I did about my life? These flitting memories I'd been having, were they nothing more than the remnants of gossip everyone shared in the shadows? Even Mrs. Worthington whispered incessantly to others about my past.

"There's every reason to think Mr. Worthington will win," Trinity said. "I mean, as long as he has the backing of Ennis, how could he lose?"

"I thought this was a democracy..." Victor lit the bowl of a carved wooden pipe, then shook the burning matchstick. "...where every vote counts."

"Oh that's true, unless you're a woman," Trinity said. "But back East, votes always follow the money. That's just how it is. At least spending summers here means I don't have to play those high-society games. Who knows whom. Which families I should associate with and all that. It's enough to drive a sane person to drink—" Trinity flashed a wink and a smile at Owen. "Coffee!"

When Owen raised his eyebrows in return, I felt an unexpected stab of jealousy.

With the whine of a giant mosquito, another boat approached the island, rounding the point and slowing as it entered the harbor.

"Wonder who's coming?" Margaret asked. She looked to me. "You would be surprised how many visitors we host on this island. It's time to put up another cabin or two to host guests. Victor," she said, "go meet them."

Victor jumped up from his rocking chair, trotted across

the braided rug and wooden floor, and slipped out the cabin's screen door.

Margaret turned to Owen and Trinity. "Don't get Victor going on the election process. He's all worked up lately as it is, and I know he'll try to put a stop to Mr. Worthington's reelection, if he can. There's nothing I can say, either, to—" Then she drilled her gaze on me. "Now don't you go repeating any of this to your father. It will not lead to anything good."

Mr. Worthington, I wanted to say. Not my father. But I let it pass.

A loon called in the distance. Its low notes filled my chest, matching the ache I couldn't seem to shake, then its song climbed high and floated in three distinct calls.

Mr. Worthington's reelection had always seemed a simple thing. Of course he'd continue on as a senator. E. W. Ennis always made it sound inevitable. He'd "carry the concerns of all Minnesotans through these turbulent times," and he was "A Man for All People." Those were a few tried-and-true campaign slogans.

Owen cleared his throat. "You wouldn't believe the talk in Ranier," he said. "If I were Victor, I'd lay low before the election. Lots of folks think he's just stirring up trouble. I mean, I think Victor is a good fellow, but he didn't grow up here. He doesn't know how things can be..."

I thought of the men who'd met Mr. Worthington at the train.

Margaret interjected, "True, Victor did not grow up here, but he is not without his own influence. He is well connected with others outside the region who share his concerns, from scientists and authors to—"

The screen door swung wide. On Victor's heels came the familiar voice and white-haired head of Hans. "*Vel*," he said, his eyes falling heavily on me as he stepped in. "Aasta thought you might be here. I said, no, how she ever going to get so far in the rowboat? She is mad as the hornet. She finds your long hair in garbage. And then you are gone. Worthingtons—they are not happy, believe you me."

I stood to greet him and smoothed my skirt. "I didn't mean to cause trouble. I—"

Margaret butted in. "Hans, stay a few minutes for custard, fresh from the oven."

He stayed long enough for coffee and two helpings of custard, and in the conversation, I learned that he'd done carpentry work on Falcon Island, as well as dock repair and stonework at Baird's Island. I shouldn't have been surprised, since Hans worked only part-time for the Worthingtons in the summer.

"And did you all know," Margaret said to everyone with a sweep of her arm, "that Hans should be our spokesman for the Suffrage movement?"

I wanted to laugh out loud. My caretaker friend, Hans?

He pushed back from the table and shook his head, but his eyes were shining.

"Go on, tell them what you told me about women in Norway," Margaret urged, hands on her hips.

"Oh, not much. I just say that in Norway, for years and years, women own property and for ten years already, they have the vote."

Margaret nodded. "See? Only when ordinary people speak up and demand their rights do things change."

In America, the struggle for power, to hold and keep power, and keep it from others, seemed to be everywhere. Even on Rainy Lake, I was quickly coming to understand, those who held power were not eager to part with it.

I wanted to stay, to join in the discussion of important issues, as well as to tease out from Margaret whatever she might know about my real mother and father. Instead, Hans said, "Getting late."

It was pressing into evening, and shadows fell long across
the island as I stood on the dock. I watched as Owen pushed
his boat away from the dock first, doffed his cap at me, and
then started his motor. A plume of blue smoke coiled behind
him as he motored between the steep rock sides of the harbor.
When he emerged into the open water, he throttled up and disappeared from view.

"Is the boy something special, then?" Hans asked, motion-
ing me to climb aboard the cruiser.

"No," I replied, with a firm shake of my head. "No." Though
I couldn't deny a curious thrumming in my chest.

We towed the rowboat as Hans steered our cruiser beyond a
cluster of islands—some with a few scraggly pines, most cut
down to stumps. Green saplings of aspen sprouted up over the
clear-cuts. Rather than following a straight trajectory back to
Ranier, however, Hans drifted into the middle of a quiet bay
and cut the motor.

"What?" I asked, turning around. Was I going to get a scolding from Hans? He didn't need to bother, as I would surely get
a thorough reprimand from the Worthingtons.

He rummaged around by his feet, pulled out a wicker basket, and placed it on the seat between us. "Supper," he said.
"While we fish."

"Fish? But I thought you were angry with me."

He grinned. "Aasta packed us the food, so don't complain.
Maybe I am still out looking for you."

And that was the end of it. As we floated, we ate pickled
herring, slabs of leftover roast beef, hardtack, and sugar cook-
ies. And then Hans readied our fishing rods with earthworms
from his bait box.

Time passed. Hans focused on his fishing line and the red-

and-white bobber, floating quietly. He waited patiently for the first nibble on the earthworm, which took until the sun neared the horizon. I had a few nibbles, but nothing serious enough to jerk up my line.

"Hans," I said.

"Ya?"

"How much trouble will I be in?"

He didn't answer right away. "Sadie, I lost my daughter once. I was so scared, I promise myself if I ever find her, I never let her out of sight again. The Worthingtons worry mighty for you. You don't talk for years, then you start. You go off and they don't know where. They're mad with you, but they will be more happy to have you back again. And I—" He reached over and gave my hand a quick squeeze. "*Vel*, don't worry too much."

"Thank you, Hans." It was easy for him. He only worked for the Worthingtons. They weren't his only family. But they could ship me off to someone as farm help. Or maybe to the orphanage in Faribault, where runaways were rumored to be chained to their beds. The Worthingtons could do anything they wanted with me, including turning me out on the street.

But perhaps worst of all, they could act as if nothing had changed at all. They could act as if everything was the same, as if the only thing that mattered in the whole world was the upcoming election a few months away.

The sun streamed through the pine tops, casting a thousand shades of red and orange across the water.

"Time we go then." Hans put away our fishing rods, started the cruiser, and we continued back.

The evening breeze cooled my face as the boat raced back toward the descending fireball. To keep from being blinded, I kept glancing to my left at the cabins on the south shore or to the right and the waters that stretched into Canada.

Though the sun hadn't yet set, the moon found its place

in the sky, if faintly. It hung like a Christmas ornament, dangling like an orange slice from a branch. I remembered that first Christmas without Mama. The Worthingtons had decorated a tree that reached the ceiling with sugared orange slices and tiny silver bows. The rocking horse beneath the tree was for me, with a black mane and tail, glass eyes, and a red saddle painted on its back. I'd rocked, yes, on the horse. But it only reminded me then that my real wish hadn't come true. It would never come true. I would never have my mama back again.

When we drew close to the Worthingtons' dock, Hans cut the motor and we glided in silently. It was near ten or later. The neighboring house lights were dimmed, but the Worthingtons' porch and living room lights glowed as if they were having a party.

On the screen porch, two men stood talking, their cigars glowing with pinpoint embers. One was the towering frame of E. W. Ennis, hands gesturing as he talked, and the shorter, yet equally commanding figure was Walter Worthington.

Waiting for my return.

| 16 |

The night had turned chilly, and I hoped Hans and I could round the house and enter through the kitchen without being noticed.

"Look what the cat dragged in," Mr. Worthington called as we neared the porch. He swung open the porch door, as if in a wide-armed welcome, but his tone was anything but warm. "Hans, you can go on home. Thank you for returning our girl."

"You're welcome," Hans said, with a slight nod. "Sadie Rose is a good girl."

I shot him a glance, wondering what that was supposed to mean. I guessed he was trying to sweeten Mr. Worthington into not being too harsh with me. "I had to stay and try Margaret Guttenberg's custard. Talked me into staying for a visit, too. No harm done, far as I can see, Mr. Worthington. Kids need to be kids, same here as in Nor—"

"So you found her at Falcon Island, then?" Mr. Worthington pressed.

I stepped into the swirling thick cigar smoke, avoiding his scowl.

"Never can trust a German," Ennis called out as Hans walked off. "Sure that Margaret didn't poison you?"

"If that custard was poison," Hans said, "I'm going back for more."

Margaret and Victor Guttenberg were hardly the type to bring down our country for the sake of Germany. Ennis may have meant it as a joke, but it didn't strike me as a bit funny. Ever since the Great War against Germany, people acted cautious around anyone of German ancestry. That seemed about as ridiculous as worrying that Hans and Aasta might have ties to the Vikings.

I stood awkwardly, my bundled sweater wedged between my elbow and side.

The floral globe lamps glowed.

"Sadie Rose," E. W. Ennis intoned, "you've grown into such a young lady. And Walter tells me you've found your voice." He sat back heavily in the wicker chair and crossed one leg over the other.

I held my breath, waiting for Ennis to tell Mr. Worthington I'd been at Red Stone recently, too. He tilted sideways, holding his glass in his extended hand. Then he drew his cigar to his mouth, inhaled until the cigar tip flickered red, and released a waft of smoke. "A miracle."

"Sadie Rose," Mr. Worthington said, "I've been concerned. My dear Elizabeth has been beside herself with worry. And so has our family friend, Mr. Ennis."

"I'll go ... upstairs," I said, unclenching a hand from the side of my skirt. I willed my feet to move.

"Yes, upstairs," Mr. Worthington said, still standing and stepping sideways to block my path. "But first, I do believe an apology and explanation are in order."

"A-po-lo-gy." I repeated. The word came out haltingly, as if my tongue were going to freeze up again and my will to speak would disappear.

"No!" Mr. Worthington barked.

I flinched at the sharp slap of his word.

"You can't pretend *anymore*, young lady, that you can't speak!"

"I...didn't...pre...tend."

"You spoke clearly enough last night. And now what's this? Like baby talk?"

Mr. Ennis waved his drink. "Walter, just ask her."

"Right," Mr. Worthington replied. He inhaled sharply, as if he'd been working up to what he was going to say for years. "Sadie Rose," he began, "sit." He turned, walked to the end of the porch, and drew up another wicker chair for me.

I hesitated, feeling cornered in an alley.

"Sit, sit."

I wanted to escape, to have Aasta come and tell me it was time for my bath, as she had done when I was younger. But the rest of the house was quiet. Mrs. Worthington must have retired to her room early, with her glass of port and a book. Aasta was likely home already.

I sat down, the chair seeming too small to hold me. My pulse pounded in my ears like a team of startled horses. I wedged my red sweater and bundled photos beside me, and then I placed my hands over the edge of my skirted knees.

Ladylike.

Waiting for what was to come.

The train tracks were silent.

Crickets sang outside, and somewhere distant a loon called.

Mr. Worthington sat heavily, as if my very existence was a burden he could no longer bear, and then asked in almost a whisper. "What do you remember of your years before you came to live with us?"

Mr. Ennis nodded, as if to encourage the flow of this conversation. He recrossed his legs and the fabric of his pants swished.

"Some," I said, thinking of the memories that had arisen of late. At first I thought they were imaginings, but now I saw there was a pattern. The more I remembered, the more

memories arose within me and the more I recalled. Tidbits.
Scenes. But memories, I was now sure. "Um..." I had to speak.
If I didn't, Mr. Worthington would get angry with me. "Not
much...Mr. Worthington."

Mr. Ennis pressed, leaning closer. The smell of whiskey
and cigar smoke and cologne pinched my nose and twisted my
stomach. "Are you certain? What of the place where you lived
with your mother when you were little?"

"The boardinghouse?" I said.

"Yes, that's it, Sadie dear." Mr. Worthington said. "See, you
must remember something of that time. Try hard. What do you
remember?"

*I stepped into Mama's leather lace-ups...and stumbled out
the back door and down the steps...following footprints that the
wind quickly erased.*

I lied. "Nothing."

They both nodded, approvingly.

"What about anyone who came and went from there?" Mr.
Worthington asked, his voice growing thinner, as if squeezed
in a vice. "Conversations, perhaps? Certainly you must remember *something*."

I shook my head. "I was young. I don't—" This wasn't the
discussion I'd expected. Scoldings for leaving the house and cavorting again with Victor Guttenberg, yes, but not this. Hadn't
I been a thorny embarrassment to the Worthingtons over the
years? Why did Mr. Worthington and Mr. Ennis want to dredge
up the past now?

I kept my eyes on my lap, then forced myself to look up. Mr.
Ennis was studying me, as if I were sitting on trial for a crime,
and waited for me to confess.

"Sorry. I don't remember anything." I stood up. "Mr.
Worthington," I said, my voice wavering with emotion, "I'm
tired. May I—please—be excused?"

He stayed me with his hand on mine, then squeezed. "If anything comes to mind," he said, "do let me know."

Of course I understood. Hadn't he drilled it into me well that appearances were everything? The fall election must already weigh on him to be worried about my sordid beginnings. "Yes, Mr. Worthington."

Then resisting the urge to bolt, I stepped through to the living room and made my way upstairs to my bedroom. With my foot on the first step, I caught a few words.

"I told you she doesn't remember anything," Mr. Worthington whispered.

"Let's hope," Mr. Ennis replied. "I wouldn't want you to forget whose platter your position rests on."

Step by step, I headed upstairs, hand on the railing, until I came to my room. I closed the door, locked it, and inhaled the darkness, drawing air down to the deepest reaches of my lungs. As if breathing with me, the night pulled the eyelet curtains in toward the screen window, then let them loose again. A night breeze usually signaled a storm ahead.

Without changing, I flopped back on my bed. I stared upward. Tears rolled down the sides of my face. I let them fall, not bothering if my pillowcase grew wet. Or rumpled. Or in need of a second ironing.

Damn the ironing of sheets and table napkins anyway.

I couldn't make out the puzzle pieces, but without a doubt, Ennis and Mr. Worthington knew something about Mama's death. But what exactly? Would I be haunted forever with wondering, but never know?

My mind drifted, plagued with questions. My stomach rolled with a strange wave of nausea. I wanted to sleep and stop thinking, but the minutes turned to hours. I rolled and turned until thunder rumbled with the beat of Ojibwa drums. Lightning cracked overhead and flooded the world beyond my

curtained window with white. In the next moment, the sky un-
leashed a torrent of rain, and I jumped up, flung the damp curtains wide, and pulled my window shut.

I listened as rain pelted my window and the tiny village of
Ranier—the village that held so many secrets.

| 17 |

I woke to the Worthingtons arguing in their bedroom next to mine. The sun wasn't quite up yet. I wondered if they'd stayed up all night. Words floated in and out of hearing range. I left my bedcovers, tiptoed across my floor, and pressed my ear against the wall.

"I'm afraid she's become a liability," said Mr. Worthington.

"Walter, she's like a daughter," Mrs. Worthington replied, her voice cracking. "You just can't do this to me. You can't just send her away like this."

His voice grew quieter, and I struggled to make out his words. "Izzy...an orphan...warned you from the start not to get too attached...a temporary situation..."

"But Walter—" She stopped crying for a moment and raised her voice. "It's Ennis, isn't it? You two talking late into the night. He plants so many ideas in your head, Walt, that sometimes I wonder if you think for yourself anymore. It's E. W. this and E. W. that! You're a senator now. I want to know for a change, what does Walter Worthington think?"

"I'll pretend, Elizabeth," he replied, his tone ice cold, "that I didn't hear you say that last bit. We owe him a great deal, and you know it. You think your social circles would be what they are—"

"Oh, Walt, I just want you to consider . . . Please, Walt, don't walk away."

Their bedroom door opened and closed. Mr. Worthington's footsteps sounded down the stairs. The entry door shut behind him. With a crank and a rumble, the Model-T started up. I glanced out my window as Mr. Worthington drove off.

A dullness settled in my bones. If I stayed to find out their plans, I would be subject to their choices for me—dismal plans, with the Faribault orphanage at the worst, or at best, a boarding school—and in any case, a situation in which I would have little say or freedom until I reached eighteen. I thought again of Victor and Trinity—even Owen—and how they seemed to choose the lives they wanted, despite whatever constraints they were born into. But I had choices, too.

I just hadn't realized it—until now.

I didn't want to wait around to see which train the Worthingtons would put me on. Rather than be sent away, I would rather leave on my own. If things turned out poorly, then I would have no one to blame but myself.

But where would I go?

And how would I get there?

The small wooden chest on my dresser contained all the money I possessed. I emptied it on my bed. Four dollars and sixty-five cents. A train ride to St. Paul cost at least $5.20. I would have enough for a few meals, if I was lucky. I would have to find work of some kind. *Any kind.*

With a determination I'd never felt before, I made a quick inventory of what I would need to take with me. My traveling satchel, a floral carpetbag large enough to hold a week's worth of clothing, lay on the top shelf of my armoire. I pulled it down and started packing undergarments, comfortable dresses, two skirts, a few blouses and sweaters, comfortable shoes, and a new green wool swimsuit I had not yet worn. Mrs. Worthington had insisted I buy one in May before we left from St. Paul for the cottage. In the middle of it all, I tucked the photographs I'd found. I left enough room in my bag to add a few books, my knitting, and a small stack of sheet music.

My clock's hands stood at 5:35 a.m. I still had time to catch the 6 a.m. steamer to somewhere—anywhere on the lake. Instantly I knew. The Kettle Falls Hotel, of course. It was remote, held work possibilities, and might possibly give me some answers. And I had enough money for boat fare.

I wanted to say good-bye to Mrs. Worthington, and to Aasta and Hans, but I didn't dare. Better to simply leave a note. I wrote neatly—and stretched the truth—and left the pink stationery folded at my bedside table:

Dear Mr. and Mrs. Worthington,
    I cannot thank you enough for your kindness to me over so many years. But now that I am sixteen, I feel ready to set off on my own. I have employment arranged and must start immediately in Duluth.
    Most gratefully and respectfully yours,
    Sadie Rose

I turned my bedroom handle and waited at my threshold for Mrs. Worthington's door to open. But there wasn't a stir in her bedroom. On the landing, I carefully avoided the creakiest steps.

My slate board lay on top of the desk in the living room. I stared at it, wondering. If I brought it with me, I would be tempted to use it, to fall back on it for security. I lifted it, as if weighing it. Then I set it down. .

Before Mrs. Worthington stirred—she must have dozed off—and before the Johannsens arrived to begin their work, I raided the kitchen for bread, sausage, milk, and cheese.

As I slipped out the porch door, I interrupted a beaver's

peaceful cruise of the bay. At my intrusion, he cracked his flat leathery tail against the water—whack—and dove defiantly away. I rounded the cottage and made my way to the road.

The village was just stirring as I neared the landing and the *Emma Louise,* her engine idling. Head high, shoulders back, I pretended I had already been hired on at the Kettle Falls Hotel. Though the morning was still and already turning muggy, with a haze above the water, I carried my traveling coat in the crook of my arm. I knew how quickly the weather could turn cold and didn't want to be without it. And I had no extra room for it in my satchel.

"Excuse me," I said, tapping a young towheaded deckhand with a missing front tooth. "Will this boat get to Kettle Falls today?"

"Hop on," he said, unaware that speech was anything out of the ordinary for me. "Won't get there 'til late afternoon. But we get quite a few customers who like to stay at the hotel pretty regular like."

I climbed aboard, paid forty-five cents for a ticket, and found a seat on the lower decks. Until the steamer pushed off, I avoided eye contact with any other passengers, a wide assortment of common men and women, a handful of children, and an upper tier of tourists and businessmen. I held my breath, hoping that the Worthingtons would not appear in their Model T and demand that I climb off the boat. Once they found my bedroom empty, Mr. Worthington would brush his hands together with an "all for the best." Mrs. Worthington would cry but soon make her husband's sentiments her own.

As the steamer picked up speed through the channel, I exhaled and let my shoulders relax. I almost wanted to pinch myself to make sure I wasn't dreaming. I wasn't on my way to Duluth, nor did I have employment yet. But by leaving the note of mistruths, I hoped they would not bother trying to find me.

If I'd said Kettle Falls, I feared Mr. Worthington would come for me and retrieve me—out of duty—only to ship me off elsewhere. So a little stretching of the truth seemed for the best.

The water route became familiar with stops at lodges and protected harbors, traversing a large bay between Falcon Island and stopping at Red Stone again. When the boat pulled near the Red Stone Island docks, I left my knitting on my bench and turned below to use the head. I closed the door and locked it. I didn't want anyone at Red Stone to recognize me. Below, in the belly of the steamer, the combined smells of fuel and the bathroom made my stomach queasy, but I stayed below until the engine reversed and we were under way again. When I feared I was getting seasick, I stepped out past crates and barrels and climbed up the ladder to the deck, grateful for fresh air.

As the steamer headed beyond E. W. Ennis's island, my mind turned to my late-night encounter. Why were they so concerned about what I remembered from more than a decade ago? What were they hiding? I didn't have any answers but was certain it had something to do with Mama.

By midday I'd eaten half the white cheese and sausage and bread. My bottle of milk was warming as the day heated, and rather than wait for it to sour, I finished it to the last drop. As the steamer covered mile after mile, I was reminded of the man behind the scarred and logged shorelines.

From International Falls and Ranier to Kettle Falls, E. W. Ennis—King Ed—harnessed the power of the flowing waterways to his world-renowned paper mill. Said he was one of the wealthiest men in America. Rumors said he might be worth $100 million. It was unthinkable that someone like Victor Guttenberg could stop the plans of such a powerful lumber giant. King Ed did what he wanted; he got what he wanted. He controlled everything and everybody. I wasn't truly heading out on my own. I was merely heading to another end of the kingdom.

After all, Ennis owned the dam at Kettle Falls, too. If I'd been thinking, I should have found a way to buy a ticket to Duluth, or Chicago, or San Francisco—somewhere far beyond his reach.

The steamer cut through water as it traveled through Brule Narrows, zigzagging between shallow reefs and boulders. A wooden fishing boat puttered by with two men and two women, who waved.

Uncharacteristically calm, the lake stayed glassy until early afternoon, when a light breeze fluttered, helping to keep the black flies away from my ankles, which they bit, despite my cotton socks above my boot tops.

An unshaven man with reeking body odor sat too close beside me. I scooted away a few inches. "Hi, young lady," he mumbled, alcohol reeking from his mouth and skin. "Going to Kettle Falls?"

I nodded, glancing his way at his yellowed teeth and hand missing two fingers.

He held up his hand, for closer inspection on my part. "Logging accident. Happens all the time. I was lucky. Could have lost the whole arm. I got by with just a couple o' fingers lopped off." Then he reached in his pocket and pulled out a wad of dollar bills. "But now I get some time off—and I'm going to have a good ole time! Join me." He tucked his money away and pulled a flask out from his jacket, offering it to me. "Wanna nip?"

I shook my head and looked away.

Finally, he got my message, tipped his mildew-scented cap, stood up, and ambled toward the stern. I half expected him to fall overboard, but he managed to stay upright.

I got up, left my bag and knitting under the bench, and walked to the bow to watch. Between two peninsulas, a bald eagle swooped from the bare top branches of a red pine, dropped toward the water, talons and legs outstretched, then lifted—

without its catch of fish—and flapped slowly before landing on the other side of the channel.

In the distance, a rumbling sound grew. At first I thought a storm was brewing and thunder booming in the distance, but the noise grew steadily louder as the steamer slowed around a bend. Trapper shacks and small log cabins appeared, plus a scattering of Ojibwa teepees. A few children watched the boat go by and waved. I waved back.

And then, the roar from the dam became deafening, as water poured from Namakan Lake and into Rainy Lake. I gripped the railing, inhaling air thick with vapor as it thundered toward us from the twenty-foot drop. Water cascaded powerfully over immense concrete and rock walls, billowing white as it fell. Water swirled and rushed headlong toward the steamer, which the captain steered away toward the sheltering cliff and harbor.

Aiming for one of three long docks, the steamer reversed its engines to slow its speed, then eased closer, deckhands ready, tossing ropes and shouts of greeting. The dock boy hurried toward me and began to loosen the nearest line.

I tried to calm my nerves. I'd felt determined when I stepped on the boat, but as I scanned the remote community at Kettle Falls, my confidence dwindled.

Stacks of empty wooden crates labeled *burbot, sturgeon,* and *whitefish* waited to be filled. Fishing boats lined the docks where a crowd waited: lumberjacks in plaid shirts and suspenders, businessmen in fedoras, and Native women displaying beadwork belts and pendants. On a rocky point, two women with their skirts hiked to their bare knees dangled their feet in the water. So much like the photo of Mama.

The shoreline was rutted and pockmarked with horse hooves, wagon wheels, and footprints. Clear-cut forest stretched from the harbor area up to the distant Kettle Falls Hotel, a long, two-story white building. I sucked in a deep breath.

I hoped they had a job for me—or I would have to take the return voyage back in one short hour. Satchel in hand, I headed up the boardwalk.

"Why, hello, hello!" a man old enough to be my father sang out as I passed by. I fixed my gaze on the boardwalk, which extended from the harbor a quarter-mile to the hotel. Behind it, a wall of rock and a few spared pines separated the hotel from miles of wilderness. Lowland on either side of the walkway gave way to cattails, wild violets, leafy ferns, and deep mud.

Another group of men, some with shirts, a few without, jostled one another near the hotel steps, studying a map.

For a brief second, I expected one of them to offer to carry in my luggage for me. But before waiting—as Mrs. Worthington may have done—I hoisted my satchel and my courage, and started up the ten steps to the hotel's wraparound porch and lobby.

One of the young men said as I passed, "Betcha she's a new girl here. Fresh outta the oven."

I winced, kept my eyes on the steps, and headed inside the Kettle Falls Hotel.

| 18 |

Satchel in hand, I stepped into the sweet tobacco-scented hotel parlor. At my left, a black bear rug hung above two red velvet sofas, a wooden rocker, and an overstuffed leather chair. Behind the glass display case and counter, a bulky woman set down her silver pipe. Her auburn hair was piled high and ringlets fell, softening her sturdy features. "Miss, do I know you?"

Her shoulders and hands were built for heavy work, and yet her midnight blue blouse was femininely ruffled and cut to reveal wrinkled cleavage. She was heavier than I remembered, yet under her commanding owl eyebrows her eyes were the same. Stern and kind. Just as when I had been a child, my wariness mingled with pleasure at seeing her. But my caution won out. I couldn't tell her who I was. If she realized I was connected with the Worthingtons, she might send me packing.

I willed my voice to work. "No, I don't believe so."

From somewhere behind me, a woman cleared her throat in a singsong fashion. I twisted around. From halfway down the staircase, a woman of no more than twenty wearing a stylishly short nightgown leaned over the railing. "Darla, I'm sorry, but he won't wake up. He's not dead, I know, because he's snoring."

"I'll send Howie right up. And, Linnea," Darla said, her tone stern, "get *dressed* before coming down those stairs. This is a ho-*tel*, understand?"

"Yes, ma'am."

Darla held up her finger to me. "Wait here. I'll be right back."

Seeing Darla unnerved me. I should have hopped the train to Duluth. If it turned out that Darla had work for me, I'd stay long enough to earn a railway ticket from Ranier to anywhere at least three hundred miles away. And yet where else could I learn more about Mama? I needed to stay long enough to know what really happened to her.

Out of the corner of my eye, I spotted a couple standing beside suitcases on the screen porch, drinks in hand—so similar in appearance to the Worthingtons—top hat and suit coat, heels and parasol.

While I waited for Darla to return, I took in more details: smoking stands, a round coffee table covered with newspapers and magazines, a set of fine china teacups on a shelf. Through an open doorway to my right was the restaurant. Red gingham-checked oilcloths covered the tables. At one, a man read a newspaper, but the restaurant was otherwise empty.

Beyond, swinging doors opened to the kitchen as a narrow-shouldered waitress came out with a tray of food. She was close to my age, which gave me hope of a job. Her button nose, ivory skin, and narrow shoulders seemed mismatched with her extrawide hips.

"Oh, that's Juju," Darla said, returning through the door behind the counter. "She's a real hard worker." Then she looked beyond me. "Oh, excuse me. I thought you were someone else. May I help you folks?"

I stepped aside, as if perusing the contents of the glass case.

"Just in from Minneapolis," the man said. "We'll be here for a few days of fishing, which I wrote to you about earlier. I'll want to ship crates of fish back to my restaurant before leaving."

"Of course," Darla said, pulling out a large ledger. "If you'll sign the guest book. I assume you're, um...Abernackey?" She ran her finger down a list. "Mr. and—"

The man answered, "Missus." At the word, the woman at his side giggled.

He set his tumbler with ice cubes and strong-smelling whiskey on the counter. I marveled at the luxury of ice, here in the middle of nowhere. Maybe these visitors took it for granted, but I knew that to get ice here, it would have been cut from the lake last winter, hauled out in blocks by a horse or mule, and stored in an icehouse under piles of sawdust, the old-fashioned way. I remembered, being held in someone's arms, watching this once long ago.

The display case brimmed with carved pipes and tobacco, caramels and hard candies, cigarettes, Indian beadwork and leatherwork, postcards, an assortment of magazines, medicines, combs, brushes, toothbrushes, small containers of shampoo, liniment, and face cream.

While I pretended to be interested in such items, Darla explained to the guests, "Breakfast is served between seven and nine, lunch between eleven and two, and dinner between five and eight. The bar," she said, pointing beyond the parlor, "is open around the clock. For those who desire more serious late-night cards and such, we have a party house behind the hotel, to contain the noise a bit so guests can sleep."

"Very good," Mr. Abernackey replied. He took his key and left his luggage where he had dropped it. Then he wrapped his arm around the woman's small waist, guiding her toward the stairs.

"I'll see that Howie delivers your things shortly," Darla said with a commanding smile. "Enjoy your stay at Kettle Falls."

After she finished writing in a ledger, she reached across a stack of Kettle Falls postcards and rested her warm and weighty hands on mine. For a moment, I was sure she recognized me. "Now, how can I help?"

"I'm here to find work." My voice wasn't as clear and strong as I would have wished.

"Yes, I thought so." She surveyed me from head to foot, then met my eyes, as if waiting for me to clarify.

"Not *that* kind of work," I said with a shrug of my head toward the staircase. "Cleaning, cooking, anything like that—if possible."

"Oh, I don't know," Darla said, her eyelids half closing. She wound a locket of hair around her finger. "This is a special hotel, dear to my heart, and anyone who works here needs to appreciate *all* that Kettle Falls has to offer. I wonder if you understand what I mean?"

"You mean, am I willing to look the other way?"

She raised her eyebrows. "Yes, that's precisely what I mean."

"Please. I need a job."

"Well, we *are* in the height of our season," she said, glancing in at the restaurant, where Juju was setting tables, "—and getting busier every year. I could use you. Sort of a fill-in-where-you're-needed job, at least to start with."

My shoulders lightened. "Oh, Darla. I can't thank you—"

"Don't go thanking me yet. I don't even know your name."

My mind went blank, until I flashed on my favorite novelist, Willa Cather.

"Oh, it's Catherine. Catherine Willer."

"Well, Catherine. Do you have a nickname? Something less formal?"

I shook my head. I wasn't practiced at coming up with lie after lie.

"Okay then. I betcha you'll be cursing me after you discover how hard I'm going to work you. There will be sweeping, dusting, water to haul, laundry, kitchen work, maid work, you name it. Show me your hands."

Palms up, I hoped to prove her wrong. But my skin was soft and pale, and my long fingers appeared more suited to playing sonatas than scouring pots.

"You don't have any calluses. I'll give you one week. One week of hard labor, and it might not look so bad to return home, wherever that is."

I hoped she wasn't right. I couldn't go back.

"Promise. I won't disappoint you," I said.

At the boardinghouse, Mama never spanked me; but the flat of Darla's hand had smacked my bottom several times, when Mama was busy upstairs and I had spilled something in the kitchen or started whining. Darla didn't put up with "nonsense." That much I remembered.

Now she held up her stocky finger at me. "Don't *promise* me anything. Just take your things to Cabin 3 on the east side of the hotel. It's for staff, and lucky you, there's one bed open. There's not a stitch of bedding on it, just an old blanket on the springs. But it will have to do until we get something more from town." She glanced at the wall clock, which read 1:25. "You've got until three o'clock to be back in the kitchen. That's when Agnes will need help peeling potatoes and such."

"Yes, Darla."

"Here, you call me either 'Ma'am' or 'Mrs. Jonas.'"

"You're married?" I blurted. I couldn't recall a Mr. Jonas or a regular man at the boardinghouse, except for a man that frightened me who dealt with unruly customers and tossed them down the back steps if they were being too rough or too drunk. His teeth were rotten to stubs, and he seemed to only appear when summoned.

She leaned toward me, nearly spilling her breasts out of

her blue dress and whispered, "Mr. Jonas, well, he's not here too often as he has his other business interests in Chicago." She winked. "Now go on, Catherine."

As I left the parlor for the front porch, she corrected me. "Wrong direction, honey. If you're working for me, you use the back door from now on." She pointed to the door behind her. "The entrance is for customers, and unless you're sweeping it clean or assisting with luggage, I don't want you out here."

"Yes, ma'am. Mrs. Jonas."

| 19 |

I wound past the parlor counter and headed out the door leading to the back screen porch, where two young men leaned
against the wall, smoking. From the end of an adjoining hallway
came the thumping and high-pitched sounds of a player piano.

"Come by for drinks," said the one with narrow eyes and a
sandy mustache.

"And dancing," the other added, tipping his fedora as I
passed out the screen door and down the steps.

"Thanks," I said, "but I'm working here."

"Ha! All the better, sweetheart!"

I ignored them and stepped into the shade of the hotel. I
hoped that I wouldn't at every turn be taken for a "fancy lady."
But what did I expect? This was a hotel built in the middle of
the wilderness, geared toward fishermen, loggers with pocket
change, businessmen, and bootleggers. Sitting on the edge of
Canada and Minnesota, the hotel, I surmised from everything
I'd heard, provided a perfect location for all kinds of trade. Not
always legal, but logical. The law was at a distance, and international borders provided easy refuge. All anyone had to do was
know where to cross by foot, snowshoe, dogsled team, or boat.

The path wound past a white clapboard building with
a plaque above its door: Gaming Room. Beyond sat a host of

storage sheds, where an orange tabby cat slipped out from a half-open door. She arched her back, then stretched out on a rock slab in the path, revealing one white front paw.

I paused and leaned down to pet her. "Hi, pretty kitty."

In a flash of motion, she kicked her back claws into my hand, torqued her body, and bolted, leaving my skin slashed and bleeding.

"That's Brandy," a man said with an English accent.

I jumped and looked to my right. In the shade and on a bench next to the hotel sat a man resting both hands on a walking stick. He peered out from under a lopsided leather hat. His clothes were rags—more dirt than fabric—and he was barefoot. His toes were knobby as tree roots, his toenails amber-colored. It was if he had grown out of the earth. No wonder I hadn't noticed him.

"Oh." I didn't know how to respond. "Hello."

He reached into a basket at his feet and pulled out a gray folded handkerchief. "Here," he said, flapping it open as if to show me what it was, then extending it to me. I stared at him, uncertain.

"Dear girl, you're *bleeding*. Take it."

I looked at the stone path, and, indeed, I was leaving droplets of blood on the walkway and on my dark skirt. I stepped close enough to accept the handkerchief and blotted my hand. "Thanks. I'm Sa—. Uh . . . Catherine. I'm starting today at the restaurant."

"You look mighty familiar . . . Miss Catherine," he said, tilting his head, studying me for a moment. "Well, they call me Caveman," he offered.

His right shoulder tipped awkwardly toward his chest; he might have been seventy, or a terribly old-looking middle-aged man. I couldn't honestly tell. "I, on the other hand," he said, his left eye constantly twitching, "am *finishing* life here. But why not? I have lived to see whole continents and a good number of decades. The important thing is that breakfast is from seven to nine, lunch from eleven to two, and dinner from five to eight. But you probably already know that, if you've met Darla."

"And the tavern," I added, "is open around the clock."

"Ah, now you are catching on, Miss Catherine. What are you looking for, by coming here?"

His question caught me off guard.

"Everyone comes here—this place at the end of the earth— either running from something or looking for something. Which is it for you, dear girl?"

I couldn't answer, and I felt caught in his probing stare, until he nodded at the handkerchief I pressed over my hand. "You can return it to me when you are finished with it. Laundered, of course."

I did a slight curtsy. "Thank you. I will." I gathered my bags and headed toward a row of six small log cabins.

At every turn, I was meeting someone unexpected, and Kettle Falls was like a little ship that drew its passengers from the fringes of society. I would prove Darla wrong. I would not run back to the Worthingtons. My back stiffened. Victor and Trinity would be proud of my stand. I wondered if Owen would notice me gone.

The staff cabins each boasted one small window and a wooden door. I found the one marked Number 3 and knocked. When no one answered, I entered. Immediately, my nose itched and my eyes attempted to adjust to the semidarkness. Two bunk beds, two wooden dressers, a coat rack, and a washstand with a basin and pitcher filled the room. The unlit kerosene lantern mounted above the washstand left black soot on the white-painted ceiling boards. A few pairs of boots lined one wall. And in the corner, next to a broom and dustpan, lay piles of mice or bat droppings.

Each side of the cabin held a bunk bed. Three mattress-es were covered with quilts and clothing—one folded neatly—and I found mine, the top bunk on the left, with a scratchy horse blanket and a mattress of metal coils. Hardly the bed I'd left at home. My traveling coat would come in handy until I could find better. At least I'd found a place to stay and work.

For now.

Exhausted from little sleep, I tossed my satchel on the end of my bunk, then climbed up the wooden ladder, and stretched out on the blanket. With my coat rolled into a pillow, I dropped into sleep.

I dreamed I bought a ticket on a passenger ship, much like the *Titanic,* its fate sprawled across every newspaper several years ago. Its rooms opened to upper cabins for the wealthy, with fresh sea air to cool their bunks, and coffee and small cakes de-livered to them on silver platters by waiters. I, however, was ordered belowdecks. As commanded, I crawled down the lad-der as the ship swayed, and I kept descending step after step into darkness and stench. The boat groaned and creaked and rocked—and hands, too many hands, grasping and touch-ing—were suddenly on me as my boots touched the ship's floor, meeting a man's murmurs of pleasure and groaning. And then I woke up.

I tried to scream, but a hand was on my mouth, blocking my voice and ability to breathe. This was no dream—a man was on *top* of me! The one smoking on the back porch with the sandy mustache. "Get off me!" I tried to scream, but he didn't remove his hand, even when I bit into his flesh.

"Don't worry, little whore," he said, panting. "I'll pay when I'm good and finished."

He pressed his weight on me, pinning me. I tried to hit at him, but nothing stopped him from fumbling with my skirt, lifting it, lifting it.

Someone knocked on the door, and he pushed harder against my mouth. They knocked again, then shoved until hardware snapped.

"What the hell is this?" A young woman stood in the doorway, silhouetted in shadow.

The man scrambled off me.

"Darla doesn't tell us we have a new roommate? And then we find her here with a boyfriend? Get out of here, both of you!"

"She was asking for it," the man blustered, nearly falling off the ladder. "I was gonna do her a goddam favor."

I pulled my skirt back over my legs. I could barely breathe, let alone talk. It had happened so fast. All I'd done was lie down for a quick nap, only to find a man trying to overpower me. My whole body began trembling with shame and anger.

I sat up. "He's lying!" I tried to yell, pointing at him as he tucked in his shirt on his way out the door. But my words stuck in my throat. The young woman at the door let him by and, glaring, turned her gaze from him to me. She was short with a long draping ponytail of red hair, and I took her to be in her late twenties.

"I was napping," I finally managed in a whisper, my face crumbling. "He forced himself on me!"

She studied me as if she'd heard this before from previous roommates.

"Better not tell Darla. She only keeps girls on who can handle themselves out here. Men come lookin' for a good time—she doesn't want to ruin the atmosphere, so I wouldn't say anything. She'll send you packin'. You need to keep your wits about you, that's all. Darla says she wishes her fancy ladies would wear red skirts like they used to in the old days. It would make things easier for the rest of us." Then she thumped her chest with her forefinger. "I'm Meg."

"I hope you believe me," I managed, tears welling as what had just happened started to hit me. If she hadn't come when she had…His arms were steel and my efforts to push him off me were completely useless. Even biting his hand didn't stop him. I shuddered. What if Meg hadn't shown up?

"I was sent for you. Darla said you're already late. It's five bells, and you better get your butt in the kitchen if you wanna work here."

I smoothed my hair with my hand, climbed down the bunk ladder, and followed Meg, who limped, her right foot shaped awkwardly to the side, like a trailing croquet club. She spun suddenly, halfway between the cabin and hotel. "I won't say what I came upon," she said, "as long as you promise never to call me what others call me around here."

"What's that?"

"Peg Leg Meg," she said, spitting out each word. "Call me that—I'll knock your head off. Got it?"

"Got it."

Willing my feet forward, I followed her every halting footstep toward the back door of the kitchen on the hotel's east end. I glanced across the hotel's strips of lawn.

The late afternoon sun pierced my eyes.

Everything felt too sharp.

Too bright.

Too loud.

Bantering and guffaws shot out from the hotel screen porch. Outside, along the length of red-and-white striped awning, men clustered with drinks; women in colorful skirts and parasols laughed gaily.

To my dread, I spotted him near the badminton net. The man with the mustache—nearly doubled over in laughter with his friend.

A gray pain spread, pulsing in the center of my head, but I followed Meg inside, wishing more than anything that the cook's name was Aasta—not Agnes. I would bury my head in her shoulder and sob. Instead, I held my head high, drawing breath after breath.

| 20 |

For two days, I forced myself to focus on work. Agnes, the cook, was short on words, but good at pointing. With her jiggling birth-marked arm, she'd point to the twenty-gallon crock and the giant wooden spoon beside it and order, "Stir." I stirred vats of bread batter, waited for it to rise, and then tamped it down with my fist until it rose again. In another vat, I added the beginnings of sauerkraut: sliced cabbage, vinegar, sugar, and fennel. I cut up piles of onions until tears flowed. I washed, scrubbed, and peeled mountains of carrots and potatoes.

When Agnes didn't have an immediate task for me, Darla did. I hauled water from the well, two buckets at a time, back and forth, until blisters broke in my palms and knives stabbed my shoulder blades. The hotel's water was heated on top of the kitchen cookstove, and when Howard, the hotel's skinny handyman, was too busy, I was asked to carry water upstairs. I used the dark and steep backstairs passageway instead of the parlor staircase and stopped repeatedly to keep steaming water from sloshing on my skirt.

More than once, after knocking on a bedroom door, I would enter, only to find one of the fancy ladies stark naked, or nearly so. I learned to avert my eyes and do my work: filling pitchers, emptying washbasins, and (holding my breath against the stench) dumping thunder mugs (a smaller version of honey buckets) down outhouse holes.

A dozen women worked the hotel rooms, and I often wondered as I came and went how similar Mama's life had been to theirs. As a rule, after a night of dancing in the tavern and entertaining customers in the game room and hotel bedrooms, the women slept until noon or later.

One afternoon, when I was changing bedding upstairs, Franny, who was plump and pale as a dumpling, sat at a vanity, applying makeup over her sallow skin and dark shadows. "One of these days," she said, "no amount of makeup is going to work anymore." She laughed ruefully. "Yup, Darla will send me packing, and then what am I gonna do?"

It wasn't that I didn't care, but I didn't know what to say, and it dawned on me that Franny was old enough to be my mother. Old enough to perhaps have known my mother. I risked asking. "Excuse me, but . . . did you ever know Bella Rose?"

Franny glanced at me in her mirror's reflection. Her eyebrows closed together, as if she should be suspicious about something. Finally she volunteered, "Huh. That one. What's it to ya?"

"I heard she was found in the snow."

"Hey, why you askin'?"

I paused. Why was I? I had to know what happened. Yet if I explained to Franny why I cared, that I was Bella Rose's daughter, she might alert Darla and send me home. I couldn't risk it and instead pretended to be just another rumormonger. "They say she drank herself to death. That there was an empty whiskey bottle in her frozen hand. But what do you think? Is that what killed her?"

"Huh. Darling, *I drink*. Lots of us girls drink to stay sane. But Bella? No way. Not that one. How she managed *without* drinking I'll never figure."

"That so?"

"Not a drop. She lived for her little girl, far as I could see."

Lived for her little girl. I felt faint hearing the words.

"Damn, she must have been saving every penny, hoping things would change. But you know what? I've learned you never make it out of this profession alive. I mean, you either get killed, you die of disease, or you kill yourself." She laughed. "But hell. We all die someday, right?"

Tears threatened to flow. I turned back to the mattress, my vision blurring as I pulled off pillowcases and bedding and added them to the growing stack. Then I left with the wicker basket to the next room, before Franny would piece things together and identify me.

The next morning, as I swept cobwebs, spiders, and bugs from the outside walls, I listened to conversations of guests. As fishermen ate blueberry–wild rice pancakes and fried walleye on the screen porch, I worked out of view below, sweeping off the whitewashed clapboard from ground level.

"Guess she went missing a few days ago."

"Most folks are glad to have their birds fly the coop."

"Not in this case. I mean, we're talking the senator."

"Yeah, when our train pulled in, his missus was crying and fussing at the ticket counter. Fella there told her he never sold the girl a ticket, no matter what that lady wanted to believe."

"I say, they want to go, let 'em go!"

Then their conversation turned. "Hey, what's going on with Ernie's blind pig? Heard he was up here producin' like gangbusters, and then no sign of him. He was back thataway last year. Did he keel over or run off with the booze?"

"Bootleggin' has its risks."

"And its rewards! Ha!"

I had no idea who Ernie was and didn't care, so I quit listening. Toward the bay, the sound of an auctioneer's voice floated out from a megaphone as he sought to command good prices for boxes of fish. "Whitefish, fresh this morning from Eckhart's Fisheries! Packed with ice and ready to ship, guaranteed fresh..."

I moved along down the eastern side of the hotel, sweeping high and low, my neck aching. This morning the dandelion spiders were enjoying the sunshine on the siding. I swept them down, along with an occasional wolf spider, and round-bellied spiders and flies caught in their webs. The day before, the building was covered in a fresh hatch of tiny, gray moth-like bugs. Every day, the lake delivered up a new hatch of something or other.

I kept sweeping and mulled over the men's conversation. So the Worthingtons—or at least Elizabeth Worthington—cared that I was missing. This news surprised me. Her concern touched me, and a pang of guilt pinched my conscience. But I doubted Mr. Worthington cared. I couldn't see how I could be of concern to him. Except for that late-night conversation when he and Ennis had worried about what I'd remembered.

And then as I swept, a memory nudged and pushed from deep within, like an earthworm burrowing through dense decayed matter to reach the surface. I felt lightheaded. I set the broom against the building and rubbed my temples, trying to shake an impending headache. Shadows licked at the edges of my memory. Surfacing, surfacing, surfacing. And then, there it was, in the light of day.

Behind the parlor stove—sometime earlier that same night—I had peered out from my corner to see two men alone in the parlor, speaking in hushed tones.

"She drank too much and she hit her head," Ennis said, kneading his large hands. "Can't let this trace back to me. Understand?"

"Got it."

"And what about the kid?"

I burrowed under my blankets, pretending to be sleeping. I stayed put, eyes closed, still as ice. Someone stepped closer to my hiding place, breathing, looking down on me, then retreated by a few steps.

Worthington replied. "Don't worry. She's out like a lamp."

I picked up my broom, in case Darla or Agnes could spot me from a window and scold me for not working. Franny said Mama never drank. Then why would Ennis, who must have been there when Mama died, say otherwise?

I swept, brooding.

No matter how many details I pieced together, no matter what injustices I uncovered, I never would be able to prove anything. No one would listen to a girl of sixteen recounting her memories as a young child in a brothel.

Just last night Meg, whose upper bunk was directly across from mine, leaned toward the edge and told me about some of the secrets she'd learned since she'd started at the hotel. She witnessed Daisy one morning last summer with bright red finger marks around her neck after a night's work. Darla made Daisy wear silk scarves until the marks healed. "Someone thought it would be entertaining to choke her," Meg said. "And then just last fall, they found Scarlett—another working lady here—facedown in the woods one morning."

"Dead?" I asked reluctantly. We were whispering over Agnes's snoring below and Juju's random talking in her sleep.

"What do you think? Think she was on the ground sniffin'

slugs? Of *course* she was dead! Some jerk had taken a knife to her after he did his business and then just left her there to rot."

My stomach rolled. "Did they ever catch who—?"

"You bet. Wasted no time stringing him up out here from a tall pine."

"So when there's trouble, the sheriff must come out here—" I ventured, relieved that there was justice for such crimes.

"No, it was frontier style. You bet. Only sheriff or law enforcement that come out here are the ones who want to spend their dimes on the ladies and booze. Or check in on their investments. How else do you think blind pigs and rum running are going to happen? That's why they don't see a thing, even though it's right under everybody's noses." She huffed. "You sure don't know much of anything, do you, Catherine?"

I didn't know what to say. She was right. My life had been so protected with the Worthingtons.

Time after time, when I'd sat in the corner reading at the lake cottage, Mrs. Worthington would sip tea with her friends and explain how I'd come into their lives. "Oh, Walter made something right out of that tragedy," she would say. And then she'd go on about how he'd reformed Ranier after they'd found 'that woman pickled with alcohol.'"

Reaching the hotel's eastern edge, I swept down the last remaining cobwebs and fish flies, and then headed in through the kitchen's back door.

| 21 |

I did my utmost not to draw attention to myself. When I was asked to set tables at the restaurant, I made sure I finished before serving hours. When I was asked to deliver an item to a hotel room, such as a bowl of soup or a pot of tea to one of the working ladies or a customer, I kept my head bowed and stayed clear of questions. My skills at not speaking came in handy. All I had to do was not open my mouth, and soon people stopped their attempts at small talk.

One afternoon, when a steady rain soaked the earth and dampened the air, I found an excuse to deliver water to Franny's hotel room. She was without a customer, and I closed the door behind me. I filled her water pitcher and then put my water pail next to the door. I didn't want to risk telling Franny the truth about my interest in Bella Rose, but my need to know burned in me like white coals. I had to take a chance.

"Franny, my name's not really Catherine."

In a lavender robe, she sat on the edge of the brass four-poster bed, her legs crossed. "You think that's big news? None of us girls uses our real name. It's too personal, if you know what I mean."

"You're not Franny?"

She rolled her eyes. "No. My given name is Chastity."

"Chastity? You're kidding."

"Don't laugh, and don't ever tell a soul."

"I promise. I won't say a word. But then you have to keep my secret, too."

Like an impatient cat flicking its tail, Franny wiggled the toes on her crossed leg. "So, you gonna tell me or what?"

I glanced up at the tin ceiling, then met Franny's eyes. "I'm Sadie Rose, Bella's daughter."

Silence filled the space between us. Not even Franny's toes moved.

"That's why I need to know..."

"Well, what d'you say." Franny began coughing, deep and retching. I waited until she regained herself. When she did, she reached for a pack of Lucky Strikes on her nightstand, put one between her fingers, and lit it. She inhaled, studying me, smoke billowing around her. "Now that you say it, you *do* resemble her, you know. I'm surprised Darla hasn't figured out who you are by now. But—lots of people come and go around here—and that was a long time ago. So you wanna know..."

I nodded and swallowed around the dryness in my throat.

"Okay, you asked for it. For starters, she was Ennis's favorite."

"Ennis? You're sure?" Though I was relieved to have Franny confirm my memory of Ennis and Worthington talking in the brothel parlor that night, my stomach rolled at the idea that Ennis had taken extra interest in my mother. His *favorite*.

She glared at me. "What? You think he's above a little pokin' around? Hell. He's been Darla's biggest supporter. It was E. W. Ennis who kicked your mother out of her own house after your father died. They'd been renting one of those little bungalows near the grocery store in Ranier. But with her husband suddenly gone, she couldn't pay the rent to Ennis. She had just had

a baby—well, I guess that would have been you, wouldn't it?"
She scowled at me. "She was skinny, scared. It was the middle
of March, and she was kicked out into the street."

I didn't remember sitting down, but there I was, sitting in
my skirt on the rug near Franny's unmade bed. Trying to absorb what I didn't want to hear.

"Of course, she had no money. No place to go. No family.
What I know is that it was Darla who eventually offered her a
place to stay and work."

Forced onto the streets, with a new baby and grieving her
husband, who could say what anyone would do? What if I suddenly had a baby to feed and clothe? For years, I'd tried so hard
to distance myself from her, but now I realized . . . if it hadn't
been for a baby, hadn't been for me, Mama's situation might
have been different. Over the years I'd absorbed Elizabeth
Worthington's judgments against her. I wanted to apologize.
Forgive me, Mama. Forgive me.

"That Bella Rose. We wanted to hate her—he had her all
dressed up like she was upper crust—but she was no better than
the rest of us. And then, because she never drank, well, she
seemed a little too good for the rest of us, y'know what I mean?"

Franny turned back to her vanity, pulled an amber bottle
from one of the small drawers, took one swig, then another,
and put the bottle back.

"But I don't get it," I said. "If Ennis kicked her out onto the
street, why would she later have anything to do with him?"

She shrugged. "Hey, Darla sends us our customers. You
think we have a say? Hell, we're so in debt for every stitch of
clothing, every meal, every drop of liquor. Oh yeah, she knows
how to keep us close to her skirts, she does. Honey, all I know is
that in time, Ennis took to that Bella and made sure he was her
only client. But then one night, they had this huge fight. Oh,
he took her down a notch all right. She must have thought she

could get out, because he was raging like a bull at her. 'You can't leave!' he kept yelling. And 'I own you!' But she was shouting right back. 'Your money can't stop me this time!' Well, maybe his money didn't do it, but he stopped her. Lots of crashing and knocking around, and then it went quiet. Awfully quiet," she said, letting her meaning sink in, "if you know what I mean."

I closed my eyes.

"Hey, kid, you okay?"

Arms clasped around my knees, a familiar pain, the color of blood, seeped in at the periphery of my brain. My head began to throb.

"Listen, this isn't something you go telling anyone. I figure, you're her daughter, you deserve to know. But you aren't going to bring your mother back from the dead. And you'll only get a shitload of trouble for yourself—and me —if you start talking about Ennis. It's water under the bridge now, got it?"

I opened my eyes.

It wasn't that I hadn't known but, rather, what I found so strangely unsettling and reassuring was that something deep inside me already knew.

Had somehow known all along.

"What brought you out here, anyway?" Juju looked over my shoulder as I prepped chickens for baking. As Agnes had ordered, I rubbed their skins with butter and stuffed the birds with a mixture of breadcrumbs, herbs, chopped celery, and onion.

I didn't want to make up an answer, so I just didn't answer. I kept stuffing chickens as if I didn't hear.

"I think she's a little slow," Juju whispered to Agnes.

I was glad to have work.

That evening turned warm, humid, and sticky. Where my apron strap tied at the small of my back, a tiny river of sweat flowed. The kitchen steamed as I emptied hot water into the sinks and washed the last of the supper dishes. As I wiped my red hands on the cotton towel, hoping to call it a night and head to my cabin, Agnes held out a bowl of green olives. When the Worthingtons had set out tables of food for holiday entertaining, I sneaked olives as greedily as a squirrel after acorns. I wondered where this year's holiday would find me. Certainly not helping to decorate the Christmas tree at the Summit Avenue home.

"Before you leave," Agnes said, her thin hair plastered with sweat, "bring these to the tavern. They're going through 'em faster than candy!"

In the small mirror by the kitchen's back door, I shot a glance at myself. I looked like I had been standing in a downpour. My fasionable bob clung in strands to the sides of my face. Swell. I mopped sweat droplets from my forehead and neck. Then I carried the plate through the parlor to the back hallway toward the sound of pounding piano keys.

Caveman, barefoot as always, tipped his hat at me in the dim hallway as we crossed paths.

When I stepped into the tavern, I felt dozens of men gaze in my direction. I kept my head down, but in one peripheral glance, I took in the long mahogany bar and rows of glistening liquor bottles; the bartender with his shiny bald crown; paintings of topless women looking down from the walls on a room filled with men of all ages and hotel ladies with sleeveless, short dresses. I expected to see a piano player but instead music blared from a nickelodeon—like an armoire with stained-glass doors, from behind which notes were struck on rolling sheets. I'd only seen them advertised in Mrs. Worthington's magazines.

And that's when I spotted E. W. Ennis at a high table, sitting tall and proud as well-fed royalty, along with another man and two women.

I nearly dropped the bowl.

"You're a cherub!" the bartender said, meeting me at the end of his counter. "We're cookin' with gas tonight!"

With shaky hands, I released the bowl into his. I couldn't move, couldn't speak, couldn't turn away.

Mr. Ennis was smiling and gesturing grandly. At his side was Linnea, her blonde hair in tight curls, one arm loose around Mr. Ennis's shoulder, and leaning in close, as if living by his every word. He patted her rump, then grabbed his drink. He was married with two daughters. I didn't want to see this any more than I wanted to think that Mama had once been his favorite. She, too, had been forced to act as if she enjoyed his company.

Before he could spot me, I forced myself away, pivoted, and hurried out into the hallway, ignoring a low whistle and a pinch by one of the men near the doorway. Face flushed warm, I walked down the wainscot-paneled hallway with amber glass lamps toward the back porch. I couldn't get back to my cabin fast enough.

Caveman, however, now occupied the wicker chair near the door. He stretched his walking stick across the door, as if to keep me prisoner. He was a most curious fellow. Just the day before, Meg had led me beyond the hotel to show me where he lived. His home was a cave in the ground covered with boards and canvas. And like so many other bootleggers around the hotel, his moonshine still was visible through the brush. Its barrel and stovepipe were almost in plain view. She said Caveman had originally come from England and then went off to volunteer in the Great War, despite being older than any other soldier. He returned changed, lost all feeling in his feet from being gassed by the Germans, and that's why he now roamed shoeless and in dirt-soiled clothes. But no one knew his story for sure, so Meg said it was pieced together since Caveman refused to talk about his past.

Now he studied me. "You're in a bloody hurry, Miss Catherine."

I nodded. I thought he might start joking with me, but his tone was weighty.

"Better to face what's chasing you," he said, "than to flee."

He had an uncanny way of knowing what was going on around the hotel. I eyed the door and frowned.

"Unless it's Brandy that's after you."

I forced a weak smile.

"Dear girl, you look like you've seen a ghost."

"Maybe I have," I whispered.

"Ah, let me guess. The famed industrialist, am I right?" Caveman lifted and lowered his walking stick, as if taunting me. "Some say he's responsible for murder. Did you know that?"

My legs nearly buckled. "You know about Bella Rose?"

Caveman shook his head. "I've heard about her. Who knows what happened in her case?" He shrugged. "No, I meant the photographer. Her husband."

"What?" I glanced over my shoulder, hoping E. W. himself wasn't going to suddenly appear. I recalled Fred Foxridge telling me he'd bought photography equipment from my mother after her husband had died. But murder?

"What are you saying?"

"Frank Ladovitch—that was his name. You might say his subject matter changed. You see, he started photographing the landscape, too. He took photos of shorelines before and after they'd been logged. And he sent those photos off to magazines—big ones. And it didn't go over well, you see. Some thought he was interfering with logging, and they didn't want photographs changing public opinion—which has a way of changing laws. He was found floating in the middle of the lake. The local paper said suicide, even though he was a fine swimmer."

"Why are you telling me this?" I wanted to cry. It was all too much to take in. And who was Caveman but a crazy war veteran who lived in a hole he'd carved out of the earth. As far as I knew, he could be making everything up, just to upset me. The air was thick and damp, and I desperately needed to step outside to breathe.

"I have to go. Please." I lifted his walking stick away from the door and allowed myself to pass. Whether he said so or not, I worried that Caveman had figured out who I was. Strange as he was, he had a way of being, of knowing things. I stepped outside to the sound of cricket song, frogs croaking, and mosquitoes whining.

But Caveman's voice followed me through the screen.

"I know about running," he said under his breath. "It kills you."

When I reached my cabin, though Meg and Juju were already under their covers, I withdrew the photographs of Mama and studied them under the lamp. I thought of Victor's words the first time I'd met him. He'd said, "Everyone has a last name." He'd offered to help me find mine, but I'd found it on my own. Bella Rose was Mama's name, but I had always sensed it was her working name—not her full or real name.

Ladovitch.

That was a real last name.

And there in the photograph was Mama, smiling, bare feet dangling, her dress halfway up to her thighs, perched on the rock ledge by Kettle Falls Dam. She had been here. I'd been here, too. And sometime before that, my father, Frank Ladovitch, had been a photographer who died before I was born.

"Sadie Rose Ladovitch," I whispered, staring at the image.

"What was that?" mumbled Meg, one arm hanging over the edge of her bunk. "Get to bed, will ya? Cut the light!"

I put the photographs away, changed into my nightdress, and climbed up to my bunk. Even though Darla had managed to find a mattress for my bunk, I tossed and turned. The night was still and mosquitoes found their way in through poorly sealed door and window frames. "Meg, are you awake?"

"Yeah."

"How's this cabin going to keep out the cold this winter if it can't keep out mosquitoes?"

"A few people stay on at the hotel, but the cabins are only for summer staff. I'll be gone by late September. So will you, I'm sure."

I'd felt so smug about landing a job that I had never considered that it might come to an end so soon. I thought I'd be able to settle in, and my biggest worry would be that I'd be discovered. "Oh," I said. "Where will you go?"

"Back to Ranier to waitress at the Empire Club."

I knew the two-story building on the corner of River Street and Main. It kept a steady stream of customers. I'd asked Hans earlier that year about how the Prohibition would change things in Ranier. I'd written my question on my slate board, and taking me just as seriously as an adult, he said that nothing in Ranier would change. Only difference was that places like the Empire Club might officially serve only soda pop, until you gave the right password. Then they'd "open up the gates of heaven" to whatever anyone wanted. I would miss Hans.

"Well, there's no way I'm returning to Ranier to work," I said.

"You're above that, eh?" Meg laughed. "Never say never."

I didn't answer. I wished I could speak freely with her, but as much as I wanted—needed—a friend, I couldn't trust her with my secrets. Even Darla, who could be a valuable ally, made me feel skittish. After all, she made money from her ladies' customers. Men like E. W. Ennis. For all I knew, he'd financed the Kettle Falls Hotel, too.

I mulled over my options in silence.

I needed to find a way to work outside the area. Darla hadn't paid me anything yet, but I hoped that before long I would earn enough for train fare to somewhere far beyond Ranier. I had few skills, with one exception. I could play the piano. Quite possibly, if I settled long enough in an affluent area, I could give piano lessons to children. Beyond that, I wasn't sure what I would do.

By the time dawn broke and seagulls began calling on the bay, I had fallen soundly asleep, only to be woken sternly by Juju. "Agnes sent me to wake you," she said. She yanked on my bare foot. "C'mon, lazy bones. Time to start chopping. Agnes is fretting cuz we have a whole gang of fishermen coming in for a late-morning breakfast." Then she ambled back out the cabin door, her hips nearly reaching the frame. As far as Juju was concerned, I never spoke. She always slept hard during my late-night whisperings with Meg.

In the kitchen, my eyes were tearing up from chopping onions when the delivery door opened. To my surprise, Owen Jensen pushed in a wooden dolly with crates of milk and blocks of cheese. "Dairy fresh! Good morn—" He stopped smiling when he saw me. "Sadie Rose?"

I glared and lifted my forefinger to my lips. Then I returned to chopping, careful not to lose my fingers—now that I would need them to teach piano lessons somewhere. I watched Owen out of the edge of my vision, in shock to see him.

Delighted to see him.

Agnes didn't turn from frying bacon and called to Owen over her shoulder. "Could ya put it away for us this time in the icehouse, dear? We're mighty busy this morning and a little short-staffed. You know where it is?"

"Yes, ma'am. I sure do," Owen replied.

I mouthed "I'll meet you there."

I chopped faster, wiped my hands on my apron, and after a few eternal minutes blurted, "Sorry, but I have to run to the outhouse. Be right back."

"You better be," Agnes replied, without turning. Since I'd stepped into the kitchen to work, the smells of bacon and sizzling French toast made my mouth water, but with Owen's arrival, I lost my appetite.

I slipped off in the direction of the outhouses, just in case Agnes had stepped outside for a little fresh air and to smoke. There were two three-holers, side by side. One marked "men" and the other marked "women." But I veered off to the icehouse, which was uphill a few yards and cut into the slope. The wooden door was closed, and Owen's empty dolly sat outside.

Only yesterday I'd been asked to haul the last bottles of milk into the kitchen's icebox. In the day's heat, I'd found the icehouse wonderfully cool. Not only was it built into the rocky hillside, but it was filled with cedar shavings over giant ice blocks from the lake. Against the blocks stood crates of produce and foodstuffs. Already the morning sun beat down on the path and on my shoulders. I welcomed its cool shadows.

I glanced both ways, then pulled on the handle and stepped into the hillside log structure.

In complete darkness, hands went to my hips, pulling me close as someone leaned his head toward mine, his breath warm on my face and his lips suddenly brushing mine. Instinctively, my mind went to the man with the blond mustache.

I grabbed his hands and flung them off of me and backed up toward the door. "No!" I shouted. I wasn't going to be taken advantage of a second time. Just as quickly, I realized it was Owen. What was he thinking?

"I didn't come out here for *that*," I said and pushed my rear against the heavy door, allowing a little light between us.

Owen hung his head. "Heck, I thought when you said you'd meet me—"

"You thought wrong," I whispered. "I need your *help.*"

"Oh," he said, his eyes like a puppy's looking for reassurance after a good kick. It wasn't that I found him unattractive. "Sorry," he said. "I just thought maybe—"

I put my hand on his forearm. "I like you, I do. But I ran away. I'm using a different name here. Catherine, not Sadie."

"Last place I expected to see you. Thought you were long gone from the area. And working for Agnes? She's a piece of tough steel." Then his eyes teased, and he tilted his head. "Is there a reward out for you? You know, I could use the money."

"Not that I know of. Mr. Worthington's probably relieved I'm gone. But Owen, there's so much I need to tell you."

And then, talking rapidly, I told him a bit of what I'd stitched together. How my father might have been silenced by Ennis for stirring up trouble with his photographs of clear-cut shorelines. Of how I remembered Ennis and Worthington talking that night my mother died.

"What a pile of rotten fish," he said.

I nodded, relieved to tell someone, even though Owen could do little more than listen. "And I can't stay here long. Just last night Mr. Ennis was here—might still be for all I know." I thought of Linnea and how if she was doing her job, she would have danced with Ennis and then led him upstairs for paying pleasures. "It's a matter of time before I'm found out. And I can't exactly tell Darla to pay me early so I can catch a train. I don't know what to do—and I better get back to the kitchen before Agnes takes her broom after me." I turned to go.

"Wait. I have an idea," he said.

"What?"

"I have one more delivery at this end of the lake, and then I'll swing by and pick you up."

"But where? I can't go to the main docks. Too many people come and go from there—including Mr. Ennis."

"Meet me just north of the point, north of the docks. There's a natural harbor there—right beside a trapper's cabin. I can get in and out of there without my boat hitting rocks."

"When?"

"A half-hour from now."

"You're joking."

"I have a plan. Trust me."

I knew I had to. I was a sitting mouse waiting for a cat to put its paw on me. If I didn't leave, I'd soon find myself delivered to the Worthingtons, who in turn would ship me off to who knew where. Thirty minutes wasn't much time. But all I had to do was to gather my belongings from my cabin—precious few—and find an obscure path to the point.

Grateful not to feel so alone, I stretched on my tiptoes and planted a kiss on his cheek. "I'll be there."

| 22 |

Owen left the icehouse first.

Near my feet, a centipede crossed the dirt floor as I counted to sixty. A zillion legs scuttled across the thin shaft of light from the cracked door and then disappeared into the dank shadows. If Owen was true to his word, I could be away from Kettle Falls in a half-hour. I would have to wait and see what kind of plan he had in mind. *Trust me*, he'd said.

I opened the door a few inches wider, hesitating. Out of duty, I felt I should return to the kitchen, but if I did, Agnes and Juju would press me into a morning of tasks, and I'd miss my chance. Still, I hated to leave them when they needed help. I was useful. I worked hard. I wished I didn't have to leave a job I'd just started.

Though the morning had launched sunny with a light breeze, now a green hue hung uneasily over the motionless air. A pileated woodpecker drummed on a nearby gray tree, riddling it with seeming bullet holes.

Found floating in the middle of the lake. The photographer. My real father. That's what Caveman had said.

I swallowed hard and stepped outside.

Somewhere beyond view, a boat motor hummed, an ax

struck wood with a rhythmic thunk, and a push lawnmower whirred.

I glanced up, praying that Mr. Ennis wasn't at one of the upstairs bedroom windows, looking down at me. Beyond the roofline, a long ribbon of purplish gray marked the western sky. Bad weather usually came from the west, but storms hit in the afternoon more often than the mornings. I hoped that Owen and I wouldn't get caught in foul weather, which could turn open water into deadly waves.

Hurry.

At my cabin, I shoved my books and knitting back in my satchel. Just as I grabbed my traveling coat and rolled it into a tight ball and tucked it under my arm to leave, someone entered the cabin and closed the door behind them.

I panicked, feeling trapped again.

Darla faced me, scowling, hands on her hips. "Franny told me, and now I see it plain as day. You're Bella Rose's girl, aren't you?"

I was dumbstruck.

"Aren't you?!" she shouted.

I nodded.

"What kind of game do you think you're playing with me, coming in under a fake name, thinking I wouldn't find out, huh? Are you trying to threaten my establishment in some way? Is that it?" She took a few long strides toward me and slapped me hard across the face.

Reflexively, I crisscrossed my arms across my stinging face.

"Who do you think you are? Coming around, asking questions, lying to me. Stirring up trouble about some of my customers. You're a liability, and I won't have it."

I waited for another assault, which didn't come.

"From the start, you were nothing but trouble for me," she said.

I lowered my arms. "Yes. I'm her daughter." My voice shook, but I stood to my feet and forced myself to speak louder. "And no, I didn't come to cause you trouble. I needed work, just enough money to catch a train away from here."

"Looks like you're packed to leave—"

I opened my mouth, thinking of some sort of excuse. "I was just—"

But she stopped me with her outstretched hand. "No more lies."

"And I had to know," I whispered, "more about my mother."

"I advise you to forget about her. Lock everything you think you know or don't know about her in a closet..." She pressed her lips into a stiff line, then spoke, her voice dropping to a rough whisper: "...and throw...away...the key. Because if I *ever*—and don't underestimate me when I say this—if I *ever* find you putting your nose into my business again—*mother or not*—you'll wish you hadn't been born."

She inhaled deeply through her nostrils, wheezing with the intake, her bosom rising beneath her ruffled blouse. Then she exhaled heavily and adjusted a silver pin that held her curls high. Then she opened the door. "Now you get the *hell* out of here." Then she strode off toward the hotel without glancing back.

Rattled, I followed one of several paths behind my cabin. Had I told Darla the truth when I'd first arrived, maybe she would have thought differently of me. Perhaps she would have told me willingly about my mother. But I doubted it. More likely, being the businesswoman that she was, I would have been back on the steamer the day I'd arrived. Now that she knew my identity, would she report me to the Worthingtons? Or would she hope that I would simply disappear—pretend she'd never heard of me?

"Catherine!" Juju hollered from a distance. "Catherine Willer! Get in here!"

Though I was well beyond view and hidden by trees, I picked up my pace, careful not to trip over the gnarly and rocky terrain. I felt pin pricks of guilt, not answering Juju, but I had no choice. The path curved toward the lake, yet far enough from it for me to stay out of view.

I passed several teepees, the temporary shelters used by traders. Outside one, a woman leaned over a fire, stirring the contents of a cast-iron pot. Three children played with long sticks and a tin can. They looked up.

I waved and they waved back.

Not a leaf of the nearby scrub oak or maple, the birch or aspen, rustled. The grove of cedars didn't stir. In the absence of a breeze, gnats gathered in a speckled cloud around me. One crawled behind my ear, another into the corner of my eye. I brushed and batted them away as I walked.

At a high point in the path, I tucked behind the trunk of an old white pine and surveyed the bay and docks below. The bay was never still: the dam forced water through at breakneck speed, sending droplets into the air that caught in the light, like jewels flung high. Below, water swirled in a constant pattern of circles, tight and forceful near the dam, then ebbing out into wider and wider arcs. The steamer had yet to arrive. It was only midmorning.

At the docks, too, people came and went in perpetual motion. Most of the fishing boats were already gone, leaving more open dock space than later in the day.

And then, my stomach dropped. A familiar cruiser rounded the bend and approached the harbor, slowing its motor until its wake became a thin white plume. It was the last boat in the world I wanted to see. I recognized the wooden boat with the red-and-white trim, the bright American flag flying from its stern. My stomach dropped. Walter Worthington was at the wheel in the bow.

I suddenly felt torn. To be wanted—wanted in any way— pulled at me as strongly as the current beneath the dam. It felt so powerful that I wondered if I could resist. In that moment I felt I could do anything the Worthingtons asked, be anything to them, just to be wanted. I nearly waved my arms and shouted, "Here! Here I am!" Instead, I held myself in check and watched.

His boat slowed and pulled up to an open slot at the dock, just behind the long, two-decker houseboat, complete with its wraparound screen porch. This was E. W. Ennis's houseboat, which I'd seen in our bay and on the lake.

A dock boy hustled from the gashouse near shore. Mr. Worthington tossed him a line, which fell short of the boy's reach and disappeared like a snake in the water. The boy fished it out with a gaff hook, then pulled the boat close and secured it.

From the houseboat, a tall man stepped off and greeted Mr. Worthington. At first I didn't recognize him, though few people possessed the height of E. W. Ennis. That day, instead of his usual three-piece pinstriped suit, he wore brown pants and a white shirt, the sleeves rolled up. He met Mr. Worthington with a handshake. Mr. Ennis pointed over his shoulder toward the wooden walkway that led to the hotel. I had to believe that he was telling Mr. Worthington right where to find me.

My heart sped. I thought I'd left the tavern last night unseen, but perhaps I hadn't been that lucky.

I scanned the bay for any sign of Owen. He said he had one more delivery and to meet him in thirty minutes. I didn't wear a watch, but it couldn't be so terribly long until he returned for me. Ten minutes. Maybe fifteen.

Miles off, a low ripple of thunder sounded. I glanced to the west, where the clouds had built and darkened. A flicker of lightning lit through dense, charcoal clouds and then vanished.

I turned away and followed the path. It wound along the shore, out to the edge of a peninsula, and then back north toward a tiny log cabin nested in the V of the protected harbor. It had to be the place.

The trapper's shack sat hunched near the rock harbor. The only boat in sight was a wooden flatboat near shore, turned upside down, a few hull boards missing. I kept my eyes on the water, waiting for a sign of Owen.

Minutes passed.

I lingered at a crook in the path, between moss-velveted boulders and wild iris on thin graceful stems. Tall cedars concealed me from boats, and when rain began to fall in droplets, the fragrant branches kept me dry. Small gnats crawled into the hair at the nape of my neck and behind my earlobes. I swatted at them, some blood-filled. What if something happened to Owen? What if he ran out of gas? I couldn't return to the hotel and into the hands of Walter Worthington—no matter how great my ache was to be needed.

When a gust of wind blew, I was grateful. At least the gnats would leave me alone. But within seconds, the wind turned to a gale, and twigs and leaves lifted from the ground and swirled past me. Trees creaked and groaned. Waves built and sloshed in the protected harbor. Soon, beyond the trapper's cove, whitecaps formed waves that scuttled ahead of the wind. A commercial fishing boat bobbed up and down, bow into the wind, pointed in the direction of the dam and Kettle Falls, but still no sign of Owen.

Like a sledgehammer, lightning cracked the slate sky, followed by a downpour. I ran for the trapper's shack, hoping it was unlocked, as most of the region's cabins were said to be. Better to let strangers enter and take shelter, people said, than to have them get angry and destroy your place. Bucketsful of rain poured down, soaking through my blouse and kitchen apron to my skin. I knocked on the squat door and then pushed on the wooden log handle, which gave way, and I rushed inside.

"Hello?"

But the one-room cabin, dimly lit by a tiny window, offered no reply. The wind howled at my back and blasted into the cabin. Dripping, I closed the door behind me.

On the square kitchen table laid a local newspaper, a teal-blue kerosene lantern, and an empty bottle. A coffee mug and a dinner plate—the same white heavy plate with green trim as at the Kettle Falls restaurant—waited for their owner's return. A barrel stove sat in one corner, sending off faint wafts of smoke from an early morning fire, its stovepipe bending at a right angle out the nearby wall.

My attention was drawn, for reasons beyond my understanding, to the gray rumples of the old quilt on the bed. It was a faded wedding-ring pattern: a series of quilted overlapping circles. Like the one Mama and I once covered ourselves with at night in those early years, this one, too, was mostly pinks and blues—so at odds with this trapper's shack. But unlike Mama's white quilt, this one was gray and dingy.

I felt nauseous.

"Couldn't be."

Of course it wasn't Mama's. Mama had been gone eleven years. Would I never stop looking for her in every corner? Stop, I told myself. Stop it. It was too old and musty with streaks of mildew. It was out here in a dank and seldom-used trapper's shack.

But there was something in my memory—something about the quilt's edge.

I couldn't stop myself.

I stepped toward the quilt. Gingerly, I turned back each edge of the rumpled quilt. First the edge near the nightstand, then both edges at the foot of the bed, and finally, I stretched across the bed—hoping not to pick up a batch of lice or bed bugs—and reached toward the head of the bed. The quilt was tucked firmly between the mattress and the wall. I yanked it free and held the corner in my palms.

On its edge—the same neatly embroidered letters I'd seen as a small child—the bumpy stitching I once ran my fingers over, but of course, couldn't then comprehend. Until that moment in the trapper's shack—with lightning crackling overhead and rain finding its way into cracks in the cabin roof—I had completely forgotten the stitching on the edge of the quilt.

Now I could read the words on the quilt, so finely stitched with needle and threads of blue and green:

JOINED IN BLESSED UNION

FRANK AND SIGRID

JULY 1, 1904

| 23 |

I yanked the quilt off the bed and gathered it in my arms. It was evidence of Mama; proof of my memories; the only artifact of her I had left. Had it read "Frank and Bella" I would have understood completely. But who was Sigrid?

And then I recalled my last visit with Franny. She said all the girls changed their names. Maybe Mama, too, had changed her name when she started working for Darla. Why else would she have kept this quilt with another woman's name?

"Sigrid."

It was possible.

I replayed last night's conversation with Caveman. He had been telling me the truth. I said aloud, "My name is Sadie Rose Ladovitch, daughter of..." A sob built in my chest. I wanted to give in to it and let out all my years of questions and fears and aching to belong—but instead I swallowed hard. I stepped over to the small square window, rubbed dust away with my thumb until it turned black, and peered out.

Waves hit the rocky shore of the little bay and sent plumes of water into the air. Trees flailed in the high winds, which built to a deafening roar. There wasn't a chance Owen could pull into the harbor now. He was—if he had a working brain—

taking shelter along with every other fisherman on the white-frothed water.

I clutched the quilt and drifted . . . floated back. . . .

Above snowbanks and endless white, I floated outside the community building, watching, disconnected from my body below. In the pale dawn light, the sky and snow merged as I watched a man toss his shovel aside and then drop to his knees in the snow. He yanked at the oversized boots, which came free in his gloved hands. Then he tugged at the legs and out came layers of the navy wool coat and cotton flannel nightdress, all intertwined with tiny legs, and the body of a girl. Waves of dark hair fell around her face. With his gloved hand, he brushed back her hair, then scooped her up in his arms and raced into the town hall.

Strange as it was to be watching him carry my body, I followed with curiosity from somewhere above.

The man murmured to himself, shouldered the door open, and stepped inside the town hall.

Inside, I floated above and observed a long table that held stacks of papers and empty strewn chairs. The man holding me yelled, "Somebody get the doctor!"

A few yards off, a half-dozen men gathered near another body—that of a woman with pale blue skin. Her body was frozen and propped upright in the corner, standing beside the American flag. Her hand clutched an empty bottle.

The group of men spun away from the woman.

I jumped back.

Across my vision at the tiny window, a bone-thin man walked by under the awning of the cabin roof. He was so close it felt as if he'd touched me. He was soggy wet, narrow-shouldered, with his head bent under a workman's cap. I'd seen him

before. He was at the train depot when the Worthingtons had
returned. Bigler. Bigly. Bigby—that was his name. Within a
second, he was at the door and pushing it open. It opened with
a creak, and I didn't have a moment to hide.

"Holy crap!" He slammed the door behind him, unaware
of me. He pulled off a long-sleeve shirt and hung it on a peg,
and then pulled a ladder-back chair toward him from the table. With a gray long-sleeve undershirt, he sat down heavily
and yanked off his wet leather boots—then his cap, revealing greasy white hair. This was one of the men who'd met Mr.
Worthington at the train station. The smell of well-seasoned
body sweat—rank and sour—met my nose.

"I'm sorry," I blurted, starting from my post by the window
toward the door. "The storm. I needed shelter."

Eyes saucer-wide, the man jumped up.

The bed, the table, the man...were nearly within arm's
reach. I held the dingy quilt tight to my chest, dreading being
stuck inside four walls with this stranger. He was closer to the
door than I was. If he tried to harm me, I would have to get past
him to escape. I should run for the door and not take my chanc-
es with this lunatic, but something made me hold my ground.

"What in God's name?" With a sharp nose, stubble-haired
face, he made the sign of the cross a second time. "Are you—
are you—Jesus, Mary, and Joseph!"

I had no plan for the conversation that followed. "I'm certainly not any of them. I was supposed to meet—"

He fell back toward his chair, missed it, and hit the floor
with a grunt, his big toe protruding from his fraying sock. And
then, like a crayfish scurrying backward, scrambled to the
wall—not taking his eyes off me—and drew his legs up to his
chest. "You're a goddamn ghost, then? Here to haunt the crap
outta me?"

Either he was a lunatic or entirely too drunk to remember

me. All I had to do was run for the door now, open the handle, run out.

"I should have left well enough alone," the man ranted. "Never shoulda got involved with that whole *goddamn* mess!" He wrapped his arms and veiny hands around his legs and body. He reached inside his undershirt and pulled out a rosary of brown beads and a brown wooden cross. He let the small cross dangle between us as he fingered the beads, one by one. His chest rose and fell quickly, like bellows working hard over embers.

Rainwater fell steadily in holes through the roof, leaving growing puddles on the cabin's uneven wood floor. My brain was so busy assessing my predicament that I almost missed what he'd asked.

"Haunt you?" I said. "Why do you think—" Then I glanced at the quilt in my arms. "This was Mama's quilt."

"Your mama?" he whispered.

"Yes, and I want to know," I started to ask, tears building unexpectedly. I forced myself to sound more commanding of the situation than I felt. I glanced at the quilt in my arms, then back at the man. "I want to know how her quilt ended up here."

He glanced at the floor, then back up at me. Dark circles gathered beneath his eyes, and white flecked the hairs at his chin and at the sides of his face. He had to be nearly fifty or sixty years old.

"Ohhh, holy crap." He leaned his knees to his elbows and rested his chin in his hands. Second by second, the lines in his forehead dissolved as he appeared to rationalize his situation. He let his gaze leave me and studied the floor for a moment before looking back up. "So you're not her. At first, I mean, you look so much like her. There was a child."

I nodded.

He peered at me, as if his vision was failing. "No, wait." He studied me. "So you're the girl the mayor took in?" Then a mixture of embarrassment and relief crossed his face. "Oh. Wait. Huh." He shook his head. "I gotta cut down on the booze. Now I remember. I seen you...the other day...with the Mayor."

I watched him, not answering. Everyone for years had called Mr. Worthington "Senator" but never "Mayor" after he left that tiny post for a grander political career.

"Sure," Bigby went on, "you're her, but when I first met you, you was nearly dead. It was like pulling a calf from a cow, just as I used to do on the farm as a boy. But you was no calf. I didn't expect to find a girl, half-dead in the snow." He shook his head. "And ever since, I've regretted..."

I listened without moving.

He swung his head slowly back and forth, dropping his gaze to the floor. "I thought it would be the best joke —just a prank. But all these years since...seems I can't go a night without seeing her staring at me, those eyes! Looking straight at me—straight through me! Bigby, I say to myself, you dumb-ass *fool*. The joke, you see, has been on me ever since."

I counted on my silence to prod him on.

Then he glanced up at me, like a man who has been serving a sentence for many years. "I was the handyman for the village. I showed up early that morning, after a big storm blew through, cuz I knew I better get going on shoveling sidewalks. You see, that storm had dumped a bundle. The council members were meeting that morning. So I was just doing my job when I came—"

With the rosary woven between his fingers, he swiped his palm down the length of his face. "I came upon this woman— in the snow. Frozen. With an empty whiskey bottle in her hand. I knew that many of the red skirts around Ranier used to end their own lives. Some jumped off the high tower by the mill. Others drank themselves to death. I figured, that's what happened. She was already dead, you see, and that's when I figured no harm would be done if I played a little prank.

"So before anyone arrived, I hauled her inside—and she kept gripping the neck of that bottle—and I stood her up in the corner. Thought it would be a big joke, you see, because there had been plenty of heated talks at those meetings then about things being too corrupt. About too many fancy ladies bold in broad daylight. And so, I thought a few laughs would come of it. You know, something they'd tell over and over for years at the saloons."

Quilt to my chest, I closed my eyes, flooded with memories.

I floated above the man who held me . . .

"Somebody get the doctor!" the man with the beak nose shouted.

In suspenders over a crisp shirt, a mustached man pointed over his shoulder at the woman in the corner. "Bigby! You oughta know! How the hell did this woman get here?"

I hovered, strangely distanced from Bigby, and the limp five-year-old body he held in his arms. "I dunno, Mayor!" Beads of sweat formed on his forehead. "But this kid here's nearly dead!"

While the council members drew closer to Bigby—a thud!—and the sound of glass shattering came from the corner. They glanced toward the frozen and lifeless woman.

I drifted toward her.

Now her hand gripped at empty air. Around her bare feet lay pieces of a shattered glass bottle. I didn't feel sad, glad, anything then.

Mama.

Bella Rose.

Frozen stiff.

And all in that suspended second, I knew it wasn't her, wasn't the voice that had called to me. It was merely her body, upright but tilted, wearing a silk nightdress. She stared out somewhere beyond. Glassily. Accusingly. I wanted to follow her voice then, to go where she was...

But like a hooked fish speeding away, I was reeled back...back against my will, back toward the men now clustered around the man who'd found me.

"Damn, Miss. I'm sorry now, I really am. You're not getting sick now, are ya? The way you're drooping there, I better get ya a basin if you're gonna puke."

I felt numb—suspended between the past and present—and watched as he rose slowly to his feet, let out a sigh, and then grabbed a bottle from behind the cookstove. He lifted its amber contents to his lips and chugged until the bottle was half empty. Then he lifted it in the air toward me. "Want some?"

I shook my head, not sure what I needed anymore. "You stood her body up?"

"That, I'm ashamed to say, I did. But it wasn't me who put her out in the snow. God, no," he said with a snort. Then he grabbed a washbasin and slid it across the table toward me. "Just in case," he said, dropping in his chair. He pointed to another chair. "Please Miss. Sit. I won't harm you. I promise. Don't go yet. I need to get this out. I've been carrying this 'round too long as it is."

I sat with the quilt over my lap. I hardly needed the extra layer for warmth; sweat dampened the curve of my lower back.

Bigby took another swig, then continued. "That mornin' when the men came to their meetin'—many who I know for a fact frequented those cathouses themselves—anyways, I was hiding in the coatrack, you see, and waitin' for the moment when they'd notice...And they were sure surprised. She was almost saluting them from beside the flag."

This man, Bigby, I realized, was now talking more to himself than to me.

"So this was the joke," I said beneath my breath, "that you told through the years? Told it from barstools?" My anger simmered and heat built behind my eyes. "How could you?"

He met my eyes, winced, and took another drink. "I've prayed to God about what I've done so many times, but I can't change what I did. See, Miss, first, that was my plan back then, to tell it as a big joke." He leaned onto his elbows and peered at me, hard. "Until I found you."

I stopped breathing.

"So durin' that big hullabaloo at the meetin', I slipped back outside and returned to shovelin'. I didn't want the prank traced back to me, you see. Just told around town, like a legend of sorts. Stupid." He closed his eyes, and I worried that he was going to doze off.

"And then you found me," I prompted, sensing that the liquor was starting to soften him, and I didn't want him to forget any details.

He chugged another gulp of booze and continued. "That's right. And then nothin' about it was funny at all. You see, I couldn't figure out what you were doin' out in the snow. I mean, what child runs after its mama in a snowstorm? I was sure certain you were deader than dead. But when I pulled you out, those tiny legs in those ladies' boots, and then I heard a breath. And you weren't dead after all."

Beyond Bigby, a few pots lay on a wood shelf. I had to move, do something. I stood up, left the quilt in the middle of the table, and grabbed a few pots and set them one by one under the holes allowing the rain to pour inside. At first the droplets tinked like cymbals against the steel pots. Then the sounds shifted.

Tink, tank, tank,

Tank, tunk, tunk.

I sat down again. "And so you carried me in your arms and went back inside the building. And you shouted for help, right?"

He leaned back against the slats of his chair. "That's right, but how do you—"

"Mr. Worthington," I lied, "has told the story many times. Of how you *saved* me. How otherwise I would have died in the snow, if it hadn't been for you finding me there."

Beneath his beak-like nose, his whisker-flecked chin wobbled, and I worried he was going to start crying. "Why, I guess that's so, ain't it? I guess I never really thought..."

I placed my hand on the quilt between us. "But this quilt. It was hers. And now it's at your place here. That still doesn't add up to me. Why do you have it? You didn't mention it when you told about finding her body."

Lightning illuminated the sky outside the window.

"You see, that's another weird thing. I found it behind the town hall in the burn barrel. Someone stashed it there. Way too nice to burn. Hate to see good things go to waste, if you know—" He studied his rosary. The beads were flying through his fingers, and I knew he wasn't saying a "Hail Mary" or "Our Father" with each bead. "So I took it home." He exhaled. "And now *you*—of all people—find it. That's the strangest. Almost like she meant for you to find it."

He stretched toward the table and buried his forehead in his crossed arms.

I pulled the quilt back into my lap. Rain pummeled the rooftop, and beyond the window, water fell in sheets of gray.

With everything in me, I wanted to avenge my mother's death. To salvage something from her life. But she'd been gone so long. I couldn't change what had happened to her any more than I could prove that someone had silenced my father. I couldn't prove anything in a court of law as to what happened between Ennis and my mother that night in the upstairs bedroom. I couldn't change the choices she made that led to her pitiful end.

I'd been frozen ever since... like Rainy Lake through the long, dark months of winter when ice grips its shores. Rock-hard, thick, and impenetrable. Until a southerly wind loosens its edges, melts the top layers of snow, and sends trickles of water along foot-deep cracks and fissures, breaking the massive lake into tiny icebergs, setting them adrift. The beginning of the thaw...

It had started, I realized now, with finding the photographs.

With facing the past—a past I could not change.

But *I* could change.

I would not allow *others* to direct my life, to dam it up like a flowing river, directing it to fit their needs.

| 24 |

Bigby lifted his head from the table and started talking again. "The Mayor, well, after that, he promised to clean things up in Ranier. Used that tragedy to advantage, if you get my meaning. Me? I left my job within the year, just couldn't stand to look at that empty space in the building by the flag. I'd always see her, and it tore at me, 'specially when I knew she had a child. Came out here. Started runnin' a trapline. I get by."

My eyes grew hot, and I blinked back my tears.

"Thank you," I whispered.

"Wait. You're goddamn thankin' me?"

"For telling me." I paused. "For finding me."

He rested both hands on the table—ragged fingernails, white hairs curling above tan and spotted skin. "Never figured I'd see this day."

"No," I agreed. "Me neither."

I studied the large four-legged pelt on the wall. It was silvery-black with a tail as long as a yardstick. Such a beautiful animal once, no doubt, but all I knew of it now was a dried leather hide and holes, from which eyes once peered.

"Timber wolf," Bigby said, following my gaze.

Then, from his trouser pocket, Bigby pulled out a gray and rumpled sheet of paper. "Had a real good season right up through May when I sold off pelts," he said, as a new wave of raindrops struck the roof.

He read from his list: "Two otter, twenty-seven muskrat, nineteen wolves, fourteen fox, two lynx, seven pine marten..." As Bigby talked about his trapping techniques and knowledge of each animal, I studied him.

This man. This man who had stood my mother's poor lifeless body up as a joke. I should be raging inside, and yet he was the same man who had found me. I wouldn't be alive now if he hadn't brought me in from the snowbank. Life was so completely unpredictable. This man, Bigby, was intertwined with my past, both prankster and rescuer. And yet here I sat with him, as if he were Hans.

When Bigby finished, he hobbled two steps to the cookstove, started a fire in the chamber, then set an iron teakettle on top. "Who knows when this storm will pass?" he said. "Better make yourself comfortable. Got some black tea and a little sugar. Would that suit you, Sadie Rose?"

"Yes, I'd like that."

We drank tea out of stained and cracked cups.

When Bigby staggered to his bed, flopped back as if dead, and filled the shack with snoring that rivaled a braying donkey, I stepped outside.

At last, the storm had moved on. Trees straightened their backs, the sky lightened to a soft gray, and waves sloshed softly in the rock-lined bay. Long grass and weeds lay bent. Under a faint drizzle and pervasive gray, a pair of loons popped up in the bay, their star-studded backs beading water. They looked at me with their unusual red eyes, then dove underwater and disappeared.

Just as I began to fret that Owen had forgotten me, his boat appeared, its slim bow cutting through the dark water. He waved, but something about his face looked wrong.

When he pulled up to the short dock, he motioned me in, swinging his arms frantically like a baseball player cheering a teammate to steal home.

But his face was all wrong.

Beneath his wavy hair, his right eye was a thin slit, almost swollen shut and sporting a grayish-purple plum. Remnants of blood smeared his upper lip, and he'd clearly wiped away whatever blood had been there with the sleeve of his denim shirt.

I looked from his face and torn knee of his trousers to the condition of his boat. It looked as if someone had taken an ax to it. The wooden compartments where he stored his dairy products had been smashed apart. Cracked boards and splinters crisscrossed the base of the boat. "Good Lord. What happened, Owen?"

"I, uh—" He shook his head. "Just get in."

Careful not to slip on the algae-slick boards of Bigby's dock, I tossed my satchel into Owen's boat, followed by the quilt.

"What's *that*?" He nodded at the quilt, glaringly filthy in the daylight. Many of its quilted pieces—once so carefully stitched together—were ripped and curling away from the pattern of large interlinking rings.

How could I answer in a word or two? My encounter with Bigby was inexplicable as stars, as if our meeting was somehow orchestrated. I shrugged and sat down near him as he motored out of the bay. "I'll explain—sometime."

He pushed the throttle down and sped through the channel toward the open lake.

I looked back at the tiny shack as it dissolved into a palette of greens. How strange that in one man I would discover the one who had made a joke of my mother's death and yet pulled my body from the snow . . . like a calf, he'd said. Yet there it was.

I wanted to be enraged at Bigby, and instead I promised myself I'd return someday to see how he was getting along.

Owen steered us through the tight, curving channel, then between shorelines toward open water. Islands and shores of clear-cut timber with their scatterings of broken limbs and stubby trunks appeared tinder-dry and brown, despite the heavy rain. And then in contrast, some stands of timber had been missed—or spared. In the towering branches of one pine, an eagle perched atop its massive nest.

The storm left giant swells on the big lake, and Owen maneuvered his boat to ride up a crest and down again, without crashing up and down. I studied him. The bruising around his mouth was deepening in color, and his upper lip was puffed up. He either had a collision with his boat, or someone had beaten him up good.

"Did you get in a fight?" I shouted.

He stared straight ahead.

"Did someone steal your goods?"

He reached up and scratched the back of his neck, ran his tongue over his upper lip, and winced. He shook his head slowly left, then right, as if moving quickly was too much of a strain.

"Do you have any ice somewhere—for your face?" I shouted.

Owen shook his head, glancing halfheartedly around at the destroyed coolers. "That's the last of my worries."

I let it go. I had enough to worry about for the moment. No destination. No place to call home. Barely five dollars to my name. But I had gained some things in the past weeks.

My voice. I couldn't imagine life now without it.

A sense of the pieces of my life. I knew my real father had cared about the changing wilderness, capturing its beauty and devastation in photographs. His name was Frank Ladovitch. Possibly murdered. Silenced. His first name was stitched on the quilt.

And memories. Memories of Mama, of hovering outside my body—all were true. I hadn't imagined it. Bigby had found me. Haunted by the shame of standing Mama's frozen body in the corner, he'd spent his life regretting.

Owen and I traveled on for nearly two hours, straight west toward Ranier, following the waters that carved a portion of the international border. There was so much I had thought I'd known and understood.

Suddenly, a few pieces fell into order.

I smacked my skirt-covered thigh with my hand. "Owen! You weren't delivering dairy, were you?"

He glanced at me, his face ashen, his usual lighthearted expression absent. He turned his gaze back at the water.

"I'll bet anything you were bootlegging, weren't you?" I'd heard the Worthingtons talk about it. How Koochiching County had already been dry for a few years, so that when Prohibition went into effect last January, area bootleggers were ahead of the game, in full swing, operating stills and selling booze. "They're tickled pink to welcome Prohibition," Mr. Worthington had said. He'd explained that now bootleggers could charge more for their goods and sell them clear across the country. Supply and demand. The border opened up opportunities for locals, as well as growing crime from influences as far away as St. Paul and Chicago. Last fall, it had seemed far-fetched.

But now, seeing Owen's beautiful wood coolers smashed, his face swollen and raw from someone's rage—he must have gotten himself into more than he bargained for.

"Promise not to tell a soul?" He glanced at me, keeping his hands on the boat's wheel.

"Promise."

"Yeah, bootlegging. Just a little. First, just to local folks with homemade brew that I'd pick up from blind piggers around the lake. But last March, I came across someone's dumped cargo. I was driving the new delivery truck when I noticed wheel tracks going down into the ditch. Thought maybe an automobile had gone off the road and somebody needed help. All I found was a caved-in root cellar and cases of scotch whiskey. Somebody's stash. Not a soul in sight, so I hauled it out, one case at a time. Figured if I didn't haul it off, someone else would. I managed to hide the cases in our warehouse."

"How many?"

"Seven."

"And how much is a case worth?"

"Fifty bucks."

"Owen! Then why haven't you left Ranier? You gotta have enough money by now."

"I was saving it, but I have to return the money I made— along with the unsold cases. The message was real clear. I have to leave the creamery door unlocked and an envelope with the cash. Then they'll forget all about it."

"I hope so."

I was stunned, though I shouldn't have been too surprised. Passing laws doesn't change people's behavior. The Eighteenth Amendment had pushed the making, selling, and consuming of liquor underground, that's all. The customers hadn't gone away. Even someone like Owen Jensen had been drawn to the quick and easy cash.

He pointed to his face. "This—just a warning. Next time, they said they'll make an anchor out of me. One of my customers must have talked."

"Oh, Owen. I'm sorry."

"Hey, don't be. I'm lucky I'm not *dead*."

As the sun neared the horizon, I recognized our surroundings. Off to the right, King Ed's Red Stone Island appeared. Straight ahead, in the distance beyond a small reef, Victor Guttenberg's cabin graced the eastern point of Falcon Island.

Owen veered wide around the bay's central reef, where a great blue heron stood one-legged on a rocky shoal. As we drew closer, it jumped to the air, glided, then rose to the sky on long wings, its stick legs trailing behind. "So you're taking me—to Victor's?"

"Too obvious. Besides, Ennis pays Victor visits—they sip tea—just like good fellows."

"Tea? They do?" I smiled at having tea with Bigby.

"Yup. Once a year, Ennis and Victor sit down for a gentlemanly tea."

I couldn't quite picture it. Victor seemed so staunchly against Ennis in every way. Why would he want to waste an ounce of time on his enemy?

"Hey, don't look so surprised. They may seem different as night and day, but Sadie, don't you get it? They come from the same world. Money. Upper crust."

I shook my head. "Victor's not the same."

"Sadie, Victor's not from here. He's from a big city. He went to Harvard. Think he's just like the rest of us? C'mon. Open your eyes."

All I could see was poor Owen's puffy and injured face. I looked away toward Victor's island. "Owen, he's not like Ennis at all. He's canoed way up north. He's gone on expeditions."

"Yeah? Did you know his Ojibwa guide, Billy Bright, got him up to Hudson Bay and back alive? On the way home, ice was forming, and Victor was in the belly of the canoe, straw stuffed in his boots and pants to keep him from freezing to death. Billy saved his life.

But who gets the credit for the expedition? I mean, who goes and speaks in London and shows photographs of moose? Billy Bright? You think he speaks to high society? Victor gets all the credit. And oh, he talks about being accepted into some Explorers Club, to be finally recognized along with the likes of Amundsen and Shackleton. There's lots of locals who have done courageous things, who know the wilderness—they don't go around looking for honors."

"Owen." I felt the need to defend Victor, especially when he'd stood up for me. "Victor stands up to Ennis! That's big."

"Well, sure, but with all his standing up, he's still around, isn't he?"

"I don't get what you mean."

"He's not dead or *beat up,* is he?"

I gazed out at two seagulls, dipping toward something on the water. I imagined seeing the lake from a high point in the sky, looking down at a body, floating facedown, a speck in a giant body of water. *Frank Ladovitch.* What Owen was saying...was it true? If Victor had been another local spouting off and causing trouble, would he have been silenced by now?

"Listen, Sadie, if you want to steer clear of Worthington and Ennis—then I'm taking you to Baird's. Trinity'll hide you, I'm pretty sure, at least for a few days 'til we figure out what's next. You just need to lie low for a few days while they're watching for you to catch a train."

"But—" I started to protest but realized I didn't have a better idea. I had to come up with some other plan for leaving the area. And I could learn from Trinity. She knew something about how to maneuver in the world.

"Now slip down in the bow. There are more cabins this way, and you don't want to be spotted."

I ducked down and crawled into the bow, amid fragments of wood coolers and a few life jackets. "I'm working on trusting you, but you've tossed me a few surprises, Owen Jensen."

He kept glancing at me, where I sat hunched in a ball with my arms around the quilt. "Look who's talkin'." A slow smile eased into his eyes, but then he winced and looked back to the water.

I studied his Adam's apple riding up and down as he swallowed. Despite the bruising and swelling, despite the lesson someone had tried to teach him, my mind replayed meeting up with him in the darkness of the icehouse, the air sweetened with the smell of fresh wood chips. The way he'd leaned down to meet my lips, his mouth confidently on mine, and the way he'd assumed I'd wanted to kiss him.

I hadn't then.

Now I wasn't as sure. But Owen *had* been all goggle-eyed over Trinity. Maybe he was willing to smooch with anyone he thought was willing. Still, I was drawn to his waves of thick auburn hair—the way he seemed to take charge of his own life. Of course he could be independent. He was a man. When I tried to think of women who had found a way to claim their own lives, I came up short. Mrs. Worthington had grown up with money, but everything she'd inherited was funneled through Mr. Worthington, despite the fact that she'd come from St. Paul's Kresler family. She waited on Mr. Worthington's every decision, as if she didn't have a voice of her own. She couldn't stand up for me and yielded instead to him.

And there was Darla. She ran her own business, hired out her own fancy ladies. She was a businesswoman, yes. But the price of such independence was high for her girls. Meg's tragic stories had helped make that abundantly clear to me. I wondered if Darla slept well at night.

"What are you staring at?" he asked, glancing at me. "Do I look that bad?"

"No, I mean...yes."

In reply, he reached down and tousled my hair, and I went soft inside.

"Owen," I said, "you could have gotten killed."

He reached down for my hand and held it in his own for several moments. "You care, even a little?"

It struck me that I'd lost not only my mother but my father as well. No wonder I'd been willing to go along with the Worthingtons' wishes for so long. As thin a connection as they were, they were all I'd had. Of course I cared what happened to Owen. I nodded and swallowed back emotion.

"Y'know," he said, "if my dad hears about any of this, I'm sunk. After I drop you off, I gotta clear out the last few cases from the creamery." He pointed to his face. "And I better come up with some kind of story to explain this—and the boat."

"What about the truth?"

He laughed without conviction. "What do you mean?"

"I mean, why not try telling him the truth?"

He shook his head. "No. I don't want him involved in this. He's a good man. It was my stupid-ass idea, not his. I'm the one who has to straighten up the mess."

"Well, then how about the storm? Your boat was battered on the rocks? It could have happened, right?"

"Brilliant. That'll work."

| 25 |

Jonah in the belly of a whale—that's how I felt, scrunched down in the bow—until Owen slowed the boat and we drifted.

His right eye was completely swollen shut. Once he returned the cases of whiskey to their rightful owner, I hoped he could walk away without any more injury.

"Sadie, there's no dock on this side of their island, but you better hop out here anyway."

I emerged as the boat bobbed toward an island's rocky shoreline and the small log cabin, its cut ends painted apple red. A petunia-filled box hung beneath two paned windows, closed shut and curtains drawn. It was Trinity's artist studio.

I hesitated. I didn't really want him to leave me. I'd be stuck again.

"It's just 'til you figure out what's next."

"As if I have a clear plan," I said, trying to laugh.

He must have read the doubt on my face. "Listen, Sadie Rose, if..."

Then he craned his neck, looking back at the channel to the east, as if expecting someone to be following from the direction of Kettle Falls. He pivoted back, grabbed my hand, and tugged me close. I wondered if he was going to kiss me.

"If I spend any more time with you, I might be tempted to—"

"To what?" I asked, knowingly. Flirtingly. "To turn me over to the Worthingtons?"

"Never," he said. His hair formed curls behind his ears and at the base of his neck. I felt the odd urge to reach out and touch his hair, to see if it felt soft or coarse. Heat rose to my cheeks as a boat motor sounded from the west.

He jumped to his feet.

"Okay, go," he said, taking my satchel from me. Then he tossed it high over the bow of the boat and sent it soaring. It landed in a low-creeping juniper bush. "Hand it here," he said, nodding at the quilt. "Sheesh. Why you want this—" He threw it as well, but it floated like a lily pad, until one edge dipped and it started to slip deeper.

"Oh no." Then I half-crawled, half-walked over the bow and stretched my boot toward the nearest boulder. I teetered but managed to right myself. I grabbed a corner of the soggy quilt and tugged it toward me, and then pushed his boat away. "You'll come back?"

"Of course," he said. "Soon as I can. At least now I know where to find you. When you disappeared, I hated to think I'd never see you again." He shrugged, then put the motor into forward, steered out into the channel, and shrunk on the horizon.

Scooping up water in my hands, I drank, satisfying my thirst. As his boat motored away without me, my heart buzzed like a trapped fly. What if Trinity wasn't on the island? Perhaps the Bairds, for all I knew, had left to travel to Europe for the month. I stood there, staring at the cabin.

Just then another boat appeared beyond the bend, and I scuttled back into the undergrowth with my satchel and wet quilt. When it passed, I walked to the cabin. Unlike Bigby's cabin, this one was built solidly atop four boulders, sitting high and dry off the earth, not growing into it. With Mr.

Worthington's advice to steer clear of the Baird family due to their social class, I knew there had to be more to their island than this small studio cabin. A cabin just for painting. *Imagine.*

I ducked down and hurried around to the cabin's front. The windows were latched. The door, when I tried its handle, was locked.

And I was starving. I hadn't had anything to eat since before my morning shift at the kitchen, which felt like ages ago. On top of that, I was utterly exhausted. Why had I thought I could set off on my own? My confidence dwindled. I sat on the cabin stoop, chin in my hands, feeling sorry for myself. "Stop it," I finally scolded myself. "You'll find a way."

Before long, the sun would drop below the horizon and night would settle. As I debated within myself, mosquitoes found me and started to land on my arms, which were bare to my rolled sleeves. Another landed on my neck, and I swatted it. When I examined my palm, it held a bloody, thread-thin bug. "Yuck."

I hoped Owen knew what he was doing, dropping me off here. He'd asked me to trust him. His rearranged face and news of bootlegging gave me reasons to doubt. But what other option did I have after fleeing Kettle Falls?

I left my satchel and the sopping, heavy quilt in the crook of two nearby moss-topped boulders. Then I followed the path away from the cabin, in hopes of finding Trinity. But the island was still.

Soft-sweeping white pine lined the path, as stately and towering as old presidents. If it were my island, I might name them Lincoln, Washington, Jefferson... I brushed the rough bark of their trunks with my fingertips as I walked along the needle-layered path. Soon I was standing on a small ridge overlooking the island's horseshoe cove with a white-sand beach. A thin peninsula of sand connected two small islands into one. In the cove, a long dock held a fishing boat fast; the boathouse near shore appeared freshly painted in nautical red.

Floating within the boathouse, with its stern visible from my vantage point, a white boat—a small yacht, actually—boasted one word in golden scrolled letters, TRINITY.

Trinity Baird had a boat named after her? I couldn't believe it.

We couldn't have come from more different worlds. I pictured Bigby pulling my legs from the snow, my eyelashes frosted together. My mind raced over a collage of images and memories. Mama, with her chin tucked so tightly into the top of my head that at times it hurt. The smell of her dense perfume, which often made me sneeze. Franny's words about Mama and Ennis, and the brutal fight Franny had overheard before Mama's death.

Mama, I wanted to ask, why did you think you could bring me up in a brothel? Why—a prostitute? Didn't you know, couldn't you look ahead to see that it was a shackle I'd wear around my ankle?

I longed to talk with her, to shout, to scream at her. What were you thinking, Mama? Surely you could have found another way to make money. You could have tried. Did you try? Did you ever try to sew for people and mend their clothes? Or work packing fish in ice during the summer? Or help out at the general store? You had been married to someone you loved, so how could you then sell your body?

From my vantage point on the ridge, I looked down on the narrow center of an hourglass, where the islands were joined by a thin sand beach. To the west, the sun rode low on the water beyond Baird's Island. Beyond Ranier and the river that led to the paper mill in International Falls, smoke and steam chugged in a pencil-thin cloud. I burst into tears.

"Mama," I whispered. "You promised someday things would be better..." And look where I'd ended up. Without a home. Without a plan. Running.

Waves murmured softly in the boathouse below, echoing off its walls. I felt ashamed. Was I jealous of Trinity, that she had a boat named after her? Was that how simple-minded I'd become? No. I didn't need wealth or a boat with SADIE ROSE burnished across its stern. But at that moment, I didn't know what I wanted—my needs ran as deep and wide as an underground river.

I wiped my eyes and, pinching off one nostril at a time, blew my nose into the undergrowth. It wasn't ladylike, but it worked.

I recalled Trinity's words when she'd sat with me at Red Stone. "We could try our hand at friendship." At least her words gave me momentary courage to search for her.

Beyond the boathouse, pines stood protectively above a scattering of cabins and a larger lodge. Waves lapped at granite boulders. Faint voices sounded from the direction of the larger building. Relief. Someone was around who might help.

I continued along the ridge, then down a few well-placed stone steps to the sandy shore, past the boathouse and cemented rock walls toward the lodge and its voices.

"Hello?" I called, just loudly enough so someone might hear. "Trinity?"

No one answered. Instead, the voices continued, back and forth—with moments of silence between.

At the base of the wide stone steps I cleared my voice, ready to try again.

But at that moment, the heavy wooden door opened. And clearly rattled, Victor emerged, his blue eyes focused somewhere over my head. He flinched when he saw me.

"Sadie Rose? I didn't hear you—"

I flushed warm, certain that I'd just upset something romantic. "I'm sorry," I said. "Owen dropped me off here, thinking it would be a good idea, and he didn't think your island would be the best since—"

"I don't know what you're talking about," he said.

"I ran away from the Worthingtons."

"You've been crying."

"I'm fine," I said, a lump returning to my throat.

He looked away toward the dock and boathouse. "Was Trinity expecting you?"

"No." I felt stupid. Ashamed again. "No, she's not."

"Well," he said, exhaling long and hard. "She's . . . inside." Then he ambled down the steps, patting me lightly on the shoulder as he passed. "It's awfully good you're here. She might need a friend." And then he continued on toward the dock and his canoe.

"Sadie Rose?" A watery voice seesawed from inside. "If that's you, just come in."

I scaled the five stone steps and stepped into the lodge of massive logs. As I entered, I nearly tripped on a dustpan filled with shards of orange and pink painted glass. A broom leaned nearby, as if apologizing for not finishing up a task.

"Better keep your shoes on," Trinity said. "Oh! I'm glad you're here."

Curled in a tight ball on a leather sofa, covered by a cotton blanket, Trinity Baird rested her head in the curve of her bare arm.

"Trinity," I said.

I pictured again the man who'd found his way into my cabin, had crawled on top of me. But I couldn't imagine that Victor . . .

"What happened?" My heart teetered, not wishing to have my admiration for Victor crash at my feet. I'd trusted him and felt so completely at ease in his company. Safe. I'd canoed out to his island with him. But then I had misjudged so much of the world around me.

Trinity wailed. "I want to hate him!"

I kneeled beside her on the braided rug. I waited for her to explain, if she was willing to.

She pulled the blanket around her and sat up on her elbow. "I'm so glad you're here," she repeated. Then she wheezed in a gulp of air. "Not that I care to have you see me this way, but I'm just feeling so terribly alone right now."

"What happened?"

"Oh—this is embarrassing! You've seen how I've been throwing myself at Victor."

I couldn't deny it.

"My parents are away at a concert in Ranier. Some big fund-raiser for your father's campaign."

"Mr. Worthington," I said. "He's not my father."

The campaign. How could I forget? In November he would be reelected, or voted out. I had always assumed he'd continue to be in office, year after year after year. But maybe that could change. Beyond worrying about me, he had to keep his reputation beyond reproach. He couldn't afford to get caught up in accusations of murder.

Trinity continued. "I knew Victor wasn't going to support Senator Worthington tonight, so I invited him here." She rolled her neck, stretching. "Yes, well, that didn't work. I thought Victor and I just needed some time alone. I know how things work. Men need to see what they want sometimes before they know."

I nodded, though Trinity was surely ahead of me in such things.

"I surprised him, said I was going to get something from the game room," she pointed to the open door. A long, green Ping-Pong table filled the window-enclosed room. "When I stepped out, I was, well, naked as a newborn baby."

"You were?"

She sighed. "I was."

"And? He did more than you wanted? Is that what that broken glass is all about?"

Then she laughed, a little too loudly, a little shrilly. "No! He looked, I don't know, embarrassed. And confused. And the more I wore my heart on my bare ass, so to speak, the more he backed toward the door. 'Friends.' That's what he said he only wished to be. I was so damn hurt, so humiliated—I threw the vase. Nearly hit him in the head. Wish I had!"

"Oh." I'd overheard Darla say, "Men are simple. All they need is a good romp now and then, and they're happy." Were men all that simple? Victor wasn't. Still, I couldn't deny that plenty of men were willing to part with their hard-earned money for time with a woman. And the money, for the girls, as Meg had been quick to point out, was a hundred times better than what we earned in the kitchen.

Victor was passionate, but not in ways Trinity apparently hoped for.

"I just don't get it," she said. "I thought we were heading for something more." Then she seemed to see me through her reddened eyes. "And what on earth are you doing here, anyway? I overheard a little of your talk outside."

I explained briefly how I'd ended up on her island.

Trinity brightened and sat up, wrapping the blanket around her torso. "You can stay in my studio! It will be perfect! No one, but me, is allowed in there. Not even the maids. So you can hide there as long as you like. I'll sneak food to you. It will be a wonderful diversion from my current state of rejection and utter despair." She managed a wry smile.

I wanted to offer her words of comfort but wasn't sure what to say.

"Thanks. I need to stay low until I can get out of town." People, I didn't add, seemed to disappear if they went up against Ennis and Mr. Worthington.

"Good," she said. "Settled then." Her chin quivered in her heart-shaped face. I thought of Owen. If Trinity stepped out naked for him, I was certain he wouldn't be able to take his eyes off her. But I decided not to tell Trinity that. I didn't want to give her any ideas.

With a burst of determination, she sat straighter, gripping the blanket fast, and then she stood. She laughed. "You certainly found me in rare form!" She wiped at the edges of her eyes. "Now I feel perfectly embarrassed and silly. I think I'll get dressed." Then she strode out like a Roman queen in a toga.

The first night, Trinity pointed to the gray, wet mound outside her studio cabin. "What's that thing? It should go in the burn barrel." She pinched off her nose in disgust.

"It's an old quilt," I said, as she led the way inside the cabin. And then I explained the strange manner in which the quilt had reentered my life.

"Oh," she said, nodding. "I'll see that it gets thoroughly washed and mended. If anyone asks, I'll say it floated up in the lake and I can't possibly live without it."

I squeezed her hand. "Thank you."

Trinity took on her role of hiding me with the seriousness of a headmistress. "We can't let anyone know you're here," she said, "or the Worthingtons might send you off to the Bastille!"

"Well, probably not the Bastille—"

"Or like Marie Antoinette," she whispered, leaning uncomfortably close to me as I sat on her painting stool. "They'll—" She made a slashing motion with her finger across my neck.

She must have noticed my alarm.

"Oh, Sadie Rose. I'm just being dramatic."

An easel sat in the middle of the room, with a half-finished oil painting. One glance told me who it was. The face weathered with sun and water and miles of canoeing, the light playing off hair and eyebrows the color of sand. Trinity wasn't finished yet, but it was definitely Victor. I wondered if he had posed for this portrait, or if she'd painted from memory. Either way, she'd caught his likeness, including the shadows that lingered at the edges of his blue eyes.

Beyond the easel, a tall stone fireplace rose like a mast through the cabin. In its hearth, birch-bark logs were set, ready to be lit. Small sketches lined the mantel: the Eiffel Tower, an outdoor café, a stone archway, and another of the towering Wrigley Building in Chicago. I remembered being there with the Worthingtons when I was twelve, pleased with my cranberry dress and matching coat. I'd felt happy as we rode the clattering elevator clear to the top and scanned the shores of Lake Michigan and the city below, peppered with trees of red, yellow, and amber. I'd forgotten that memory and ached with something bittersweet.

The rest of Trinity's cabin was amazingly bare: a chaise lounge and several hanging paintings, and more resting against the log walls and on the glossy maple floor. There was a floral arrangement of deep reds and purples. A small painting captured a young woman's silhouette at the end of a dock, hands over her head, ready to dive into black water. Another caught a cheery blue ceramic pitcher and single lemon in a ray of golden sunlight.

Trinity's skills put my own efforts at painting flowerpots to shame.

"But first..." Trinity said, tan arms crossed over her petite frame and staring at the canvas painting of Victor. Her bobbed waves fell fashionably in her eyes as she tilted her head, concentrating.

"First, this." She squeezed black paint onto a stained painter's palette, grabbed a large brush, and dramatically made thick Xs all over his image. When the Xs began to meld, she filled in each and every spot of color until the blues and tans disappeared.

"Voilà! I'm done with all of that," she said, standing back as if to admire her work. "Now I feel perfectly fine."

And then, as if her crying over Victor had never happened, she didn't say another word about him. She left to find bedding and returned with a towering stack of blankets. "I took one from here and one from there—that way no one will notice anything missing."

Sweat formed on her brow, but she went about making a many-layered bed for me with a pillow near the hearth. "In case someone comes, you'll be able to climb out to get away."

"Up the chimney?" I asked, with a laugh.

"Where else?" With eyes of flickering green, she replied gravely. "Of course, the chimney. You have to be looking ahead. They'll stop at nothing, you know, to get to you."

I didn't know then whether my assumptions about Trinity had been wrong, or if she knew more about the far-reaching tentacles of E. W. Ennis and his trusty dog, Mr. Worthington. The part about the chimney wasn't logical, but her words made me shudder.

As the sun set, a boat hummed near the island. Trinity pulled the red curtain back a sliver and peered out. "I'll bring you food, but first I better go and say hello. So my parents think everything is normal."

And then she was gone.

That first night, my thoughts drifted to Owen. All he had to do was leave the creamery door open and leave the cases and the returned cash from sales he'd made. It was a fair deal. By morning, he'd know if he could start over. I hoped.

I thought my stomach would gnaw itself from hunger. I was starving, and I kept hoping that at any time Trinity would return. When I needed to use the outdoor privy, I was grateful to find a honey pot in the cabin, because Trinity had locked the door shut. The windows, fortunately, locked only from the inside, so I could have made my way out by cutting through the screens.

Trinity never brought food that long night. My mind bounced over miles of worry. Over being found, over Owen getting hurt again, over Trinity's peculiar behavior. Since I'd arrived at her studio, I'd felt myself descending into something dark and nameless. I wished to leave and hoped Owen would return for me soon.

I didn't see Trinity until the next day. I peered out between the curtains at the lake: the sun arced like a baseball struck high.

The key turned in the door with a clunk.

I jumped.

Barefooted, her hair and navy swimsuit wet, Trinity stepped inside, a basket in her arms.

"Please. Don't lock the door!" My voice sparked with anger. "What if a fire started and I needed to get out?"

"Oh, you're right," she said, hurt tainting her brow.

The picnic basket she carried was filled with corn muffins, slabs of ham, tiny clusters of red grapes tied together with yellow ribbon, two slices of chocolate cake, and a bottle of red wine. "I'm in such a habit..." Trinity frowned.

I collected myself, like puzzle pieces scattered. With so many hours alone, maybe my imagination was overstretched. "What's all this? And wine?"

"From the perpetually well-stocked cellar."

No wonder Owen had found it easy to be in business delivering liquor when well-respected families like the Bairds disregarded the Prohibition law. I'd only had a few sips of wine before the law went into effect last January. Mr. and Mrs. Worthington had allowed me occasional small glasses when they served wine with dinner. Now with the law in effect nationwide, the Worthingtons never openly served any kind of

alcohol, though I knew the tumblers Mr. Worthington and Ennis shared weren't filled with water.

From a cupboard, Trinity drew a wine opener and two cut-
crystal glasses, skillfully uncorked the bottle of burgundy, and
poured. At her urging, we finished off the bottle that afternoon
as we ate and talked. I sipped, rather, and she talked and drank.
A warm numbness gradually spread from my head to my fingers and toes. She never quite caught her breath between telling me about growing up poor compared to everyone else in
Greenwich, Connecticut. "We were the last to get a second automobile," she said. About how her mother had a baby, a boy
who only lived to be two weeks old, and how after that her
mother decided never to have children again.

She explained how her mother never went by Mrs. Samuel Baird but insisted on using her first name—Mrs. Beatrice
Baird—now that women could hope to gain equal status with
men. "She even opened up a bank account in her own name,"
Trinity said, "and shortly after she did that, she opened one for
me in my name, too."

I pictured Elizabeth Worthington and the way she defend-
ed a woman's place in the home and beside her husband. I
couldn't imagine her demanding her own bank account. She
couldn't muster up enough resolve to spit if she had to. If it
came down to a choice, she always sided with Walter Worthington. She loved me, I guessed, as long as it was easy. But if it ruffled the rooster's feathers, she was quick to go clucking away,
head down and pecking at imaginary specks in the sand, to
avoid a confrontation. Better to let him have his way.

Trinity talked on about being sent to boarding school from
the time she was eight and how she was always in trouble. "I
had tantrums," she said, staring off into her wine glass. Then
she looked up and stated matter-of-factly, "They don't *allow*
tantrums at boarding school. I was kicked out. A few times.

But they never can turn away good money, so eventually, they always took me back."

That night, after I had tuned out the scratching of bats in the attic and fallen soundly asleep, the door swung open, and Trinity stepped in. "It's midnight," she announced, as if we'd had a plan. A kerosene lamp hung from her hand, casting an amber light around her feet. "Wake up."

"What? Why? Is something wrong?"

"How else will you see the island if I don't give you midnight tours?"

Groggily, I followed her into the night. In her nightgown, she fluttered like a moth ringed in ethereal light down the shadowy path.

I did my best to follow, stubbing my toes on tree roots.

Under scattered stars and dancing milky-green ribbons of northern lights, she whispered, "Sometime I hope you can sleep on the boat. It's so dreamy to be rocked to sleep."

I wondered why the boat wasn't in the boathouse to protect it. As if Trinity read my mind, she replied, "The boathouse shingles need replacing, so it's under construction for a few days. That last storm just about took my socks off!"

"I know. I had to wait it out in a trapper's shack."

"Oh, yes. Well, this will be a change from that!"

We stepped onto the boat and under its canopy roof. "First, the galley kitchen," she said and led me down a short flight of vertical steps. Beyond the stove and sink, seats upholstered in velvet graced a small table. I sat down in the lamp's glow, smoothing my nightdress over my knees, feeling like royalty.

From a silverware case, Trinity lifted up a silver table knife by its sharp point, as if to fling it at a dartboard or perform a dangerous circus act.

Not until that moment did I realize the circus would have come and gone from Ranier while I was at Kettle Falls. I'd missed it, but it barely mattered now.

"See the *T*?" she asked.

I noticed the letter scrolled into the knife handle.

"Every fork, knife, and spoon," she said, "and every towel and pillow. Need a robe? There are two in the stateroom, monogrammed, of course. Don't you think my parents went a little overboard?" She laughed. "The boat was a welcome home present." Between her palms, she rolled the knife handle around and around, the way I'd rolled clay into coils to make clay pots.

"Home from Paris?"

She shook her head. "From my last stay at the hospital. But it wasn't really a hospital at all, more of a resort, really. I wandered around in my bathrobe all day. They say fresh air is so good for you. And you should have seen the rose bushes! Every variety you can imagine!"

To my relief, she put the knife away, grabbed the lantern from the table, and continued the tour. Back on the main deck under the canopy roof, she pointed to the large steering wheel. "Henry, our caretaker, drives the boat. Guests love to hear him tell stories about the lake. He's a local, and they find him so primitive!"

The guests would certainly find old stories of Ranier interesting—especially if they heard of the prank once played with a frozen prostitute. *Primitive.* I supposed that was one word for it. I thought of Caveman and Bigby—who both lived their lives close to the earth and soil, choosing to live away from society's scrutiny.

"After the *Titanic* went down," Trinity whispered, speaking fast, "Daddy insisted we have a lifeboat on board." She pointed out the lifeboat, turned upside down, which sat under the roof behind the bench and captain's wheel. "As well as life-saving rings. Can you imagine, not enough boats on that gigantic ship? Sinking down…down…down…into that icy blackness, nothing to cling to but ice."

I wanted to change the subject. "Guess I've never much wanted to think about it."

"Oh, I have!" she said. "Over and over! I can imagine every terrible second of it. Out in the middle of those icebergs, in the middle of nowhere, and sinking into that cold, dark water…knowing no one can save you—"

"Trinity, I'm tired." I faked a long yawn. "I want to head back."

With each day that followed, I managed to wash, eat, and sleep in Trinity's cabin. And she encouraged me to paint while she was gone. Not that my attempts at still life were good, but I kept busy trying to paint dragonflies. When I found one in the flower box outside the window, I carefully set its lifeless iridescent body and delicate etched-glass wings on a display table. I painted it over and over, trying to capture its beauty. But I never could get it quite right.

It was so different with the piano. My fingers knew how to find the right keys and translate them into something artful. It was one thing that came naturally to me, and I missed playing. With deep regret, I doubted I would have access to a decent piano again.

Each day, small fishing boats and larger passenger boats came and went in the channel beyond the cabin, some occasionally rounding the point and heading to the island's main dock.

Midweek, when the sound of a deep rumbling boat engine floated over the island, I was curious—and restless. I slipped out of the studio cabin and crept to the overlook above the beach and boathouse. Stretching on a carpet of dense moss and under a Norway pine, I watched the fifty-four-foot yacht TRINITY get under way.

A U.S. flag fluttered from a pole at the stern, where Trinity now stood and chatted with her parents. She had one hand on a brass pole, next to a short flight of stairs leading to the stateroom, "a fancy word for two beds and a dresser," she'd explained to me the night of our boat tour.

On the stern deck, beside a round, red wicker table holding glasses and bottles, her parents sat in chairs against the stern railing. They were a nicely matched couple, both well padded with rounded faces. Samuel Baird, with no hat and gray hair trimmed neatly at the sides of his head, leaned back and reached over and squeezed his wife's hand. I'd never witnessed such a display from the Worthingtons. Under a straw hat with a scarf, secured at her chin, Beatrice Baird smiled at her husband, patted his hand, and then adjusted the creamy shawl over the shoulders of her summer dress.

I so wished I could join them and not be hidden away like some castoff. But I kept to the ground until the boat reversed into the bay, then carved a path toward a sky of pink clouds softly layering the horizon and the promise of a fiery sunset cruise.

When I returned to the studio cabin, to my shock Owen was waiting for me, stretched out on the chaise lounge, arms crossed behind his head.

I had to catch my breath, and when I tried to speak, the words momentarily froze in my head. "Owen, you scared me!" But what I really wanted to say was that I was so relieved to see him, to see his face mending, not worse for wear.

"Didn't mean to," he said. He swung his long legs over until his boots hit the floor. "I tucked my boat in a little spot just around the bend. Hoped to find you. There's a big article in *The Press*. It's about how you've gone missing, and the muckraker reporter is raising questions about Mr. Worthington and how he's using your disappearance and tugging on heartstrings for political gain." He pulled a folded newspaper out from his shirt. "Here. You can read it for yourself."

I looked at the paper, but my eyes wouldn't focus. Refused to focus. I looked at Owen and felt a delicious swirling dizziness running through me—better than wine—my body felt remotely connected to my brain. I would study the paper in my quiet hours after Owen left. "I'll read it later. You're okay? Everything went smoothly?"

"Yup. Left what they wanted and hurried back the next morning. They didn't touch anything else. Didn't burn down the creamery. I'm lucky."

"I'm so relieved. I was worried."

He smiled. "Hey, you look good," he said, with a slight tug on the rim of his cap. "Great, in fact."

My heart would not keep a regular beat. "Well, your face isn't as puffy." Now the bruising had turned a mix of purple, green, and yellow. I pointed to Trinity's artist palette resting on the floor by her easel. "But it's that colorful. I feel bad for you."

He raised his forefinger and pointed toward his good eye. "A little kiss, then, to make it better? Just here?"

I stepped closer to where he sat. He kept his hands to himself as I leaned over and kissed his eyebrow.

"Ah, better already," he said. "But maybe here, too?" He tilted his head and placed his finger on the side of his chin.

"Owen," I said, the soft scolding in my voice sounding just like Elizabeth Worthington when she tried to correct me. Half-hearted and unconvincing.

He gave me a puppy-eye sad expression. My hand, almost as if it acted against my will, dropped to his shoulder, and then my fingers explored the curls of hair at the back of his head. Soft and coarse. I leaned closer and placed my lips on his chin. He turned his head slowly, questioningly. Our lips met, softly at first, and then with increased longing. His kiss took me far beyond the walls of the cabin, beyond the island's shores.

Suddenly, he pulled away, his hand over his mouth.

"What?" I asked, bracing myself to be rejected, as Victor had dismissed Trinity.

He put his hand to his mouth and bruised jaw. "My mouth is too sore."

"Oh, sorry," I said, stepping back. "That'll teach us."

He gently reached for my waist and rested both hands there—as light as feathers—as if waiting to see if a scolding would follow. He looked up, smiled, and held me with his eyes. "Us?"

"I believe, um, that's what came out of my mouth."

"Hmmm. I figured once you learned I'd broken the law— with your living with the senator and all—that you wouldn't have anything to do with me."

"You thought I'd look down on *you*?"

"Hey, you have a fancy life in St. Paul, the biggest house in Ranier—and that's just your summer cottage. I mean, everyone knows Mr. Worthington designed the lift bridge. I can't compete with any of that. Not now anyway. But someday—things could be different."

"Owen Jensen," I said, loving the feel of his name on my tongue. "You don't know much about me, do you?"

"I think I know enough."

"About my real mother, I mean." I gathered my courage and continued. "That she used to work in Ranier, for Darla. One of her girls."

"Yeah, I heard that somewhere. Guess I didn't believe it. There's enough gossip on any regular day in Ranier to fill a barn, floor to ceiling. It's all manure, far as I'm concerned."

"But if it's true, wouldn't that change how you think of me?"

"Sadie Rose," he said, lifting his hands toward my face, his warm palms against my cheeks, "you are *not* your mother."

I flinched and wanted to look away. I worried tears would start. But Owen's eyes, brown as a beaver's pelt, wouldn't let me go.

"Listen, whatever your mother was or did, she must have had a whole lotta good in her to produce someone as fine as you."

My eyes brimmed hot, and I bit down on my lip.

He whispered. "I mean it, Sadie."

Then he pulled me close and pressed his face against my chest. Standing over him, I removed his cap, dropped it to the floor, and tucked my nose into his head of thick hair. I breathed in the tang of cedar boughs, the heartbeat of whitetail deer, the waters of a vast and flowing lake—all in that one deep breath with the creamery boy.

| 27 |

When Trinity returned at midnight, I was wide awake, thinking of Owen. She lit the gas lamp, and I sat up from my blankets.

In her arms she carried my mother's quilt, now folded neatly. It smelled of bleach and soap, and was now a soft winter gray and mended with light blue stitching. It seemed the nicest gift I could ever hope for. "Oh, Trinity. Thank you!" I said, rising, but she stopped me with her hand.

"No, don't get up. And thank the help, not me." She set the quilt on the chaise lounge.

Then she tilted her head and crossed her arms, gestures I'd seen many times from her before, but this time her green eyes flashed. "There's something different about you. You're glowing."

I couldn't tell her about Owen. I wanted to, but something in me held back, unsure.

"Owen came to see you, didn't he?"

I was stunned. "How—" I began. Then I realized she must have seen his boat somewhere after he departed the island.

The delight in her eyes vanished. "I knew it," she said, accusingly.

I wanted to tell her about my first real kiss—one that counted—about how Owen said he'd return to gather me at the end of the week. About how he knew someone who was going to drive the long, muddy road to Duluth and that he was willing to take a rider for free. About how Owen said he'd accompany me, to make sure I found a place to work and stay. That he had showed me an ad for lace-collar jobs from the *Duluth News Tribune*, employers advertising for on-the-job training for stenographers and secretaries for "girls of good reputation."

They were jobs relatively new to women, jobs that could offer me freedom and independence. Perhaps if I worked hard at saving what I'd earn, I'd be able to put myself through college. It might take me forever, but it would be worth it. Besides, Duluth was a big port city on Lake Superior. I could imagine myself there—a modern young woman living on my own—maybe someday with Owen, too.

"Well, aren't you going to tell me what happened?" She glared at me.

But I didn't want to tell her anything. I didn't trust her—trust this streak of jealousy. "Oh, nothing much," I said. "He said he'd come for me in a few days. He dropped by to let me know. I can't stay here forever, after all."

"Oh, so nothing happened between you two then?" Her tone shifted, softened.

I shrugged.

She studied me. "You're a terrible liar," she said and then laughed.

"Oh. I didn't want to make you feel bad, especially after—"

"After?"

"You know, Victor. When I arrived."

She looked at me as if she had no idea what I was talking about. "Silly Sadie Rose. You have a wild imagination, don't you?" Then she pushed her blonde curls back out of her eyes. With childlike enthusiasm, she motioned me to join her on my thick layering of blankets. She plopped down, cross-legged. "So you and Owen! Tell me every detail!"

Her sudden warmth primed me like a pump, and everything I'd only one second earlier decided not to share with her flowed out in a gush of words. This time she seemed to soak up my good news, smiling.

She hugged me. "Sadie, I'm genuinely happy for you! I truly am."

The next day passed, and with it, Trinity's mood.

As trees cast late-day shadows, I was getting hungry, wondering if Trinity had forgotten me again. I hated being a burden for her. She arrived, but this time with a single slice of bread between her fingers. She thrust it toward me, as if I were a tiresome prisoner. "Here. And don't complain. Some fare far worse than you."

Her words and actions left me tottering, uncertain what she might do or say next. I wanted to take back every precious secret I'd shared with her about my time with Owen. I wanted to leave Baird's Island and wished I'd insisted on climbing in Owen's boat when he'd left.

The next day she didn't step foot near the cabin. I kept watch at the lakeside window, feeling much more a prisoner now than guest or stowaway. If only Owen would arrive early. I moped about the studio cabin until I'd memorized each and every sketch and painting, every chink between the logs. I'd already come to expect the same red squirrel each morning in the petunia box, where he ate a pinecone half his size. The flaky seeds he didn't eat he buried in the soil.

After sunset, I slipped from the cabin to a sandy nook sheltered by overhanging branches. If I waited until after sunset, the mosquitoes died down. I hung my nightdress over a branch and eased my body into the cool water. Washed, then floated under dazzling pinpoints of constellations and waves of milky light. An occasional boat ventured along the channel, but no one could see me as I rubbed the chill away with a towel.

But that night, a white moon rose—just shy of full—spotlighting my bathing area. I hurried and returned to the cabin in my nightdress.

On my extravagant pile of blankets, I pressed my palms against my belly, which had grown thinner. I couldn't survive long on a slice of bread and water. My stomach rumbled and complained, echoing off its empty chambers.

But thinking about hunger didn't make it go away.

Instead, I imagined a big dinner of pork roast, glazed carrots, and mashed potatoes with gravy. I drew a deep breath and pressed my belly outward, pretending I was incredibly full.

And then I imagined a different kind of full belly. My hands smoothed over an imaginary swollen womb, wondering what it might be like to someday carry a child. I'd felt so wronged being brought up in a brothel that I'd never imagined that I'd someday want a child of my own.

But if I could offer a good home, a sense of belonging.

If it were Owen's child...if he and I were to become something more...not that I was in a rush...I longed to continue my education before I married and thought about a family...but for the first time, I realized I could warm to such dreams. Someday.

For now, I certainly could warm to Owen's fingertips, his lips and tongue on mine, his hands...the way he had of building a slow fire of deep embers within me.

I breathed in the truth of Owen's words—*you are not your mother*—and the way they were more than words. A key that set me free. Free to live my own life. I would always be linked to my past, as everyone is, but I wasn't bound by it any longer. Now I had a better understanding of my real mother. She'd been in love once, married, had a child, and out of desperate circumstances, tried to keep herself and her child alive. I would hold fast to the good in her.

I breathed—deep, long, grateful breaths—and let my thoughts return to Owen.

I was falling all right. Tumbling in a sweet free fall.

But so far, Owen was proving a sturdy and welcoming net.

That night, I dropped into a peaceful sleep.

I woke to a whistling wind, to branches scraping at my window, and to something more...a single, low, and soul-piercing howl.

I sat up, waiting to hear it again.

I'd heard wolves howl before, their ancient chorus of voices rising into a melancholy whole, penetrating marrow, reaching an eerie crescendo, then dropping off, voice by voice, into silence.

Once, right in the middle of the day, when our passenger train from St. Paul had stopped for repairs after hitting a bull moose, howling had sliced through the cold fall air. Everyone in the passenger car stopped talking to listen. And another night, on a sleigh ride with the Worthingtons when I was six, wolves had sounded so close that I'd huddled closer to Mrs. Worthington, and she'd wrapped her arm around me until the howling—shrill and shuddering—stopped.

I surfaced from a cavern of sleep, but the night was quiet. I sat up, waited, then lay back down again, questioning if I'd been dreaming.

Again, the soft-pitched howl.

This time I recognized the voice.

I wrapped the quilt around my shoulders and nightdress and rushed out, following Trinity's voice, which carried on the sharp, northerly wind. I dashed along the twisting paths, through stretches of darkness and patches of moonlight. I ran toward the ridge and peered down. Trinity, bathed in streams of milky light, stood on the roof of her namesake boat, her hair silver and blowing across her face.

"Trinity?" I called out in a whisper, but I was downwind and too far away. I had to get to her before anyone else found her this way. Before she hurt herself.

I hurried down the path, slipping once and skidding on my bum, and then started off again across the beach and onto the dock.

I whispered as loudly as I dared. "Trinity! It's me. Sadie Rose. What are you doing?"

She tilted her head back, her nipples pressed through her sodden nightdress, and howled at the moon. Then she glared at me, her hair wet to her scalp. "Go away," she said. At her side, a knife glinted in her hand. I thought of the way she'd shown me the boat's monogrammed silverware, the way she'd lingered over the knife. I'd felt uneasy then, but I never imagined this.

"Help! Trinity needs help!" I shouted at the top of my lungs.

"I won't let them send me *back*," she snapped. "Not ever again!" Then she tilted her head back again and let out another moaning howl. Stiff-armed, from shoulder to wrist, she swung the knife back and forth, half-circling her body. Not only was her mind not right but her movements were awkward, as if her mind were making threadbare connections with her limbs.

In seconds, lights flashed through the trees.

Voices broke the night.

Screen doors whined on sleepy hinges.

Footsteps pattered.

I could have ducked into the shadows of the boathouse, lowered myself into the water, and swam around the island and back to my hiding place. But not with Trinity in this condition.

I couldn't leave her like this. She'd said we could try our hand at friendship, and if that's what this was, what kind of friend was I to flee and leave her now?

"Trinity, honey," called a man, soothingly. "Come down from there, sweetie!"

Emerging from the path, Trinity's parents ambled onto the dock. In a dark smoking jacket over pajamas, Mr. Baird headed for the boat, his stricken face so fixed on Trinity that I thought he might fall off the dock. Mrs. Baird hurried, buttoning her robe over her ample middle. Her hair was so thin and short that I realized her daytime hair was in reality a wig. When she spotted me, her voice and finger raised at me. "Hell's bells! Who are *you*?"

I opened my mouth to explain, but she put up her hand. "Oh, I'll find out later. My knees are bad. Get on the boat and get a blanket from the stateroom!" she ordered. "Hurry!"

I pulled the quilt from my shoulders. "Here. Use this."

Now others gathered near the shore, some in moonlight, others in shadows.

"Look! I see a toad!" a child said, holding an adult's hand and pulling toward the sandy beach.

"Children, go back to your beds!" someone ordered.

"Quick!" Mrs. Baird advised me, pointing upward. "Hand it up to my husband."

I tossed the blanket toward Mr. Baird, who despite his stoutness, had managed to scramble up onto the boat's canopy roof with his daughter. I hoped it would hold them. He caught it by its edge.

I stood on the dock beside Trinity's mother, so I could see.

Now Trinity stretched her arms, palms braced, like a preacher envisioning hell.

"Oh, I thought this was coming on," Mrs. Baird said, wrap-

ping her arms around her plump waist. "She had been doing so
well, and then these past few weeks—"

Trinity was screaming now, shouting. "No! You come one
step closer and this time I'll do it. I will not be taken captive
alive!" Then she pointed to me, standing below on the dock.
"She's the only one who is on my side!"

Trinity held her knife high, wielding it as if she were some
warrior. Mr. Baird stepped in slow motion toward her with the
edges of the blanket stretched wide, a large shield.

"Don't!" she shrieked, her voice the color of pain. "Come!
A step! Closer!"

He dropped the blanket, arms at his sides. "Darling, Trinity," he soothed. His voice was maple syrup on the verge of crys-
tallizing. "Put down the knife, Trinity. Come down, dear girl.
Please just come down. Whatever you're afraid of, it's okay now.
You're safe, and everything's just fine."

I wanted to believe him.

On the dock, Mrs. Baird turned to the half-dozen adults
forming an audience below. "If he can just get her wrapped
tightly in the blanket, she'll calm right down. You'll see. Everything will turn out fine."

"Oh, that's what you want me to believe!" Trinity said.
"Don't you idiots understand anything? Are you that stupid?
What kind of fools are you? They're coming! They're hiding
out there—" She pointed toward the island's silhouetted pines.
"And there!" She stretched her neck, as if she could truly see
something or someone. "They're hiding in the jungles. And
there's no way out for any of us! For once you all need to listen to me!"

"Trinity," Mr. Baird continued sweet and slow. "You know I
won't do anything to harm you. I only want to help you, sweetheart . . . now put the knife down."

"Noooo!" she wailed, her hand clamped on the knife's silver handle. Her eyes glinted, fierce as a predator after its prey, and she held the blade high in her fist.

Just as I was wishing there was something I could do, Mrs. Baird turned to me, pleading. "She seems to trust you. Can you try?"

I clambered onto the boat and up onto its roof. "Trinity," I said, my voice unsteady.

"Sadie Rose," Trinity said, softening for a brief moment as she looked beyond Mr. Baird to me. Then her father eased back as I stepped forward.

"Trinity," I said again. "I'm here ... and I'm not going to let anything bad happen to you."

Her eyes flashed wide. "Why should I believe *you*?"

I shrugged. "I don't know." The boat rocked slightly, throwing me off balance. The wind iced my back and legs. "Because we're friends. You've helped me, remember?"

Trinity lowered her arm a few inches but still clutched the knife.

I reached down and picked up the quilt at my feet. "You returned this to me, all clean and dry." I stretched it toward her. "Here. You're wet. You're freezing. Why don't you wrap up in it?"

She studied the quilt. "It was your mother's?"

I nodded. "Yes, it was."

Trinity lowered the knife a few more inches, and then her arm went limp and she held the knife loosely at her side.

And then, as naturally as a child drawn toward comfort, she stepped toward me and the quilt. I wrapped it around her thin and shivering body, and in the same motion, I reached for the knife in exchange. She let go of it without a fight, almost as if she'd forgotten it was in her hand.

I hugged Trinity close, and she buried her head in my shoulder. I sensed Mr. Baird behind me, slipping the knife from my hand and backing off the boat.

I shivered and held Trinity close until her breathing slowed. As the Bairds sent the others back to their beds and called the visiting doctor from bed, a memory tumbled back to me.

It was morning at Darla's boardinghouse. Smells of coffee and rising bread mixed with the scent of spilled blood. Amid screaming and crying, I stood in the bedroom doorway, watching the young woman in the washtub. She was flopped like a limp doll, her head lolling back, her pale wrists striped red in wash water turned dark as rubies.

I watched, helpless, relieved it wasn't my mother.

I shuddered. The wind chilled my legs and neck as I held Trinity. She'd come so close to taking her life. What if I hadn't heard her? What if I hadn't been on the island to help her? And why would she do such a thing? Why?

I wanted to make sense of her actions, of why she would raise a knife against herself. She had all the social privileges and comforts anyone could hope for. She wasn't like women who tried desperately to escape their bottom rung on the social ladder.

Despite her social standing, despite her family name, Trinity's mind wasn't well.

When Trinity began to cry, I said, "Go ahead. It's okay. You can cry. Everything's going to be fine."

And after I was certain she was in a calmer place, we climbed down from the boat, where her parents stood waiting, shoulder to shoulder.

| 28 |

Somewhere in that long night, hovering near the bed as Dr. Mary Austin and Trinity's parents came and went, Mrs. Baird said, "Oh, now I know. You're the Worthington girl, aren't you?" She had taken up the chair near Trinity's head. I sat on an embroidered stool near the foot of the bed. Until someone ordered me gone, I refused to leave.

"Yes, ma'am."

"So Trinity was hiding you under our noses?"

I nodded again.

"In her studio?"

"Yes."

"That explains her being so protective of her latest work. She said it was going to be her 'masterpiece.' Well…"

Mrs. Baird studied her daughter, and I followed her gaze. Trinity's hair was matted and clung to her head. Eyelids closed, she looked peacefully asleep.

She'd willingly walked with me from the boat to her bedroom in the lodge. Dr. Austin, the first woman doctor in the region and a family friend of the Bairds, had helped settle Trinity with teaspoons of laudanum, as if she were a baby, eyes unfocused and half-closed. "We need to keep her calm," the doctor said. "No more theatrics for a while."

Now Mrs. Baird turned her head toward me. "You're a good friend, to stay here like this."

"She's been good to me." Though I didn't pretend to understand Trinity's fearful or delusional moods, I knew from the moment I'd met her at Red Stone Island that she'd been willing to help me.

Mrs. Baird lifted her cup of tea to her lips, but without sipping, set it back down again on the nightstand. "You know, when I'd heard you'd gone missing from the Worthingtons, I thought you might have run away. Trinity used to threaten to do that all the time. She succeeded a few times and gave us a real scare. When she was four, she went only as far as the house next door to ours. But when she was in her teens, she'd hide on the island from us. She was angry, and I don't remember what always started it. I was just so relieved when she'd finally show up and I'd know she hadn't drowned." She looked at me. "This isn't the first time."

"First time?"

"She's tried to . . . extinguish her life. Once, overdosing on pills. Another time she kept swimming out into the lake in the middle of the night. I don't understand. We love her, she has all the opportunities a young woman could hope for . . . and much of the time, she's brimming with energy and life and new ideas. But when she sinks low . . ."

"I saw a girl at the boardinghouse once. She slit her wrists," I said. "When I was little."

"I'm sorry," she said, nodding. "For those girls and women . . . trying to take their own lives . . . they must not see a way out. The high tower in International Falls. Several have jumped to their deaths rather than live. Such desperation, I can almost understand, but our daughter."

Mrs. Baird reached across the floral bedspread of pinks and greens to Trinity's hand. "So many times, I've thought of her life as a rich tapestry. You know her. She's talented, has everything anyone could want, and yet there's this dark red thread that zigzags through it all."

"Mmhmm." I understood about a red thread.

Trinity moaned and tried to roll over, but her arms were strapped to her sides. A homemade rigging of socks tied around her arms joined with belts that stretched under the bed. I hated to see her restrained, yet knew it was best—until she settled back into her own mind. She mumbled incoherently, then lay still again.

Beneath her blankets, Trinity's legs and torso looked so small and frail. Without her lovely waves of hair falling toward her eyes, her forehead appeared sharp, her eyes sunken, like a stray wandering too long in the streets. When I'd first met her, I'd been awestruck by her experiences and grace. I'd thought Trinity was invincible, so free and unconstrained by society, never guessing she could ever be brought low.

Yet Trinity's mind took her down some frightening, invisible waters.

Early the next morning, I woke with my head leaning across Trinity's covers. I was disoriented, but then the events of last night tumbled back in sequence.

Mrs. Baird was tapping my shoulder. "Sadie Rose, wake up," she whispered.

I pushed hair off my face and rubbed my eyes. The whole of last night seemed a dream, but here was Trinity, bandaged and resting beneath bedcovers, and here was Mrs. Baird, talking. Her wig was on, full and dark, but beneath her eyes half-moons appeared, ink-stained with fatigue. "We sent notice to the Worthingtons about you. They're sending Hans to collect you. He should be here sometime soon."

Things were set in motion. I would have to face the
Worthingtons. I couldn't run anymore.

Trinity stirred and then woke with a groan. "Sadie Rose?"
For a moment, she fixed her dull gaze on me. "What are you
doing here?" Then lifting her head off the pillow, she tried
to sit up. "What's going on?" She struggled against the make-
shift straps holding her wrists to the bed. "For God's sake! Will
someone undo me and tell me what's going on here!" Her eyes
spiked with fear.

"Darling," Mrs. Baird said, placing her hand on Trinity's
forehead. "You had another spell."

"Trinity, you're not well yet," I said, rising from my chair.

"Untie me, will you?!"

I looked to Mrs. Baird. "No," she said, "for your own safety,
you need to be right where you are."

"Trinity," I added, "last night you tried to harm yourself. Try
and rest. I'll be back to see you as soon as I can." I patted her
ankle through the blanket. "I promise."

"Sadie!" Trinity screamed, high-pitched and angry.

Staying longer to try to reason with her seemed futile. I
had to be ready for Hans when he arrived.

I pulled myself away from her and Mrs. Baird and then
stepped into the lodge's long hallway, scented with comforting
smells of coffee and toast, wafting from the kitchen. I was hungry, but I didn't want to stop to eat. Instead, I hurried around
the island's winding paths to Trinity's studio, changed out of
my nightdress, gathered my few belongings, and carried my
traveling satchel and coat to the dock.

I glanced at Trinity's boat, its canopy roof beading with
droplets of dew. In the clean scent of morning, last night's
events now seemed more like a nightmare. I wished for Trinity's sake that it had just been a bad dream. Sometimes life

seemed more about starting again, no matter how hard, no matter how deep the wounds.

A morning haze gathered above the lake, a thousand ghostly wisps of regret, hovering, waiting to be chased off by the day's determined rays. The water was glass, the air so still and fresh that it seemed all of nature was pausing, except for shimmery black beetles dancing on the surface beside the dock, and a small bass rising up, mouth opening and closing, sending the beetles swirling. I listened, watched, and waited.

I tried to sit on my traveling bag, my hands over my knees, but I hopped up and paced the length of the dock.

"Thank you."

I turned toward the voice. Mr. Baird walked out in cotton trousers and a pressed shirt. "I wanted to thank you before you leave. If you hadn't alerted us—" He steadied his emotions. "I need to relieve my wife so she can rest now, but if there's any way we can repay you, please. Just let us know. We're indebted to you."

"There's no need to repay me," I said. "Trinity's my friend."

He nodded. "Yes. A friend. I'm glad of that. Well, then..." He extended his hand and we shook before he moved off toward the lodge, where Trinity was bound to a bed frame to protect her from herself. I wondered if she would be shipped off again soon to the hospital she'd mentioned, the one with the gardens of roses.

When a familiar boat motor buzzed around the island's peninsula, I felt a wave break over me. Maybe it was from lack of sleep, from witnessing Trinity's mind snap, like a twig in winter. My emotions and thoughts jumbled together and spilled over me, and tears fell down my cheeks.

Han's fishing boat carved toward the dock. He waved from its stern, where he straddled the seat, his hand on the motor's handle. In the bow, to my surprise, sitting tall and straight,

Aasta fixed her gaze on me. She appeared to clench the gun-wales with her hands. She never rode in boats. She was too afraid she'd drown. She'd never learned to swim. Yet here she was, joining Hans to collect me.

As the boat slowed and floated in closer, she called out, "Oh, Sadie Rose! We were so worried to death! And here you are!" With a red life jacket strapped around her neck and chest, she grabbed the dock's edge as the boat slowed. Hans reached for the dock cleat near the stern. "A sight for sore eyes," he said.

My nose ran, my chest heaved and shuddered. Hans of-fered me a hand as I climbed down onto the middle seat. I hugged him and the fishing boat tottered.

"Sadie?" he said. "What happened?"

So much had happened since that day I'd found the photos in his shed, since Victor had arrived on the doorstep, since I'd run off from the Worthingtons... I let go and turned to Aasta. Even though she wasn't one to hug and carry on, I threw my arms around her, too, ignoring the rule about standing in boats.

The boat began to sway, and in an instant, I let go of Aas-ta, worried that I'd cause her to tumble overboard. Instead, I clanked my ankle sharply against the wooden seat, lost my bal-ance, and all in an instant, toppled backward over the edge of the boat and into the lake. The water was well over my head. In my boots and skirt, I sank, but when my feet struck bottom, I kicked off and pushed upward toward the dim light.

When I broke through, I hacked up water, and then half-choking, half-crying, I started to laugh.

"Of all the things," Hans said as he fished me out with his sturdy arms and pulled me back into the boat, "you are the tro-phy muskie!"

I was dripping wet, but somehow a cold dunking helped clear my mind from all that had happened last night—and from the uncertainties that awaited me when I returned home.

Aasta asked, "You need dry clothes, ya?"

I settled, dripping, onto the middle seat. "No. I'll change when we get back."

Hans yanked on the motor's rope handle until the Evinrude glugged back to life, leaving a thin iridescent layer of gasoline on the water as we left the dock. Without another word between us, we headed back toward Ranier, our boat a diamond etching its path through glass.

Though I kept my gaze on the water, the film began again.

"What's going on here?" One man rushed over, his face crumpled with concern.

"Mayor, think the kid belongs to the red skirt?"

I hovered above, watching, unfeeling, unable to leave as the men debated.

"Bigby, hand the girl here. Send Dr. Stedman to my house the moment he gets here!"

And then the mayor, Mr. Walter Worthington, gathered my body in his arms. He left the town hall and strode straight-backed down the snowpacked street and toward the cedar-shingled house on the bay. Somewhere along his path, I slipped from above and back into the body I knew was my own.

| 29 |

Skimming along the lake, we traveled west as the sun burned off the early morning haze. A light breeze carried a perfume forest and the sweet moisture of endless intertwining northern lakes.

Halfway back, Hans cut the motor and the boat slowed to a lilting stop. I turned toward Hans. Waves piled up behind the stern, then swept past us.

"Is something wrong?" I asked.

Hans nodded. "Very, very wrong. We should have told you so much longer ago."

"Told me what?"

Hans chewed on his lower lip.

What was he getting at?

Aasta said, "Our shame was too great. We didn't know how... and the time was never good..."

I spun toward Aasta, her hands clasped together between her skirted knees.

"Sadie Rose," Hans said to my back, "I said we lost our daughter long ago. That was true. But I didn't tell you all the rest."

I remembered Hans saying something about a daughter when we'd stopped to fish after he'd retrieved me from Falcon Island. So that was what this was about. They wanted to share their lives with me, their story. They probably hoped it would somehow help me. "She was your mother," Hans said.

A ripple of electricity went through my body. "What did you say?"

He worked his lips, but nothing came out for a few moments. Emotion tugged at the edges of his crisp, blue eyes. "Our daughter was your mother."

"We stay quiet for so many years," Aasta said. "But when you disappear, we died a little every day. Not know if we ever see you again. You left and you didn't know truth. We feel so terrible."

I felt as if my head would tumble from my shoulders. I'd spent so many years not knowing, sheltered as a canary in a gilded cage. "But that makes..."

He nodded. "That makes us grandparents to you."

"Grandparents?" I repeated the word in disbelief. I couldn't draw a straight line between things. They were the cook and housekeeper, not my grandparents.

"Do the Worthingtons know?" I tried to wring some clarity from all of this, but my mind was murky as dishwater.

Hans smoothed his palms on his trousers. "Nei."

"Honest?" My voice broke. "You're telling me the truth?"

Water lapped against the boat's ribs.

They each nodded.

Anger flashed through me. "But then why hold this back from me? Why allow me to think I had no family—all these years—when you were both right there?"

Aasta leaned toward me, her elbows on the knees of her skirt. Then she grabbed my hand in hers and squeezed tight. "Oh, Sadie Rose." Her voice was a whisper. "Ya, it is true. And we want so much to tell you."

Hans nodded. "We should have long ago told you."

So much needed to be said, to be explained, and yet I felt enveloped, aware they were far more now in my life. Though the morning sun warmed my shoulders, I shivered, my garments still wet. "But why—why didn't you tell me?"

I looked to Aasta, who held back tears. "At first we didn't know anything about you. We came north to find our daughter, Sigrid—"

Sigrid. Of course. That explained the inscription on the quilt. Mama had changed her name. "You mean, Bella Rose," I countered.

"*Nei!*" Aasta said. "That was her working name. Sigrid, she left home when was your same age. We did not go for Catholic boyfriend—Frank Ladovitch. We were so angry with her. She ran off. We thought, sure she will come back. Nearly six years went by, we hear nothing. Then she sends the posted letters. So. We board the train from St. Paul to find her in Ranier. She wrote in letters that she was schoolteacher, but that turned out not true."

"Then," Hans added, "we saw a posting for a cook and caretaker. *Vel,* you can guess what happened. We took the work. But we have no idea the little girl was you. *And how could we?* We didn't know a baby was born to our Sigrid. We took the job—" He nodded. "And for that, we were grateful."

A flock of cormorants winged past, low to the water, black and angular.

Hans sniffed but continued. "We didn't know you were ours for long time. You were getting over sickness, and it did Aasta good to cook for you and help you get stronger. But months passed and passed before we found out about Sigrid. We keep looking and learn about Frank and that he died. And then we learn his wife—our Sigrid—worked for Darla. Finally, we search old newspapers and find . . . the death notice for Sigrid Ladovitch. Her married name."

Aasta added, "Poor Sigrid. She never got proper Lutheran burial."

"So—" Hans went on. "From there, we start to put things together. You were her daughter. Found in the snow. Our *granddaughter*. Living right with the Worthingtons. It seemed strange miracle for us."

My tongue lodged in my mouth. I forced myself to speak. "But I still don't understand. Why didn't you tell me sooner?"

"We wanted to, but we worried. What if the Worthingtons not believe us? We are immigrants to this country. And Elizabeth...by then, she had her mind fixed to adopt you. We thought they can give you a better home and a good life, and we are getting only older. And we worried, too, that if we said you were our granddaughter, with Sigrid falling into such a life, we worry they send us away. Say we...were...not fit to raise you since we failed our own daughter. We could not take this risk."

His shoulders rose and fell, and he hung his head.

"We not stand to lose you, too," Aasta continued, lightly pressing her fingers across her lips. "We keep to ourselves, but treating you always as our own."

I was angry with them for withholding the truth of who they were in my life. Hadn't they heard me crying for Mama in those early years? If they had told me that they were my grandparents, I wouldn't have felt so alone. Things would have been different. I felt the urge to be cruel, to treat them as servants. If they could play years of charade with me, didn't they deserve to feel pain, too?

"But I didn't *know*," I said. "I never knew I had any family at all!"

Hans said something in Norwegian I couldn't understand. Then he leaned closer. "*Vel,* now you're old enough. If we get fired, at least now you're old enough to choose your family. No one can send us away forever from you now."

But just as quickly as the morning haze burned off, my anger lifted. Too much time had already been lost.

It was Aasta and Hans, whom I already loved.

My grandparents.

A half-dozen pelicans, white wings tipped black, flapped low and hit the water with their golden webbed feet, then floated side by side, fishing in formation, heads cocked toward us.

We drifted along in silence on the vast and endless lake, in a world I'd never imagined before.

The train groaned and clattered above us as our little boat scooted through the swift-flowing passage between Canada and the States. I felt like the lift bridge, rooted to my past on one clear shore, my future cloaked in thick fog on the other. I wondered what awaited me at the Worthingtons. For the first time in my life, I didn't care. They didn't own me. I wasn't bound to them a moment longer.

Their summer cottage rose above the harbor, tall and proud. It made perfect sense that Walter Worthington had built his lake cottage directly across from the steel bridge he'd designed. It was a monument to his engineering skills, his vision, his determination to take Ranier from a rough frontier town to something more. I smiled to myself. Ironic, then, that the many brothels he'd worked at shutting down had given way to a new industry: bootlegging. There was money in it, not just in the area but in trading over the border and shipping across the country.

I pictured Owen's face, his bruises likely lightening by now, and hoped he could truly quit and find another path for his future. I didn't want to see him hurt again.

And I couldn't wait to see him again. There was so much to tell.

As the boat slowed, the sun was at the house's back, casting shadows from its roof to the lawn and dock below.

We floated toward the dock. "*Vel*, here we are," Hans said.

I jumped out and tied the bow off, then offered a hand to Aasta.

"Oh, I'm fine," she said, waving me off. "I must do what I can while I can."

I studied her long limbs, so much like Mama's . . . so much like my own.

| 30 |

From the cottage, Elizabeth Worthington gathered her skirt and petticoat, hurrying down the steps to meet us. "Walter! She's back! Sadie Rose is back! As long as you're safe, that's all I care about. You're safe. You're back home. I haven't slept well since you left!"

I had been gone three weeks. And yet a whole lifetime had shifted on its axis, tilted off center, and begun a new and uncertain orbit.

"Come," she said. "Aasta, please serve up some tea. Hot tea, Sadie? Yes?"

I nodded. "Yes. But only if Aasta and Hans join us."

"Oh," Mrs. Worthington said, as if it were a surprising suggestion, as if I were hers and hers alone. "Why, of course!" She forced cheeriness.

Mr. Worthington met us at the doorstep. "Finally," he said, swinging the door wide enough for his wife, and then stepping in. "You've put us through no end of trouble, young lady."

I pictured Trinity, threatening with a knife. Whatever angst I'd caused the Worthingtons, it seemed thin compared to the worry the Bairds shared over their daughter. Could they ever trust her to be alone again?

"I'm sorry," I said as I passed him, setting down my traveling

bag near my chair at the dining room table. I rested my hands
on the back of the chair. Out of the corner of my eye I spotted the piano, tall and proud, the last sheet music I'd played
still turned open. I felt a great need to spend hours at the keys,
to let the music wash over me, to retreat to a world without
words—with only chords, notes, rhythms, and melodies.

After an awkward pause, Mr. Worthington said, "*Sorry?*
You're *sorry?*" He'd been standing in the archway between the
living area and dining room, watching me. Then he turned to
the Chinese lacquered serving table, pulled the glass top off a
crystal bottle, paused, and then put it back on again, as if debating whether to pour himself a drink. But I knew he wouldn't. It
was a "respectably early hour." Instead he spun back toward me.

"As if that's enough. My poor wife, fit to be tied with worry.
And then blasted editorials accusing me of murder? All I can
say is it's good you're back, or I may have had to find you and
kill you myself."

He must have seen the color wash from my face.

"Go," he said. "Change into dry clothes and come back down."

My bedroom was tidied, the bed made. I felt I'd been away
for years, as if I were no longer the girl who once slept here. I
slipped out of my clothes and into a soft yellow dress and returned to the dining room.

At its threshold, Mr. Worthington stopped me.

"Sadie Rose," he said in hushed tones, "I didn't mean 'kill
you' literally. I meant it as—okay, that was an admittedly terrible gaff. It's just that pressure from Ennis, from townsfolk,
and with the campaign, little things can topple everything." He
snapped his fingers. "Just like that."

"Little things," I said crisply, aware that Mrs. Worthington,
Aasta, and Hans had joined us in the dining room, though none
sat down. I eased closer to them. "Little things," I continued,
"like when my mother said she was going to leave and Ennis

killed her?" My voice was raised, and my questions flowed like an unstoppable river. "Someone had to do something with her body, Mr. Worthington, yes?"

"You don't know what you're talking about," Mr. Worthington said, dismissing me. He turned back to the decanter and filled a goblet halfway with amber liquid. "You were only a child then. What could you possibly remember?"

I pressed ahead, as if possessed by cornering him. "She was Ennis's favorite, his exclusive fancy lady—yes?"

I reached into my traveling bag and pulled out the photographs and set them out in a fan on the table.

Slowly, he turned, his attention to the images.

Hans registered recognition. "Oh, Sadie. You should not find these. I thought someday I would tell you, but it never seemed the right time—"

I rushed headlong, aiming my anger at Mr. Worthington. "That's why when I showed these photographs to Mr. Foxridge, he nearly pushed me out of his office. He knew what could happen with Ennis if you stick your nose in his business."

Walter Worthington sat down heavily at the head of the table and tipped back his tumbler. "Oh, the hell with everything!" he raged. "I should kick you out right now! But you know I can't. I can just imagine the headlines..." He painted them with his hands in front of his face, as if he were doing the actual mockup of the newsprint. "Senator Worthington Sends Orphan Girl Packing!" Now that would tug at their heartstrings, wouldn't it? The kind of thing that friend of yours Victor would just love, wouldn't he?"

"Walt, what *are* you talking about?" Mrs. Worthington turned fragile as ice on a puddle. I felt sympathy for her. Her world had been constructed so carefully around everything her husband accomplished. Now everything was shifting, with no solid bottom. "I don't understand, Walter." She pressed her palms together, as if in prayer, and then pressed her fingertips to her lips. "Aren't you *glad* to have Sadie back with us?"

He looked at his wife, then beyond, and drew a deep breath, the way he always did before embarking on a long and cumbersome speech.

For once I had to speak up and not let them take the reins away from me. "I was behind the parlor stove," I blurted. Before my legs buckled, I pulled the chair under me.

"You remember. I pretended to be sleeping when you and Ennis were talking. Then later, I followed into the storm. I thought it had been Ennis carrying her, but then I realized that Ennis wouldn't do that kind of thing. He doesn't clean up his messes, does he? He has you to do that. Like when my father—Frank Ladovitch—started sending off photographs of shorelines after logging...started making trouble...and he conveniently drowned. Did you help Ennis with that problem, too? Or did he send another underling out to silence him?"

Walter Worthington slammed his fist onto the glossy table. "This is ridiculous. You were too little then to know what you're talking about. And I didn't have anything to do with that photographer's death. It was suicide, that's all I know. Where are you going with all this anyway?"

"I was little—it's true—the night my mother died. But I remember things clearly. The pants, the shoes, the stride, the voice." I held his gaze. "It was *you*."

"I didn't break any laws, damn it!"

He looked to his wife, as if seeking support. She only offered a bewildered expression in return. "I could have sent someone else in to deal with it," he said. "God knows I'm not the kind of man who hangs out at brothels. But when Ennis said she was already gone, I thought, why not find something positive out of the situation. And—" He looked around desperately, eyes both pleading and defensive. He pulled at fine hairs at his hairline. "Okay, if you want to know, I lugged her body outside and set her down gently in front of the town hall. And I was right. It caused a big stir. Got people thinking that things needed to change, that Ranier should be a place to raise families—with schools, churches, and common decency. No one wanted to think of such a woman, frozen with an empty bottle of booze in her hand."

"That you placed there." My voice was oak-solid with deep, sure roots.

Beyond, a train whistle sounded, one short, two long, in usual warning to clear the tracks.

"What difference does that make? She was already dead! Who cares now anyway after all these years? She was just a *prostitute*, for God's sake."

In an explosion of motion beside me, Hans jumped from his chair and pounced on Mr. Worthington, knocking him backward. The chair cracked against the floor, as Hans shouted in Norwegian, and they rolled against the hutch in a heap of arms and legs.

Then just as fast as it had happened, Hans was on his feet. He stepped back, fists up, waiting for Walter Worthington to rise.

We left our chairs and gathered around.

"Walter!" Elizabeth cried, kneeling beside her husband. "Are you hurt? Hans, how could you?"

I looked at Hans, amazed.

Then Hans was crying. "The difference is, Mr. Worthington," he said, his voice breaking, "—Sigrid was my daughter."

"*Our* daughter," Aasta whispered.

"Sigrid?" Elizabeth Worthington looked up. I felt bad for her. Her tidy world was unraveling at every seam.

"Bella Rose was her working name," I said. "Sigrid was my mother's real name."

Hans pulled a handkerchief from his back pocket, dabbed his eyes, and then offered it to Mr. Worthington as he rose to his elbow on the floor.

Unceremoniously, Walter Worthington grabbed the handkerchief and pressed it to the red seeping at the corner of his mouth. Then he stood up, chest heaving, and stared at Hans. Then he looked at Aasta. And me. "Lord," he said, his teeth streaked red.

He righted his chair and then sat back down, dabbing at his mouth. And almost as if he'd called a meeting to order, everyone sat again at the table.

Mr. Worthington sagged. "After all these years...and you didn't say a word? I thought she was just another—" He sat tall, but his jaw hung slack as he looked from Aasta to Hans to me and back around again. I'd never seen him so undone, as if his podium had been kicked over.

"Walter?" Elizabeth asked, leaning close to him. "Will you tell me what in the world is going on?"

He glanced up, his eyes avoiding hers. "Sadie Rose. Hans and Aasta. You, you wouldn't talk about this to anyone else...would you?"

For a few seconds, none of us said a word.

"If Ennis murdered my mama," I said, "how can you expect me to be quiet?"

"Shouldn't he be brought to trial?" Hans asked. "You would be witness. I know he's powerful, but if it be murder..."

Mr. Worthington cleared his throat. "No, not murder. Ennis told me they'd been arguing and that she fell back and hit her head against a sharp corner. He said it was an accident."

I held his gaze. "Do you really believe that?"

He shrugged. "There's no way to ever know for sure. All I know is what he told me. Looking back, I should have called the sheriff to deal with her body. But I didn't. I regret that now."

He looked around the table at each of us. "Soon as this gets out, it'll be the end of my career."

Silence fell like heavy snowflakes.

I looked to Hans, his fists unclenched, and then I realized that everything had changed. Before the photographs, Mr. Worthington had held all the cards, but now they were in my hands. I chose my words carefully.

"Mr. Worthington, over the years I've listened as you've negotiated lots of compromises. Made deals. I don't think this has to be the end of your career, as long as none of us talks—"

"True. Oh, Sadie Rose, you're exactly—" Mr. Worthington brightened.

"We won't need to say a word . . . about the likely murder of my mother . . . about who dragged her body into the storm. We don't need to say a word about the possible murder of my father . . ." The deck of cards felt weighty in my hands. "As long as you'll agree to a few things."

He pushed back in his chair and pulled himself to his usual straight posture. "I'm listening."

I glanced to Hans and Aasta, hoping for their agreement. "First, that you refuse another nickel from Ennis for your campaign."

Mr. Worthington removed the handkerchief from his mouth, studied the blood, then reapplied it. "Ennis," he said, then let out a jagged breath, as if seeing a wide array of complications before him. "And?"

"Second," I said, "that you listen to Victor Guttenberg's ideas. Hear him out, consider what he has to say, and offer your support."

He pushed away from the table and filled his glass from the decanter. After a long moment, he turned, his free palm up. "And?"

"And then we won't say another word about it."

The senator ran his hands slowly down the sides of his face. In that moment, I saw him not as a rising senator with increasing power and influence, but as an older man. Possibly alone, abandoned. His hands stopped at his chin, palms joined, fingers splayed, as if holding up a great weight.

I forced myself to look away—to give him a moment to consider—and turned my gaze toward the centerpiece on the table, the cut-glass vase filled with deep pink peonies. Rising from her chair across from me, Elizabeth Worthington cleared her throat and tucked her silk blouse more snuggly into her skirt band. Her tiny chin trembled. "Sadie Rose," she said, "I hope you have felt a little bit of my love for you. I know I haven't always been the best at . . . please," she said, looking around the table. "No one is getting fired. Don't leave, any of you. Please. Stay. You're the closest thing I have—to family."

Then, as the senator turned from the decanter, she challenged him. "Walter Worthington," she said with iron conviction, and I glimpsed the child she must have once been. "I want you to hear me this time! Your political life needn't come to an end. For years you have refused my family's money, saying you couldn't accept money from a newspaper baron, that it would bind you somehow to compromising political views—and to my father. But where has Ennis's money gotten you?"

Mr. Worthington sat in silence.

"You've been in his back pocket ever since you went into business together with the building of the bridge. You've sold out for his money, his help in your rise to power. But don't you see? You're not just an engineer of modest means anymore. You're no longer the mayor of Ranier. You don't have to be bound to Ennis anymore. You have options, Walter, if for once you're willing to put your pride aside." Then she smoothed her skirt and was almost seated when she bounced back to her feet. "And wait. There's one more thing since I have the floor."

"What more can you possibly have to say, Lizzy?" Mr. Worthington said, shaking his head.

"For years I've pleaded that we adopt Sadie Rose. For years I've wanted nothing more than to offer her a true home and family, but you've put your concerns first, always worried about political fallout."

"Now, wait—"

"No, this time—you wait. You've told me I couldn't get it all my way. Well, neither can you, Walt. And I've decided that we will adopt Sadie Rose and give her—if she's willing—all the privileges of family. This time you'll have to choose, Walter Worthington, between a family or none at all."

"What's that suppose to mean?" he asked, his voice barely audible. "Or you'll leave me?"

"I didn't know it until this moment, but yes. That's exactly what I'm saying. This time, I'm offering you a choice."

On the dining room wall, the German cuckoo clock began to chime. Mrs. Worthington sat back down, her head high, as the little doors above the clock's numbers opened wide, and out popped the wooden bird—in and out, ten times—until it retreated silently.

"Stupid little bird," Hans said, cracking the tension.

Familiar knocks sounded on the porch door. I guessed who it was and sprang from my chair. As I stepped from the table, I could see the visitor adjusting his glasses. At his side he held a leather satchel, no doubt holding maps, reports, and various letters in his campaign to save the waterways.

"It's Victor," I called back. I doubted Victor had yet heard about Trinity's ordeal. I would tell him about all that had transpired, when the time was right.

On my heels, Mr. Worthington strode after me.

"Victor, this isn't the best time—," he began, pushing open the screen door.

I placed my hand on Mr. Worthington's shoulder, stopping him midsentence. It was the first time I'd ever touched him. "On the contrary," I said with a smile, as if this were another carefree moment in my life with the Worthingtons. "I can't think of a better time to see what Victor has to say, can you, Mr. Worthington?"

I held my breath, waiting for another icy dismissal. If it came, I would have to make good on my threat. Above the bay, seagulls cried, swooping in wide arcs on the warm breeze.

Instead, Walter Worthington met my eyes. From the moment he'd carried my nearly frozen body home, he'd always held me at arm's length, worried that I would bring him down. Now a crack emerged in his political armor, and with it, something new—a softening in his brooding eyes. He gave a single nod to me, then extended his arm to Victor. "Come in, yes."

Victor stepped inside, tucking his shirttail into his khakis and shooting me a quizzical glance.

I shrugged my shoulders, as if I had no idea how or why things had shifted.

"By the way," I whispered to Victor, as he passed. "I found my last name."

"Is that so?"

"Ladovitch," I said. "Sadie Rose Ladovitch. My father was a photographer."

Victor looked taken aback. "Your father? I know of his work. He captured how something wild can be so easily lost."

The senator cleared his throat. "Indeed . . . it was a different era." When he motioned toward the porch's wicker chairs, I turned to rejoin the others in the dining room, but Mr. Worthington stopped me with his hand lightly on mine. "Please, Sadie Rose. Stay. Join us. You're right, you know," he said. "It's high time I hear some fresh ideas."

| 31 |

St. Peter, Minnesota
May 1922

A new driver picked me up from outside the women's dorm at Gustavus Adolphus College. I settled in the back seat with the confidence of a junior.

"And what are you studying?" the man asked.

"Music education."

"I have six kids," he offered. "Hope one of 'em can go to college someday. I never went past eighth grade."

I nodded politely, then pulled my journal from my satchel. The journal was a gift from Aasta and Hans after I had arrived in the river valley of St. Peter, Minnesota. I turned to the inscription on the inside cover: *It was your mother's. Now it's yours. Aasta and Hans.*

When I'd first held the journal, I hesitated to turn to the first page, expecting to read Mama's own words from when she was my age. But every page between the brown calfskin cover was blank. I would have to tell her story, I decided then, and my own. I found a pencil and turned toward the end of the journal; its pages fluffed wide with inserted cards, notes, and coffee stains. I wrote.

When we drove under the arched gates of the Oak Hills Mental Asylum, I tucked my journal away.

Waiting outside the entrance, alongside a nurse with a

glaringly white cap and uniform, stood Trinity, her arms folded like tiny wings over her waist, her head tipped toward the gravel driveway. I had often observed her this way when I'd visited, listless and dull, until she saw me.

On either side of the steps, lilac bushes hung heavy with pale lavender blossoms. Everything bloomed three weeks earlier in southern Minnesota than in the north. I rolled down my window, the air too sweetly scented. "Trinity, hello! Are you ready?"

Her hair caught the sun like dew on a spider's web. It was washed clean and golden, and sparkled in the light, not the way I often saw her, with it lying flat and lifeless against her head. She glanced up, startled, and her eyes registered pleasure.

"You're here! I thought I'd go crazy with waiting for this day!"

The driver jumped out and added her luggage to the Ford's trunk, and then we were off, bouncing along in the springy back seat. Trinity grabbed my hand and drew it to her lips and kissed it, then set it back in my lap.

"I'm just so glad to see you! Can you believe it? We're going up north!"

"For the whole summer this time," I said. "Not just a long weekend."

She rested her head against the back seat, closed her eyes, and let out a sigh. I knew her moods could reach the clouds and later crash to the deepest pit, but with time her highs and lows seemed less severe. I missed the unbridled enthusiasm I'd known when I first met her, but life was also about trade-offs. And Trinity, I reminded myself, was still around. Still in my life.

Three years back, when I'd returned to the Worthingtons, I informed them of my plans to look for work in Duluth. "But you're sixteen and single," Mrs. Worthington had said. "It's not right. A girl like you, all alone. Who knows who will prey on you? You don't want to land in trouble like your—"

She never finished her sentence that morning. Aasta had held her finger up. "Not another word against her mother, ever again."

That day, the Bairds came visiting with a proposal.

Mr. Baird got right to the point. "We want to pay Sadie Rose's college tuition to Gustavus Adolphus College. Four full years to study whatever she wishes."

"Oh," I managed.

"It's a progressive school," Mrs. Baird added. "In return, with Trinity at the nearby institution, our hope is you would visit her weekly and chaperone her on trips home."

If I said yes, then I knew my relationship with Owen would be put on hold. I would only see him on visits home. There was no guarantee he would wait for me. But I knew the answer. This wasn't just about furthering my education, something I had longed to do, but it was also about helping Trinity. If Owen and I were meant to be, things would somehow work out. A modern woman shouldn't have to choose between her education and marriage. Both were possible.

Not to be outdone, Elizabeth offered to share half of my expenses. Even with my new opportunity to go to college, she pleaded for me to stay connected to them and begged Hans and Aasta to continue to work for them, as well. "Our lives would be empty without you."

Now our driver dropped us at the train depot, nestled in the valley near the curving Minnesota River. Before long, we found our seats on the passenger train and settled in for the ten-hour ride to Ranier.

Every trip, within an hour of leaving St. Peter, Trinity pulls out her sketchpad. Every trip—and we've made this trip more than a half-dozen times now—allows me to write. I never intended to write so much, but the telling seemed to take a course of its own, much like this train.

We cross the trestle over the Mississippi, rush past red barns and farms—some with new tractors—most with horses in harness, pulling iron blades through black earth. We leave the trolleys and honking automobiles of St. Paul and journey north, winding between forests of oaks and maples, crossing rushing rivers, pushing on through white-pine forests, and dynamited granite passageways.

Here and there, clear-cuts lay scattered, like board games discarded by hasty children. A tall pine stands, here, there. And then we plunge into shadows between thick balsam and spruce. I think often of Victor and his battle against Ennis. The talk in Ranier against Victor continues, that he will threaten everyone's livelihood, yet even I can see that the log drives are fewer, that the virgin timber has nearly vanished. When I arrive in Ranier, I expect to see more posters and flyers luring visitors to Kettle Falls, now advertising itself as "a healthy respite from city life...a place for families to come to fish and play." Maybe Victor will find more people who value the remaining wilderness, value it enough to join his cause and keep Ennis from enacting his visions of endless dams and industry.

I will continue to help Victor as I can, writing letters, attending Friends of the Wilderness meetings in St. Paul in support of his cause. Already, several attorneys on Victor's team have been let go from their law firms for their involvement against Ennis. Who knows, maybe someday Victor will triumph despite the odds, a David slinging a stone against a Goliath.

All I know is Owen Jensen waits for me at the depot, his Adam's apple a little less prominent now that he's twenty. Though he's starting his automobile dealership—with hints of success—and always dresses smartly for work in a tie and jacket, I know he'll be waiting for me in a plaid shirt. And when he meets me at the train steps and holds me in his strong arms, I'll bury my nose in his collar, returning to my beloved woods and water.

As I've discovered in my literature classes, endings are difficult. The writer needs to wrap things up, make sense of what has come before, and point the reader toward the future. But how can I wrap things up?

My past weaves itself through my being. Every time my fingers touch the piano keys, the girl in the snow emerges, her story given voice through my music. Not a day passes without thinking of Mama, glad for the love she showed me despite her harsh circumstances and limited choices. Not a minute passes without feeling gratitude for Aasta and Hans. Though I'll never call them Grandpa and Grandma—it's true, just the same. And even the Worthingtons, with all their flaws, have continued as fixtures in my life. Like family, I don't always enjoy them, but I can't close the door on them either.

Ahead, beyond the horizon, my future stretches out like a ribbon of silver. The train clacks and sways, jolting along its winding journey . . . north.

Author's Note

For two decades I have been haunted by an account in Hiram Drache's *Koochiching* about life in northern Minnesota in the early 1900s. A prostitute was found frozen one morning in the snow; as a joke, someone stood her body up in the corner at the start of a council meeting. This, allegedly, caused quite a stir.

What it churned in me was a deep desire to understand and give a voice to this woman's life and death. Perhaps avenge it. I wanted to know more about her and the challenges women faced in one of the last settled frontiers. It took years before I started writing this story but when I did, the story's narrator stepped onto the page: the woman's daughter, Sadie Rose.

I had never before written about such an early time in Minnesota. As Sadie Rose's story began to take shape on Rainy Lake, I found her life set against the backdrop of wealthy industrialist and timber baron E. W. Backus and the penniless and emerging environmentalist Ernest Oberholtzer. Then these larger-than-life "David and Goliath" characters and their conflict over preserving wilderness threatened to overtake Sadie Rose's story. This is in part why I fictionalized their names.

I live in Ranier, directly across from the historic lift bridge that fits prominently into the story. It's easy for me to picture steamers, log booms, taverns, and brothels from the turn of the century. The home I share with my family, a house more than one hundred years old, became the natural setting for the summer cottage of Sadie Rose's caretakers, the Worthingtons. Within the string of our home's previous owners was a woman named Sadie Rose. The name fused with my emerging character, and I never considered changing it. In many ways, I felt the earlier "ghosts" of my home and area speaking to me over the years about this story's direction. My job was to listen to the story that needed to be told.

My hope is that through one character's struggle to learn of her past as she shapes her future, readers will gain a sense of the confluence of many powerful rivers at that time in Koochiching history. *Frozen* is a microcosm of what was happening on a national scale, from the Suffrage movement and Prohibition to unchecked development of wilderness and emerging environmentalism. Most important, it is a reminder that the past is filled with the voices of individuals...and many stories yet to be told.

Acknowledgments

I want to thank the many individuals who helped sustain me over the years and encouraged me to finish this story. I thank my agent, Andrea Cascardi, for her unflagging support, pointed questions, and belief in this story, and my editor, Todd Orjala, whose insight and editorial comments proved invaluable.

Thanks to Mike Williams, whose family's roots go back to Kettle Falls and who now shares his knowledge as a park guide at Voyageurs National Park. Thanks to curator Ed Oerichbauer at the Koochiching County Historical Museum, for answering my questions and allowing me to hang out in the museum basement to peruse newspapers brittle with age. I am indebted to authors Joe Paddock (*Keeper of the Wild*) and Hiram Drache (*Koochiching*) for their extensive historical research, as well as the numerous other authors whose works are listed in the bibliography.

Thanks to Jim Hanson, for welcoming me to his family's island to soak up stories and photographs, especially of Virginia. I am grateful for our time on the boat named after her, which Jim has returned to Rainy Lake and so lovingly restored.

To the Oberholtzer Foundation, for allowing me to return so many years to Mallard Island, thank you. The island I depict in 1920 hints at the beginnings of environmentalist Ernest Oberholtzer's dream—a dream the island today continues to fulfill, blending civilization and arts with wilderness. I have slept in Ernest's bed, dined in his wannigan, walked his island paths, and perused his library and some of the ten thousand books he collected. I am indebted beyond words.

I value the honorable mention this manuscript received from the McKnight–Loft judge. It was what I needed to keep going at that time.

My life is rich with good writers and good friends. Thanks to those of you in my writers' groups who listened to and read various drafts of this manuscript. I am sustained by my local writers' group—Karen Severson, Sheryl Peterson, Kate Miller, Lynn Naeckel, Shawn Shofner, and Naomi Woods. What would I do without you? To the talented writers who flock up every summer for a weeklong island retreat—thank you for your belief in this story. And my gratitude also to many others who generously waded through rough drafts and encouraged me to keep going, especially Gail Nord, Mary Dahlen, Dan Tausenfrend, Marilyn Graves, and Kari Baumbach.

And last, but never least, my family: Kate (and Chris Koza), Eric, and of course my husband, Charlie. Thank you all!

FOR FURTHER READING

Atkins, Annette. *Creating Minnesota: A History from the Inside Out*. St. Paul: Minnesota Historical Society Press, 2007.

Carlisle, Rodney P. *Handbook to Life in America: The Age of Reform, 1890–1920*. New York: Infobase Publishing, 2009.

Douglas, Marjorie Myers. *Barefoot on Crane Island: A Fond Reminiscence of Lake Minnetonka in the 1920s*. St. Paul: Minnesota Historical Society Press, 1998.

Drache, Hiram M. *Koochiching*. Danville, Ill.: Interstate Printers and Publishers, 1983.

———. *Taming the Wilderness*. Danville, Ill.: Interstate Printers and Publishers, 1992.

King, Shannon. *Kettle Falls: Crossroads of History*. International Falls, Minn.: Lake States Interpretive Association, 1989.

McQuarrie, Neil. *A Bit of Legend in These Parts: The Life of Betty Berger Lessard*. Brandon, Manitoba: NJM Enterprises, 2007.

Meier, Peg. *Bring Warm Clothes: Letters and Photos from Minnesota's Past*. Minneapolis: Neighbor's Publishing, 1981.

Paddock, Joe. *Keeper of the Wild: The Life of Ernest Oberholtzer*. St. Paul: Minnesota Historical Society Press, 2001.

Sandeen, Ernest R. *St. Paul's Historic Summit Avenue.* Minneapolis: University of Minnesota Press, 2004.

Seagraves, Anne. *Soiled Doves: Prostitution in the Early West.* Hayden, Idaho: Wesanne Publications, 1994.

Steinke, Gord. *Mobsters and Rumrunners of Canada: Crossing the Line.* Alberta, Canada: Folklore Publishing, Alberta Foundation for the Arts, 2003.

Yeager, Allan. *History of Koochiching County.* Sponsored by the Koochiching County Historical Society. Dallas: Taylor Publishing, 1983.

Mary Casanova is the author of thirty books for young readers, ranging from picture books such as *The Day Dirk Yeller Came to Town, Utterly Otterly Night,* and *One-Dog Canoe* to novels (*The Klipfish Code, Moose Tracks,* and *RIOT*).

Her books are on many state reading lists and have earned the American Library Association Notable Award, Aesop Accolades from the American Folklore Society, Parents' Choice Gold Award, *Booklist* Editors' Choice, as well as two Minnesota Book Awards. She speaks frequently around the country at readings and library conferences.

She lives with her husband and three dogs in a turn-of-the-century house in Ranier, Minnesota, near the Canadian border.